The
Other Side
of the
World

The
Other Side
of the
World

STEPHANIE BISHOP

TINDER
PRESS

First published in Australia by Hachette Australia

First published in Great Britain in 2015 by Tinder Press
An imprint of HEADLINE PUBLISHING GROUP

1

Cataloguing in Publication Data is available from the British Library

Hardback ISBN 978 1 4722 3061 4

Printed and bound in Great Britain by
Clays Ltd, St Ives plc

Headline's policy is to use papers that are natural, renewable and recyclable products and
made from wood grown in well-managed forests and other controlled sources. The logging
and manufacturing processes are expected to conform to the environmental regulations of
the country of origin.

HEADLINE PUBLISHING GROUP
An Hachette UK Company
Carmelite House
50 Victoria Embankment
London EC4Y 0DZ

www.tinderpress.co.uk
www.headline.co.uk
www.hachette.co.uk

For Boyd

'Nostalgia (from *nostos* – return home, and *algia* – longing) is a longing for a home that no longer exists or has never existed. Nostalgia is a sentiment of loss and displacement, but it is also a romance with one's own fantasy. Nostalgic love can only survive in a long-distance relationship. A cinematic image of nostalgia is a double exposure, or a superimposition of two images – of home and abroad, past and present, dream and everyday life. The moment we try to force it into a single image, it breaks the frame or burns the surface.'

Svetlana Boym, *The Future of Nostalgia*

'But of course the dream-England is no more than a dream.'

Salman Rushdie, *Imaginary Homelands*

Prologue
Cambridge, 1966

SHE WOULD HAVE walked, only Henry said no. The footpaths are treacherous, he told her, and I don't want you slipping and injuring yourself when I've just found you alive and well. The snow has come early and the cold is fierce. No, he said, I'll come and collect you and bring you back here, to the hotel near the river. There wasn't room for them all in his bedsit and Charlotte didn't want the college knowing of their situation, so Henry had booked rooms at the Royal. He'll be driving past the river now, she thinks, checking her watch. Her husband, ever punctual. The water a dark stripe in the corner of his vision. He'll see it as he drives straight ahead, lose it as he turns left then right. On the river there will be rowboats – the faint sound of blades smacking and cutting at the water, the creak of hull and oarlock, the call of boys.

Charlotte opens the window and pushes her face into the cold. Outside, the college grounds are empty – the air filled with the whirr of falling snow. There are no bird calls, no lawnmowers, no hum of the London train, no movement other than this drift of white. The wind gusts towards her and she steps back into the dim room. Although there is not much more to pack, her stamina has vanished. There is a glass paperweight from the market, a small blue vase for the flowers she gathered on her tramps through the fields, the photograph she stole from Henry. But the effort required to wrap these last things and place them in the box seems monumental. She crouches on the ground, tugs a sheet of newspaper from the pile and stuffs it into the vase. She slips the photograph of the children into her handbag. Altogether there is less than she expected, just a couple of boxes and a suitcase. Henry will be surprised.

Another gust blows snow into the room. Charlotte gets up to close the window and sees his car parked beside the hedge. How had she not heard his arrival? The purr of the engine and the slow crunch of wheels over gravel and ice. She had kept the window open so that she might catch the sound of these things. She didn't expect this. He will be here any moment now. She had meant to watch for the car and use those last minutes to compose herself. To be ready; to know what to say. She starts to sweat. There is the smell of it. This frightened animal called woman. Her hands shake as she lifts the small round mirror to her face and tries to fix a smudge of blue eye shadow. She rubs a hand against the centre of her chest and walks a nervous circle, to the door and back, her heart skittering beneath her palm. Should she let him in, and invite him to sit down, or should she wait by the window and call out – *It's open* – when he knocks? Then they'll walk towards each other. Or will he find her with her back to him; she'll turn, and each will pause, unsure of who should make the first approach. He'll brush the snow from his coat, he'll take off his hat. And the children? Where are they? The children.

Part One

DEPARTURE

Cambridge, October 1963 – December 1964

SHE CLAMBERS OVER the fence and strides out into the field. It is autumn, cold – an arctic wind blows and her coat billows behind her. Rain falls in a sudden shower, but she pushes on into the green distance and further, towards the blue rise where the woodlands begin. It is like wading into the sea, she thinks. The wind against her, the grass up at her knees. They go on for miles, these grazing lands, and the further she walks the smaller she becomes, until she is just a thin black mark against the fen. Henry must be wondering where she's got to – she could never be lost here, but she could disappear, she thinks, as she passes the slow cows chewing frozen ground, steam rising from their flanks. She passes the pond, covered now with silvery ice, the frosted hedge of brambles. Above her the sky is mottled brown and grey and the air smells of dung and grass. The leaves on the hawthorns are gone; those on the horse chestnuts are still browning and falling. She is on her way back from the doctor's, so it must be a Monday, or perhaps Tuesday. Dr Pascoe only sees patients Mondays and Tuesdays. How can I lose track of time like this? she thinks. Dates do not seem to matter; one day feels the same as the next. But they do matter, the doctor assured her, they do indeed. 'You must be mistaken,' she said. 'You cannot be right.'

She startles at the sound of a crow. The certainty – impossible – that the call is that of her child. The sound coming towards her as she moves further away, her own voice drifting back: *Lucie? Is that you?* No, of course not, it's just a bird, the baby asleep at home. Charlotte watches the crow swoop down, coast on a low current of air and land further out. She can count on one hand the times she's left the house alone, without the baby. And every time it is the same – how she startles at every long, high note, thinking it is Lucie. She feels the strange phantom sense of the child's weight against her hip, the loose stone of her head lolling, asleep, on her shoulder. The crow calls again – she sees it call, the open black beak, the silky, lifted throat – and her skin prickles. A gust of wind disperses the cry; the sound rises up then floats down over the field, coming from everywhere and nowhere all at once. Her arms suddenly ache to hold her daughter. She looks back but can't see her bike. Where did she leave it? Perhaps it is over that way, behind the hedges. But the field appears the same from every direction. She finds her way to the fence and begins to trace a path back along the perimeter.

Above her the clouds ripple and bend, moving herd-like towards a distant corner of the sky. Her stomach heaves. She stops, holds on to the fence, leans down towards the grass and vomits a string of yellow bile. She stays that way a moment, hunched over, gripping the wood and dry-retching, then wipes her mouth with the sleeve of her coat and rests her head against the railing. 'It'll pass soon,' the doctor said. 'These things always do.' She weeps then, at the memory of his words. 'All for a good cause now,' he'd said. 'All for a good cause.'

She remembers last night's dream, that the two of them, she and Henry, were looking at rainbow-coloured paintings in Vienna. They stood before a very bright canvas, and Henry said to her, 'It is the colour of your soul forming.' He looked at the painting as he spoke, and she knew he was not talking about her, about her soul, but about the soul of the child now growing inside her, the child she has not yet told him about, although it is his.

She pushes back out into the field, walking faster now, puffing a little, her breath white in the thin, cold air. Icy grass crunches underfoot, her toes numb in her wet shoes. She was supposed to ride into town and ride home again, not stop like this and disappear into the wilds. If only the doctor had given her a script and sent her home. Just something to settle her. Then a cup of tea and a lie-down. Further ahead a flock of birds lifts up from the grass, sways in the sky a moment, then swerves back down to earth. She doesn't know what she'll say to Henry. She doesn't want to have to tell him.

—

In the warmth of the living room, Lucie grunts – her arm jerking up into the air then falling back down. Henry shuffles forwards in his chair to check on her. She is asleep in her pram and he rocks it a little with his foot, pushing the toe of his shoe against the lower rung. Has it really been seven months since she was born? It seems so much longer, that Sunday dawn when the midwife set him to work, boiling water and fetching cloths. The baby grunts again, kicks her legs, squirms. Henry holds his breath and checks his watch: eleven thirty. What's keeping her? Charlotte should be back by now, he thinks, running his palm along the armrest of his favourite wingback chair. The chair is covered in gold velveteen and he strokes the smooth grain of the fabric as if petting a calm animal. Lucie settles, then snuffles in her sleep, and Henry sits back and returns to his reading, examining the brochure that came through the letterbox early that morning. *Come Over to the Sunny Side!* the brochure says. Beneath the curve of blue writing two blonde women in red swimsuits skid over Sydney Harbour on waterskis. *Australia brings out the best in you. You could be on your way to a sunnier future in the New Year. Fine for your wife. Good for your children.*

It is not that he expects Charlotte to come home and say she's perfectly well. She isn't, of course she isn't, that's why she went to the doctor's in the first place. The headaches, the nausea. The way she works through the night, sleeps a couple of hours, then gets up for Lucie at the crack of dawn. He has to clear her paints and brushes from the bench in the morning to make himself some toast.

A dog-eared copy of Yeats's *The Wind Among the Reeds* lies open, facedown, on the coffee table beside him. He's supposed to give a lecture next week on the early love poems, but every time he tries to prise one apart he finds himself lost in a tangle of memories. Reciting 'The Cap and Bells' to Charlotte in the summer, the two of them lying in the grass and watching puffs of bright cloud. Or reading the poems together, by winter firelight: 'When You Are Old' and 'To an Isle in the Water'. *Shy one, shy one, shy one of my heart.*

Someone once told him that the southern sun could cure all manner of ailments. It does look bright, in the picture. It is certainly an improvement on the Women's Voluntary Service for Civil Defence pamphlet that Charlotte keeps taped to the side of the fridge. In case of emergencies. She likes to think of emergencies. That pamphlet also came through the letterbox, a long time ago now. The paper is grimy with dust and the tape has browned and been replaced, the top right corner torn away with the old sellotape, taking with it part of the title – something about the larder and what to stock in an emergency, all that bother about the atomic bomb – but the rest of the lettering remains clear. Henry knows it by heart; from a slight distance it looks like a poem and he is unconsciously drawn to read it, over and over again, so that by now the thing has lodged itself permanently in his brain.

Suggestions for Food that would be Particularly Useful:

CANNED MEAT

corned beef

steak and kidney pudding

cooked pork sausages

herrings

pilchards

sardines

CANNED VEGETABLES

baked beans, carrots, tomatoes, etc.

peas and beans

CANNED SOUP

MEAT OR YEAST EXTRACT

TEA OR COFFEE [instant if possible]

BOILED SWEETS [in tins]

The list is followed by instructions on how to fireproof their home with various quantities of borax and boric acid. It is something they have both laughed over: Just wait a moment, darling, I hear a bomb's coming – I think I'll spray the thatch and paint the woodwork. Yes, yes, I'll dip the curtains while I'm at it. Henry can't imagine. He doesn't want to imagine. His gaze drifts back to the picture in his hand. *Any Briton who lives in the United Kingdom may apply for an assisted passage by sea or air to Australia for permanent settlement provided he is healthy and of good character.* The sea, it says, is warm enough to swim in all year.

He wonders how they might decide if he is of good character. He is educated. He has a job. He has a wife and child. Such things could be the sum of a good man. He does like the look of the sun, glinting on the water like a million little pieces of shining glass. The picture stirs a memory – something about his mother's blue dupatta, the one dotted with small circles of mirror. It smelled of violets and neroli. He remembers pushing his face into his mother's body, the circles of glass filled with shifting colour and light. This is an image, but perhaps not quite a memory. Broken, moving, far away. No, he must be wrong; servants wore dupattas. He and his family wore what the British wore.

He stares at the brochure and finds himself filled with a strange nostalgia: for the light, the colour of the sky, as if he'd already been there, to Australia. The picture makes him think of his childhood before the war, before he was sent to Southampton in the midst of battle. He remembers hiding on deck behind wooden crates while distant liners were bombed and sunk. He was eleven years old. 1945. A younger boy crouched beside him and clung to Henry's back. They sat there and cried, terrified that they would be bombed next. What was his mother thinking when she packed him off during the war? Only of his safety. India, she said, was going to the dogs and England was where he belonged – it was his ancestors' country after all. What did they used to call him? *Kutcha-butcha*, half-baked bread. There had been, before this, some discussion of moving to McCluskieganj – that promised homeland for the Anglo-Indians. But there was his father's job with British Petroleum, and his mother's extended family. Besides, they were used to the city – they were not farming people. They'd be no good living off the land, and they didn't want an enclave. 'Why would I go there?' said his mother, full of disbelief. 'McCluskieganj, that is for the Indians.' This is how they were, too British to be Indian, too Indian to be British.

Nevertheless, their future was uncertain in an independent India. 'And independence will come,' said his father, 'it is just a matter of time.' The problem was what might come with it – the violence, the unrest, at the very least the erosion of status. It was possible that Henry and his family would come to represent the enemy. They were, after all, children of the Raj.

He remembers that last conversation – they were on the verandah, near the mango tree. The monsoon was upon them. Henry was home from boarding school and sat on the ground, pushing a toy train along a track, his parents assuming that he wasn't listening.

'Better to send the boy home,' said his father, meaning England. 'Get him out while we still can.' His parents promised they'd follow later but never did, and now here he is.

The picture on the brochure reminds him not of India exactly, but of something else, something more elemental, of running through damp green space, of fine grass beneath his feet, of running fast into sunlight – *flash* – and then back into shadow – *flash* – and then out into sunlight again – *flash*, *flash*. It looks lovely. Magical, that is what people said. Why has he never thought of it? There'd be no harm in applying for an assisted passage. It might be good for them. It is so cold outside. The house is so small. And there is Charlotte. Perhaps he will suggest it to her, if the doctor doesn't have a solution. Something to lift her spirits. Truly, he's never seen the likes of it – the yellow tinge of her skin, the grey-brown circles under her eyes, and her body, how she's grown so thin, eating little more than dry toast and a bit of potato. Meanwhile, the baby cries and cries. If she is not sleeping, she cries and cries.

He looks down at the book of poems. He hasn't the heart to sit there with his sharpened pencil and decipher them, scanning the poems line by line. These days he prefers the memory of a poem to the actual reading. Could he tell his students this? He likes the way the sounds hover in the mind, merging, drifting. What does one learn from a poem? he wonders. He feels he should have learnt more than he has, or rather, if he had learnt more they would not be in the mess they now find themselves in. As if there were something he should know about love, something these poems should teach him.

Leaves fly past the window and for a moment Henry mistakes them for birds. Brown and slow, then quick and tumbling. It begins to rain. In the field across the road, children play in the drizzle. Alfred, the dog, sighs and slumps down against the door. Henry switches on the radio just in time to catch the weather. A cheerful voice tells him it will be cold but bright. Bright cloud is on the way, the voice says, merrily. It is exasperating. Surely nowhere else has so many ways to tell you to expect cloud, the forecast regularly listing several different types (low, grey, white, high). Henry adds 'bright' to the list. Rain, too, comes in more kinds than he would have liked: light and heavy showers, scattered or isolated showers; patchy, fine, light or heavy rain. Even the prediction of sun is compromised: 'sunny intervals' really means 'intermittent rain'. When he first came to England he didn't mind the weather. He liked the novelty of putting on layer after layer of woolly clothing, and he found the quick changes – from showers to wind to fog to sun – exhilarating after the predictable weather of Delhi, where you had, simply, hot and hotter, wet and wetter. But he is older now, and he has a child. The damp makes his knees ache and creak. It is no good. He is a man for a dry land. Australia is a dry land. In his mind he sees a kind of paradise: sunlight, blue sky, pineapple and steak, golf and tennis.

Henry's thoughts are interrupted by the sound of Charlotte's bike clattering against the side of the cottage. He presses himself up from the armchair and goes to meet her at the door. 'What is it?' he asks, seeing her eyes red from crying. 'What did he say?' But she only dips her head and falls against him. He bends to kiss her hair and smells the vomit. He puts his hand to her back and feels her spine beneath her coat, reminding him of an old skinny cat. 'Come along,' he says. 'Let's get you inside.'

He leads her to the table, sits her down and pours tea. He made it half an hour ago, when he expected her home, and now it is stewed and a little cool. Charlotte wraps her fingers around the cup and stares out the window. 'Charlotte?' he whispers. There is not much time. Any minute the baby will sense her mother and wake, crying. Then the conversation will be over. Charlotte's gaze drifts further out, over the fields and towards the hedges. 'Charlotte? Tell me. Please. What did he say?'

She chews at her bottom lip and looks down into her cup. 'I'm three months pregnant,' she says.

It is an announcement, Henry knows, that ought to make them happy. For a long time they both imagined themselves surrounded by a large family, but then Lucie came along and everything changed. At least it seemed to Henry that everything changed, because Charlotte changed so much. She forgot the names of people and places, forgot terms and definitions. She described objects by tracing their shape in the air. For weeks she'd struggled to remember the name for a certain kind of bent and twisted metal; unable to bear it any longer, she'd knocked on their neighbour's door, with Lucie on her hip, and tried to describe the thing she'd lost the words for. Wrought iron, the neighbour said, and Charlotte started to cry.

In those first months Lucie hardly slept, and Charlotte began to lose other things: she found her watch in the freezer, the citrus press in their wardrobe, and she put Henry's hat in the oven one night when he came home from work. 'What is a memory?' she asked him, when he found the hat and she could not recall how it got there. She meant this in the spirit of enquiry but it sounded as though her forgetfulness had spread to such a degree that she had lost the very concept of recollection. 'Don't worry yourself about it,' said Henry. 'It is a detail, a minor detail – the whereabouts of your watch or my hat.' Henry hadn't thought it possible for a mother to be sent mad by her child. And now here she is, weeping over her tea and expecting another baby.

Henry reaches across the table and covers her small hand with his larger one. She is incredibly beautiful, even like this. Her translucent skin, her wide-set eyes. They are the colour of the sea at Land's End in the sunlight. She'd chopped a fringe into her dark hair over the summer, and this only makes her eyes seem bigger, if sadder now, and somehow even more lovely. He strokes her cheek with the back of his fingers and from the corner of his vision spies the brochure lying on the carpet, beside the armchair, where it must have slipped when he got up to get the door. He does not think as he says it, the words just come out. 'We should move to Australia,' he says.

'What?' Charlotte replies, uncomprehending. He sees the shock on her face but once the words have settled he knows he is right. It is the only option. It is the only way.

'You know this means we can't stay here,' he says.

'What does? Why on earth not?'

But before Henry can respond the baby wakes, letting out a shrill wail. Charlotte leaps towards the pram, lifts the bundle to her shoulder and walks to the window, where she stands, watching a robin peck at the bird-feeder that hangs from the branches of the apple tree. Henry thinks it a barren, pointless view: all muddy fields and black hedges and more fields. A line of trees in the distance.

Charlotte says she loves the different shades of winter grey, that she loves to see the structure of plants beneath their leaves and to notice how whole trees sway at once. Great, heavy, empty branches dipping and lifting in the wind. Not the twigs. Not just the leaves, as it seems in summertime. But the whole, almost human structure, the body and the arms.

Henry, however, does not like the wind; he does not want another English winter. He had not planned on another child. He cannot bear the thought of another child in another terrible winter. Although he's been in England more than half his life, still his body rebels against the cold – too often the weather seems a kind of punishment. As a boy he taught himself to numb his limbs at will, in defence against the worst of the elements. He remembers his arrival in England – the boat trip, the long train journey, then the ancient grey boarding school by the sea presided over by a one-legged headmaster, injured in war. There, each morning, the headmaster would march the boys down to the beach and order them into the water. The headmaster always went first – he'd drop his crutches on the sand and throw himself into the ocean. 'Come along now!' he'd call. 'Tonic for the soul!' It was the only thing, he said to the row of children who stood shivering on the beach, that made his body feel whole again. Then the bravest of the boys would plunge in and do their best not to scream. Every day they did this, no matter the season – the landscape perpetually bleak and windy, snow settling over the sand during winter. For Henry, the pain of being in that freezing water was always something terrible – the cold clutching at his lungs, the slow burning loss of sensation. But so routine was this suffering that after a time he could bring the numbness on in an instant.

Henry goes to the kitchen and stokes the Aga while Charlotte feeds the baby, Lucie's hot red mouth working the teat of the bottle. She drinks quickly, making little glugging and umming noises as the milk goes down. 'We'll be all right, you and I,' Charlotte says to Lucie, to the unborn child, to no one in particular. 'We'll be all right.' But if he is serious? Once he sets his mind on something, there can be no stopping him – and everyone is talking about it, about getting out and moving somewhere else. 'Every man and his dog are moving to Australia these days,' her hairdresser said, just a fortnight ago. 'I'd do it if I could.' But it is impossible for Charlotte to even consider such a thing. This is her home – there could be nowhere else. And things will pick up again soon, she is sure. The commissions will come again.

When Charlotte was seventeen she'd won a scholarship to the Royal College of Art. Later, after she married, she had the letter framed and hung in the bedroom so she could see it from her bed. Through the last phase of her pregnancy she'd gazed at this letter as if it were a riddle. A code for a past life now irretrievable. Then for months after Lucie was born she hadn't the strength to lift a brush, and when she started again it was for the money alone, painting forgeries ('pastiche' was what they called them in the business) of

Dutch flowers that she sold to the dealers for a tidy sum. But things will change, she is certain. She can do better than this. There will be more money. They could move to a bigger house. She will make herself right again. He must believe her. If she can somehow get herself back to what she was before.

Lucie's suckling slows and becomes erratic. One-two. One. One. One-two. Her eyes blink, heavy. A few more sucks and her eyes close. The teat comes loose from her mouth and a line of milk dribbles from the corner of her lips. Charlotte stays very still while Lucie's head grows heavier in the palm of her hand, then she wipes the milk from the curve of her daughter's chin. The baby's mauve eyelids tremble. What does she see while she is sleeping? Such a perfect child. So perfect when she is asleep. Charlotte can love her well then, she can admire her then – the dimpled chin, the curious tilt of the eyebrows, the apple-round cheeks. She bends down to kiss her. When Lucie wakes, the two of them might go outside for a walk. It is lovely out there, cold and crisp and brightening; it looks like the clouds are brightening. The weather will improve, she thinks, and he'll forget this mad idea. God willing, he'll forget.

FOR THE NEXT few weeks Charlotte hears nothing of Henry's plan. She doesn't know whether this is because he has given up on it, or because he is keeping his thoughts secret. Either way, she thinks it better not to ask. The winds come and disperse the clouds, making the autumn crisp and fresh, cold and breezy. In the absence of rain they resume their morning walks through the fields, heading out early before Henry leaves for college, sometimes walking in the dark, little Lucie rugged up in her pram under the blanket that Charlotte's mother knitted. They walk at Charlotte's insistence. Henry would much prefer to stay warm under the bedcovers, but Charlotte begs him: Come on, Henry, please, you know you'll like it. And while he hates the cold he likes to be near Charlotte, likes to see her flushed and happy, out in the open air, at dawn. He knows these walks are her favourite thing and so says yes even when he doesn't really want to.

So they head out, the blue of day just lighting the edge of the fields, the trees hung in hoarfrost, the pale path curving around the grass. In an odd way Charlotte feels she has come to live for these walks, for this place. For Henry's quiet company – their voices drifting back and forth, gentle, unhurried. For the sky all about them. The land flat at first, all horizon, while the wind buffets, pushing them into the day, then the light breaking as they reach the top of the hill. She is closest to the sky then, the blue-grey air cascading down either side of the slope. Rabbits hide in the hedge shadows come springtime. Blackberries grow on the hilltop in summer. Foxes lurk. But never another human soul at such an hour as this, just after dawn, midweek, heading into winter. Now there is just the sound of their boots slipping, crunching, the wind over the grass and in the hedges. Thin branches knock and scrape.

They buried her placenta here. Carried it up in a bucket in the dark of dawn just a few days after Lucie's birth. Henry took a small shovel in his knapsack while Charlotte pushed the pram through the mud. At the top of the hill Henry crouched down and began to dig a small hole, the trees leaning towards him in the wind. 'How deep should it be?' he asked, the wind carrying his voice away from her. She didn't know. As deep as he could make it. But the ground was frozen and it was difficult to work a decent hole with the hand shovel. 'There,' he said after a while, dropping the shovel and brushing his hands against his trousers. He pushed himself up, palms against his knees. 'It's ready.' He stepped back towards Charlotte. She nodded, and he took hold of the pram, jiggling it to keep Lucie asleep, her little round cheeks red in the chilly air. Charlotte took the bucket and knelt down beside the hole. It was only shallow – no doubt the foxes would soon catch the smell of it and dig the bloody organ out. But they were burying it, that was what mattered. Marking her place, their place, together. Charlotte scraped out the loose dirt at the bottom of the hole then put her hands into the bucket and lifted the placenta; it was slick, and heavier than she expected, the colour of liver. It slipped against her fingers as she placed it gently into the earth, putting her hand to it one last time before she pushed the dirt over, covering it up and tamping down the ground as if planting seeds.

'Come,' Henry said then, 'we should go.' He was worried someone might see them. See his wife with her bloody hands.

Charlotte knelt there a moment longer, looking out through the empty branches, down to the town below. Small ancient buildings, the line of the path through the fields, the horizon beyond. She had walked up here every day when she was pregnant, the child wobbling and drifting inside her. She'd walked this way when the contractions began and thought she'd happily birth the baby out here, in the wild grass. She patted the soil down one more time. Her hands were freezing. This thing. The memory of the child moving inside her. The feeling of it turning. The weight. 'When I die,' she said, 'I'd like my ashes scattered here.'

'Darling,' said Henry, thinking her morbid.

But isn't this what one wants from a place of happiness? Such a desire is a sign of something good. Charlotte stood, smacking her hands together to rid them of dirt. From the top of the hill they could just see the roof of their cottage, the church steeple to the north of it. 'All right,' she replied. They held hands a moment, then Henry hooked his arm around Charlotte's waist and they traipsed down the hill.

That was less than a year ago, Charlotte realises now, as they make their way down the same path. A few more weeks and it will be winter again, too cold to go out so early. They must make the best of these autumn mornings. Today the furrows in the eastern field are filled with frozen water, air bubbles preserved beneath the ice. They walk over them, feeling the plate of ice splintering, the sound sharp in the air. Alongside them cows eat rosehips and apples from the low branches, their breath steaming. 'The cold is on its way,' says Henry. The cows will move and snow will arrive.

'A white Christmas, maybe,' she replies. That's what she always wants. She'd paint it this year, like Cézanne, rugged up in his fur coat, the easel sunk in snowdrifts. The different whites and greys. They always surprise her, the colours a cloud can make. She reaches out and laces her fingers through Henry's. 'I love you,' she says. He squeezes her hand. The fields always make her happy.

But when she comes inside this feeling vanishes. The cottage is small and messy, the day ahead lonely and full of chores. She turns quiet while she prepares Lucie's bottle. As Henry leaves for work he passes her a brochure. 'Here,' he tells her, putting it in her hand, 'just take a look.'

'Henry—'

'Just look.' Then he kisses her, closes the door behind him, gets on his bike and rides away.

Once he is gone the house seems very still. The baby nuzzles her face against Charlotte's chest. She puts the brochure down and moves the baby to her hip. Henry won't be home until dinnertime. The days with a baby are longer than she expected. She thinks she should know how to look after a baby by now, but does not. Lucie's body is slippery in the bath. Poo often leaks from her poorly folded nappy. Charlotte's milk didn't last. Henry says he's tired of eating baked beans on toast for dinner and can't she make something else? But she doesn't know what to cook, she has forgotten.

She makes tea, then lays the baby down on a blanket on the floor and watches it. From the corner of her eye she glimpses the brochure: women in swimsuits, on waterskis. The baby wriggles and drools. She can roll over, and tosses herself back and forth. Today Charlotte has dressed her in pink stripes. Everyone says Lucie looks good in stripes. The woman at the grocery shop. The old lady at the post office. Charlotte sits staring at her daughter for a long time. It is like watching the sea from a high window. Hypnotising, and, after a while, soporific. She knows that when he gets home Henry will ask if she has looked at the brochure and she'll say she really didn't have time, although she knows very well that this is because there's too much of it. The hours blur and stretch, refusing to break down into smaller units of action: one thing, then the next.

She reaches up and touches the hair at the nape of her neck. It is ropy, matted. Why is this? These details of her life are still new to her, unfamiliar. Then she remembers: the gush of milky vomit in the night, some of it in her hair. She has never known the nights to be so long: the endless cycle of feeding, crying, vomiting. Henry has fashioned himself a pair of earplugs from candle wax and tape, and so sleeps on, oblivious. While he snores, Charlotte rocks the baby, jiggles it, does what she can to soothe it until she realises she cannot soothe it and so just holds it tight and close while it cries. In these moments she is neither awake nor asleep but something in between, and in her mind's eye strange visions surface. There is an image of the cars parked outside the shopping arcade, of the train station in Milan where she and Henry once stood. The blue metal gate at the front of her mother's house, the bus stop on the main road, the queue for bread and cabbages on market day. All images, she realises, of places where she has waited for something to happen, for something to change. She must bathe, she thinks, looking down and seeing the same blue dress that she has worn for months now. She wore this dress in the last days of pregnancy. She wore it during the early hours of labour, and it was the first thing she put on after Lucie was born. The dress is navy and covered in small white spots. When Lucie feeds, her eyes graze the dress and she stares at the patterned fabric. It is soft with wear and smells of milk.

Meanwhile Lucie kicks; Lucie smiles. She flaps her arms in her mother's direction. Charlotte doesn't say to herself, I am a mother. Instead she finds herself thinking, riddle-like, I am a woman with a child. She reaches down and puts a pair of socks on Lucie's fat feet. They are stripy socks to match her stripy suit. Her daughter flaps at her again, gurgles. Charlotte tries to make gurgling sounds in return but she is so tired. At the edge of the field, trees bend back and forth, but she cannot hear the wind. The cup of tea beside her has turned cold. She sits a while longer then lies down next to her baby and closes her eyes. There is the feeling of her body sinking. It is not like falling asleep. It is heavier. Darker. Like being sucked into something.

When she wakes she has forgotten where she is, the time of day. She thinks for a moment that it's early morning, a new day, the next day, then remembers. Her cheek is wet with spit and itchy from the rough carpet. She knows she cannot stay in the house until dinnertime and so goes back out to the fields. She can spend hours this way, pushing the pram through the grass. Always happiest, it seems, when surrounded by these acres of open space. She does not know why, she just knows that she is. It is something about the sky, the empty stretch of ground. About being alone with her child outside. The smell of the air. It is as if the place has chosen her. The leaves on the poplar trees are flickering, silvery in the wind. What time is it? Noon, perhaps. Or later; she doesn't know. Storm clouds gather in the distance. She painted this once, a fen storm, wrapped in her black coat, her easel set up in the mud of the field. The clouds were tinged with purple, slouching diagonally down towards the hill. Roiling, Henry called it. Between the hill and the clouds a yellowish sky glowed.

She stands there, in the wild grass, rocking the pram. Lucie calls at the sound of a bird. They are fine, out here, she thinks, she and Lucie. They are peaceful together. She won't tell Henry. He doesn't like all this tramping. 'You shouldn't take her out for so long,' Henry says. 'Not in this season, she'll catch her death.' She bends over to stroke her daughter's face and Lucie smiles. Such soft cheeks. Everyone says Lucie looks like Henry – *Isn't she her daddy's girl*, they say. And it is true, already Charlotte can see that the child has his fine features, his dark hair. But she still finds this strange, to look at her child and think of her husband. The likeness is in the bones: in the slope of cheek and jaw, in the broad spread of the forehead. When they met it was what she noticed first – the beauty of him. Tall and slim, with warm, heavy-lashed eyes like those of a deer.

It was the summer of 1958: Henry was completing his degree at King's College London and she was in her final year at the Royal College of Art. Charlotte's mother, Iris, took regular holidays to India to visit a favourite student of hers who'd married an Indian man, and after Iris retired from teaching she opened up the extra rooms of the house to Anglo-Indian boarders. Henry rented the ground-floor room, directly beneath Charlotte's bedroom, and she took to making them both tea in the afternoons, when she returned from the studio. At first she simply knocked at his door and passed him the teacup, but then one day she glimpsed what was inside: the floor covered in sketches, papers pinned to the wall, books piled in a circle around the armchair like a corrugated fortress. She hadn't known what he was studying, and assumed it to be medicine or engineering – that was what most of them came for. But it turned out that Henry was writing his thesis on the use of illustrations in Charles Dickens's *Bleak House*, and the sketches scattered about the room were from that – dark little pictures of women with their faces hidden. The papers on the wall – above the bed and by the window – were drafts of poems Henry was working on. They stood in the doorway and talked fiercely about their studies and Henry gave her a chapter of his thesis to read. Charlotte brought it back the next day, covered in notes, and they took their tea out into the garden, where they sat beneath the fruit trees and talked until dinnertime. After this they were inseparable, and soon enough Henry proposed. Charlotte knew it was coming. She knew it was what she wanted, discovering this one winter night as she sat in the back row of the audience while Henry read from his first poetry collection, published earlier that year. It was the sound of his voice, how it soothed her; no one else had a voice like his, dark and breathy, the vowels coasting on the body's subtle expulsion of air.

'And what will you do, when you've finished your studies?' Iris asked her daughter when she announced her engagement.

'I'll paint – what do you think I'll do.'

'Yes, but I mean what will you do for money?'

Charlotte thought this such an annoying question. So irrelevant. 'I suppose I'll sell my paintings,' she said.

'And will that be enough to live on?'

'People make do.'

'One wants, I think, to do more than just make do,' Iris replied.

Henry and Charlotte waited until he'd finished his thesis and then they married in a registry office. After their honeymoon – a wet week camping in Devon – the two of them moved to Cambridge, where Henry had been offered a college lectureship. They signed the lease on Fen Cottage in July of that same year, and three years later Lucie was born. Charlotte had been desperate for a child but didn't fall pregnant easily that first time. The wait made Lucie extra precious somehow: a gift that was meant to perfect them.

Charlotte comes in from the fields as dusk settles. Lucie's cheeks are cold to the touch, and that night she begins to cough. Charlotte hopes it is nothing, just a dry tickle, but it quickly worsens and over the coming days the cough grows louder, short fits turn into long ones, Lucie gasps for breath. She coughs so much after feeding that she vomits. She coughs so much that Charlotte cannot sleep – the sound terrible, the incessant bark, then the pause when there is neither coughing nor breathing, Lucie's eyes bulging and watering, her face turning pink then red, the edges of her lips darkening to blue, and only then, just when Charlotte is about to shake the child from worry, or put her over her shoulder and hit her back to get her breath going again, just then comes the long, moaning, wheezing, sucking sound of an inhalation, followed by dry-retching and the first explosion of sour milk from Lucie's mouth, her tiny body squirming and shuddering with the effort.

The doctor comes and leaves a bottle of red medicine, instructing them to keep her warm. 'I told you so,' says Henry. 'I told you not to take her out in the cold. You've been doing it again, haven't you.' She needs a warmer climate, he says, beginning once more with his plan. The cure is sunshine. Life would be better. *Australians spend their weekends relaxing in the sun.* On and on he goes – rabbiting, Charlotte calls it.

Two weeks later Lucie still hasn't improved and Henry grows more determined. He travels to Australia House in London, where he watches promotional films and gathers more pamphlets. He makes enquiries and reads books, plans dates and marks places on a map. He ponders weather reports like an explorer about to embark on the greatest of journeys. 'I don't know what you're doing with all that,' Charlotte says when she comes upon him late at night, hunched over the kitchen table peering at documents and flyers.

'I'm just making investigations.'

'Nothing will come of it,' she replies, stoking the fire.

'You know it would be for the best,' he says, putting the piece of paper down and trying to meet her eye, but she slips away from him. 'Whose best?' she wants to say, but doesn't. Lucie is his excuse.

'You haven't even glanced at these pictures,' he says. 'You haven't read the pamphlets. If you'd only look—'

—

For days Charlotte paces the cottage with the sick child limp over her shoulder, Lucie's cough exploding in wet, phlegmy barks. When Lucie refuses to eat, the doctor comes again, diagnosing pneumonia. He peers at the child, taps her ribs and listens to her breathing. He weighs and measures her. Then he looks out through the window, towards the damp fields. 'This winter wouldn't be helping,' he says. 'These days each winter seems colder and wetter than the last. Keep her rested. Keep the house dry. I'll be back to check on her tomorrow.'

After the doctor leaves, she and Henry argue. 'You don't know,' Charlotte says. 'You don't know that it will be any better over there.'

'Well it jolly well can't be worse.'

'Don't exaggerate,' she replies. 'The summer will be here soon.' Red poppies will sprout out of nowhere. Teasels and cow parsley will sway in the grasses. The farmlands will be full of broad beans and wheat and yellow flowering rapeseed that grow as tall as her. There is a path running through these. The summer before last, Henry lifted her up so she could see over the top of them. On and on they went, acres of yellow. Everywhere the sound of bees.

'*Is* there an English summer?'

'Oh, Henry. Please.'

'Well, if you'd stop being so damn cheerful.'

'That's not fair.'

'No, of course not – because you're miserable, you're exhausted, which is why we should go, why we can't stay. Don't you see that?

Tell me you can't see that. Think of the coming baby. Of Lucie.'
As if that's not all she thinks of.

She looks away from him. On the far side of the room the washing hangs over the radiators. On the wall next to this the paint flakes and peels with damp. Just the week before, Henry discovered a starry pattern of black mould on the wallpaper behind the armchair where Charlotte nurses Lucie. Henry phoned the landlord and asked him to see to it, but the man explained that it was just the climate and nothing could be done. Their neighbour said he was just a miser. 'I saw him,' she told Charlotte. She'd heard Lucie was ill and so brought her a small stuffed animal. 'I saw him just before you two moved in, painting over a whole wall of black mould. Covering it all up with that glossy paint. Straight over the wallpaper, he did it. I'd come to the door for something, I can't remember what. "You can't do that!" I says when I saw him, and he says, "But look here now, it looks all bright and cheery this way!" and on he went. You just scratch that wall there and you'll see it. The nerve of some people,' she said as she stood at the front door, holding out the yellow toy and jiggling it at the baby's face. The child went cross-eyed trying to focus on the moving object. The neighbour paused a moment and glanced up, nose in the air. 'You can smell it,' she said, her pink nostrils twitching. 'Take one sniff and you can smell that mould. I'd be looking for somewhere else if I was you.'

—

Henry does what he can. He fills the hot water bottles. He gathers wood and keeps the fire burning. He makes endless pots of strong tea. Soon the roads are so bad that he can't ride his bike to the university. Charlotte shovels snow off the garden path. The water in the toilet freezes at night and they have to smash it with a crowbar in the mornings. Then the wind comes up, whistling in beneath the front door. Henry plugs the draft with a towel, but it's too late – that night Lucie's fever worsens and she vomits again. In the morning Charlotte washes the sour-smelling sheets, but there's nowhere to hang them outside, so she drapes them over the dining table and chairs and over the doors. She has a painting to finish, but it's too cold in the shed, so she sets up her easel in the kitchen. In the living room Lucie crawls towards the front door, wailing, then stops and bangs her head against the ground, over and over again. Henry picks her up and tries to calm her. 'Shoosh now, shoosh now,' he says.

He knows he has to get out of the house. The smallness of it, the damp, the feeling – so real – that at any moment he might explode. If it were summer he'd just open the door and plunge into the fields, Alfred running after him. But the house is freezing even though the fire burns. He holds Lucie to his chest and riffles about in the box by the back door, searching for hats and mittens. Everything is a tangle of black and grey. Three mittens in different sizes. Four hats, none of them Lucie's. Henry runs back and forth, fetching, carrying, searching. He puts Lucie in the pram and she starts to cry. It is cold. It is early. He has not had enough tea. He needs his scarf and a handkerchief. Alfred needs his lead. But Henry is already outside when he remembers these things. He will not go back for them now and instead marches out towards the path.

They travel a loop, down through the fields of Manor Farm, then Rectory Farm and over the grounds of Thrift. They pass the old barn, the line of ancient pear trees, the green pond and the wet black meadow ditches. He walks fast, trying to warm himself. The pram bumps along and Lucie whimpers then falls asleep. Henry puts his jacket over her. It is bright outside. Fresh and gusty. Cold and white.

When Henry returns he parks the pram by the back door and collects an armful of wood. Balancing the woodpile with one hand, he opens the door and slips in sideways, careful not to make room for Alfred, all wet and muddy from the walk. Henry kicks the door closed as he steps inside, ducks through the low doorway between the laundry and kitchen, then drops the wood by the stove. But the back door didn't close properly and Alfred runs in behind, catching Henry by surprise as he bends over, stoking the fire. Henry stands and spins round, trying to block the entrance to the living room, but as he does so the new wood, just catching alight, falls to the floor. Henry kicks this towards the hearth tiles as he lunges for the dog; he doesn't see the teapot – a smudge of blue and white – until it's too late, his forearm striking the side of the pot and sending it skidding off the bench. It smashes on the kitchen floor, hot tea spraying across the walls. Alfred leaps into the living room, runs happily towards Charlotte, jumps up and streaks her dressing-gown with muddy paws.

'Henry!' Charlotte cries, when she sees what has happened in the kitchen. Henry looks down, frozen with alarm, the marbled linoleum covered now in tiny pieces of blue and white china. Half a cornflower here. A leaf and stem over there. The teapot belonged to Charlotte's grandmother and is part of a set that Charlotte inherited. It is the only thing her grandmother left her and is, Henry knows, Charlotte's most cherished possession.

'How could you not see it?'

'I did see it, I'm sorry, it was—' He wants to explain that it was an accident, that he was trying to catch the dog, that he had been distracted by the fire, but instead says, 'You shouldn't have left it there, perched on the edge.'

'If you hadn't let Alfred in—'

'I *said* I'm sorry – it was a mistake.'

'You could have closed the door.'

'I thought I had.'

Lucie, still outside in her pram, wakes up and begins to wail. In the kitchen Alfred spins in circles of joy – his long pink tongue hanging out the side of his mouth and his wet tail whacking the doors of the kitchen cupboards. Henry kicks the wall. 'Damn this house,' he spits. 'If it wasn't so small this wouldn't have happened. Look at us,' he says, spreading his arms, 'we're like rabbits in a burrow.' Henry can't swing out his arms without hitting something, breaking something, doing damage. Even the furniture is too large and cumbersome for the space. There is the chesterfield lounge that once belonged to Henry's father, the little round feet knocked off to get it through the door. And the grandfather clock given to them by Charlotte's mother, now relegated to the small damp alcove that functions as the laundry, because it is the only space where the ceiling is high enough for the clock to stand.

Charlotte doesn't reply. The pot is broken. It can't be fixed. What more is there to say? Henry's right, though. The house is too small: Charlotte finds herself permanently blotched with bruises – arms, shins, knees, thighs – where she's bumped into protruding corners of furniture. The drip-dripping of the hot water tap in the kitchen can be heard in every room. Everything in the house is too close. The ceilings are too close. The walls are too close. The doors and windows are too close. The very air is thick and stuffy and too close.

Charlotte crouches down and begins to gather up the pieces of china. The baby is due in three months and she feels it shift. She'd once been consoled by the smallness of the place. It meant there was less to clean and less room in which to make a mess. Now it means that everything just gets dirty faster. Charlotte hates this; she's comforted by order – neatness calms her. The clutter sets her teeth on edge – the narrow kitchen bench crowded with jars of tea and coffee, sugar and biscuits. But it is the filth she can't stand. She sees it now as she scuttles about low down, gathering up the last shards – unidentifiable grime on the linoleum, hard bits of dropped vegetable, the drips of food on the cupboard doors, the residue of oil and tomato sauce on the surface of the cooker.

The spat-out and regurgitated food, the flakes of dried mud from the soles of boots, the windows smeared with thin, greasy finger marks, the debris scattered over the carpet – breadcrumbs, sand, black grit from the chimney – the grey murk of dust condensed along the skirting boards, the brownish hem on the side of the white kitchen door, opened and closed so many times by hands coated in oil, butter and flour that it has developed a varnish-like layer of filth.

Henry stands above her, too close. 'I could get another one, very similar, better. You could choose it, we could—' Charlotte feels her scalp tighten with irritation and senses the first flush of rage blooming on her neck and spreading to her cheeks. She lifts a hand to silence him. 'Just shut up, Henry,' she says, tight-lipped. 'Just shut up.'

Henry closes his mouth and looks on. Alfred has been put outside and now whines at the door, scratches. Charlotte's newly washed hair drips onto her pink robe, leaving a round stain of darker pink across her shoulderblades. Henry can smell the light scent of shampoo – lemon, lavender – a sweet, fruity aroma that cuts through the stale air of the kitchen.

Charlotte blames Henry for the broken pot. Henry blames everything else: the country, the house, the weather. Charlotte stands up with her back to him and tosses the china into the dustbin. He takes a step towards her, reaching out a hand to touch her shoulder, but Charlotte turns as he does so and he misses her. 'If we had more space,' Henry says, 'this wouldn't have happened. If we move—'

Charlotte looks away and twists her hair into a wet knot. He is blocking her exit, his body filling the space between the sink and the bench, and she thinks quickly about how to leave the room without touching him, without being touched.

'We could have a huge house in Australia,' he says. 'A garden. Imagine. We could start again, start over. We could—'

Charlotte pushes past him and takes the stairs to the bedroom. 'Fine,' she says, as she disappears into the narrow stairwell. 'Fine, I'll go.'

The day passes, hectic, apologies withheld on either side. In the evening Henry and Charlotte sit in the living room by the fire. They've managed not to speak since morning, since Charlotte said those words – *Fine, fine, I'll go*. Now Henry does a crossword and Charlotte knits. A yellow cardigan for Lucie, the collar fiddly. She's found some lovely brown leather buttons for the front and is looking forward to seeing them stitched neatly in a row and fastened tight over Lucie's little belly. But now she peers at the row she has just completed, sighs, unstitches, knits again. Charlotte is afraid of what she said. She didn't mean it. She didn't quite not mean it. She doesn't understand the new difficulty of life and wants somehow to escape it – the difficulty, that is, but not the life. The mess, the exhaustion, but not the place. She is tired of him nagging. How to unsay what she said? She is afraid he will take her statement as a clear yes. *Fine, fine*, she'd said. They each wait for the other to speak. To address the question.

It is Henry who breaks the silence. 'Clothes and linen collected before marriage. Nine letters.' He has T something O something S something. 'Any idea?' This gap bothers him – he needs to solve it before he can reach the next answer.

Charlotte never had one of those things, the linen chest. At least he doesn't think so. But maybe she did. That nice damask tablecloth now stained with gravy.

26 down: Wise man (4). *Sage*.

He drifts over the cryptic, his mind bouncing off the clues. Bury lost letters in an earthy way. Chop hard wood. Forced out. Weathers outburst. Lapse. My other. Windy, half heard. He prefers them as hints of a poem. What's the point of an answer?

'Trousseau,' says Charlotte. Very good. They sit close together, the armchairs at a slight angle, facing the fire. Their feet rest on the same footstool, clover-shaped, covered in carpet, turquoise with pink roses. Henry bends his foot to touch Charlotte's, the two of them wearing the woollen socks she knitted by that very fire some winters past. Henry's socks are blue and brown striped, Charlotte's plain red. She leans her foot towards Henry's. A strong gust of wind rattles the windows.

'I do love you,' he says quietly, catching her foot between his. She reaches over, picks up his hand, kisses it. This is the apology. His skin smells of smoke from the fire, soap. She puts his hand down and knits a little more. After a while she says, 'If you find a job. If you find a job, I'll go.'

FINE, SHE'D SAID. *Fine.* Then, on a whim: *You find a job and I'll go.* It was a token only, a conciliatory gesture. She'd thought this condition would make the move impossible. She thought, rashly, that it would be enough to stall him. But he applied for work all over Australia. Then the letter arrived, offering him a job in Perth. *Dear Dr Blackwood, we are delighted to offer you the position of lecturer in English literature . . .* They could travel as sponsored migrants, no need to stay in the hostels and take some god-awful work just to eat. Henry found them a partly furnished house, a car, even a television.

She lies in bed, thinking and listening. It is December, winter is upon them. Across the hall the children sleep. Lucie and the baby, already eight months old – a plump little girl whom they named

May. From outside comes the sound of the wind as it tears through tall field grass, their small white cottage moored in this endless stretch of weedy green. She hears the wind whistling through the keyhole, and at the gaps beneath closed doors. It passes through the worn seals of the windows – the thin current cold on the back of her neck.

What will it look like, she wonders, the new house. She'd seen the blurry black and white photograph of a place surrounded by leaves. Clear sky above. There are four bedrooms, a big garden. There are fruit trees, Henry said. The river nearby. The beach not far.

The floor creaks as the old boards shift with the gale. This is the ship, Charlotte thinks, sleepily – certain she feels the house pitch and sway under the onslaught. But no – that is tomorrow. Tomorrow they leave. Soon she will be at sea and the house empty. It seems impossible and therefore magical – the idea that they will soon find themselves on the far side of the world. One day I will wake up and I will be there, she says to herself, over and over. One day. And *we* will be there. One day.

Beside her Henry dreams, his tongue flailing about in the dark cave of his mouth, trying to make word shapes. A loose, airy string of sounds reaches her as she lies there listening for the moment when she'll need to put a hand upon his shoulder to comfort him – the moment when his half-formed words become an inarticulate cry, preceded, always, by the twitching of his legs as though he were running from something. He always dreams this way. Then she will say, 'You were dreaming,' and he will not remember of what.

Around them the bedroom air is damp and warm, smelling faintly of old apples, fermented and sweet. In the dark, the dormant garden bed bristles under frost. Charlotte thinks of the bulbs nudging the dark loam, of the rosehips and the brown stems of last season's hollyhocks left standing to provide a perch for small birds. She will miss the garden. It is a tiny plot, all mud in winter and little bigger than the rug on the living room floor, but Charlotte had planted it out, tended it, watched for signs.

She moves closer to Henry. Her stomach turns at the thought of leaving – but it is done now, she tells herself. It is done. She has said yes. She said yes because he is her husband. She said yes because she didn't know what else to do. Yes, she said, although she regrets it now – yes, it would be better for the children. She fusses with the pillows, restless, unable to sleep, her mind full of visions. She thinks of the place they're heading for: Perth, City of Light. Charlotte imagines it – a bright speck on the edge of the world, glimpsed from space. The most isolated city in the most isolated continent. 'But of all Australian cities,' Henry told her, 'it is the closest one to England.'

'And that's meant to comfort?' she replied.

She imagines it to be a city rising out of red desert, with kangaroos hopping down the main street. She imagines savages with bones through the cartilage of their noses and spears in hand coming to greet them at the port. She has read this – that such people live there – and that they themselves, the Blackwoods, may have to survive without electricity or running water. She does not tell Henry these fears. She wants to be brave. He has assured her that it will be just like England, only a little different. There will be plenty of sunshine and cheap meat.

Henry's breathing quietens. His tongue falls still, soft against the floor of his mouth. His hands rest beside his head as if in prayer. She moves her face closer to his – his breath gusts, warm and slightly rancid. She can hear his watch ticking. It is an old watch that his father gave him. It has gold hands, roman numerals. Each night he wears this watch to bed, although he cannot possibly see what time it is in the dark. She listens to the tick tick tick and when sleep finally comes she dreams.

In the dream she is in hiding. She is in an attic and outside there is a war. The guns go click click click. Distant, but still too close. The other man hiding in the attic with her had escaped through the roof, pushing out a skylight, but she was afraid that if she stood on the roof she would be shot. Eventually Henry comes for her and they kiss. It has been so long since they have kissed. Her whole body softens towards him. He puts one hand to her back and takes hold of her long hair with the other. Their mouths press hard. When he pulls away he says, 'I have brought you food and water. There is a car waiting.' She doesn't know how they will drive away and says this and starts to cry. She doesn't know where they are. How they got there. What country. He kisses her again. His mouth is so soft, his tongue laps and flicks at hers. His lips are even softer, warmer, than she remembers. Again there is the sound of gunfire. She is wearing a purple dress. His hands move up and underneath the silky fabric. 'Don't worry,' says Henry, 'there is a road.' There is a road. It is a bright hot day. They do not know where the road goes.

———

The sky is still dark when Charlotte sits on the edge of the bed in the morning, frowning into a small mirror. The house is almost empty – all that remains are the items belonging to the landlord: the beds, the kitchen table and chairs, a set of cheap crockery. They made sure to sell all the belongings that were not worth the cost of shipping, and had sold, too, many things they wished they could have kept: books they could not afford to send, a Victorian needlepoint lady's chair, an ornate mirror that Henry was too superstitious to ship. In the end they sent the sofa and armchairs, a mahogany sideboard, the writing desk, the grandfather clock and Charlotte's dressing table. They packed their wedding gifts: silver cutlery, the Wedgwood dinner set, a Gibsons tea set, floor rugs and framed photographs, a green glass punchbowl and vase.

She twists her hair into a bun then powders her cheeks and nose. Her pale hand flickers over her face, applying lipstick and fastening her earrings. The left. The right. Downstairs Henry plays with the children. Their delighted squeals ricochet through the kitchen and up to the bedroom. Charlotte checks her watch. Nearly eight. She must hurry; the taxi is picking them up at half past and driving them to the station, where they will catch a train to London, then the official train to the Port of Tilbury. She dabs perfume behind each ear then slowly buttons her blouse, broken images surfacing and cutting across her vision, distracting her. A purple dress. A dirt road. She thinks of these things as she tugs on a skirt and cardigan, then pushes her feet into a pair of sensible shoes, the dream troubling, half forgotten.

As she comes down the stairs Charlotte hears the children's happy squeals escalate and collapse into sobs. Lucie sits on the kitchen floor, clutching Alfred to her sweaty little chest and wailing; he cannot come with them and is to be donated to Frankie, the unfortunate-looking boy who lives nearby. Lucie is inconsolable and too choked up to swallow her breakfast. A lump of toast is lodged in the side of her mouth. As she cries, bits of soggy bread fall out onto the floor. 'Your turn,' Henry says to Charlotte. Charlotte takes Lucie's plate from his hands and kneels down beside her daughter while Henry paces by the front door; the taxi is due soon and he's certain it will be late. In the background May starts screaming for milk.

When the taxi still hasn't arrived by quarter to nine, Henry starts to curse. 'Damned drivers,' he mutters. 'You'd think they could have – I should have known – when the boat's due to leave—' Charlotte is in the kitchen, helping Lucie into her coat. Henry's voice rises and falls as he marches towards the door and back the other way. Here he is again, coming towards them.

'Two more minutes and I'll have to call them. I'll give them a—' Henry sneezes. He'd come down with a cold a few days earlier and now pulls a large striped handkerchief from his trouser pocket, shakes it out and blows his nose. Once. Twice. It sounds like a trumpet.

'Again? Do it again?' Lucie asks.

Henry folds the handkerchief and pushes it deep into his pocket. He is exhausted. The last months have been a flurry of train rides to and from London, organising bank accounts, arranging the sale of the car, renewing their passports, firing off telegrams, arranging removalists and accommodation, to say nothing of planning for his new job: a lectureship at a sandstone university by the river. All Henry wants to do now is lie down and stay very still for a very, very long time. He leans his forehead against the glass panelling of the front door. He feels the cold coming through the keyhole. He feels it lower down, on his ankles, as it leaks in over the floor. He closes his eyes. And then he hears it. The tyres crunching to a halt over the loose bitumen beside the front gate.

Henry dashes out with the suitcases. Charlotte ushers Lucie from the kitchen and towards the vehicle. May wails in Charlotte's arms. The driver loads the boot and Henry takes the baby while Charlotte runs back inside to fetch her handbag and Henry's hat.

On her way out she stops to take one last glance about the living room. Her footfalls echo. The sunlight plays over empty walls. The cottage feels larger, brighter. Perhaps they might have stayed. They do not have to go. She feels sadness everywhere she looks, memories everywhere she looks. It is their home. Suddenly it is not their home. She does not know how to make sense of this.

She thinks of Lucie standing on the windowsill and watching the winter birds, of May lying on her back and cooing at the leaves of the potted geranium that wavered above her head in the mild autumn breeze. Without warning her eyes start to sting with tears and her throat burns. Henry calls her name.

'Charlotte? Charlotte – we need to go!'

She steps outside, pulls the door shut and puts the key through the brass flap of the letterbox for the landlord to collect. Then she turns away.

The weather changes as the taxi pulls out from the house. It is just a light fall at first, but as the car moves into the countryside the rain comes fast, drumming against the windscreen. All about is the light hush of water: the wheels turning over the wet road, the rain on the metal roof and on the bonnet and on the glass. Silver rivulets course over the surface of the window. Inside, the mist from their warm breath begins to swallow up the view. Charlotte pulls the sleeve of her cardigan down over her hand and wipes a circle clear, then opens her palm and presses her fingers against the passing scene: the waterlogged fields, the haze of winter trees in the distance – apple and ash, hawthorn and hazel. Past the greenery – the hedges of holly and common box, the ivy strangling the high walls of the occasional cottage and the low walls of the villages, of Saffron Walden and Harlow. Lights shine in some of the windows. Just a small yellow blur and they are gone.

Charlotte shifts May onto the other side of her lap. Lucie turns the pages of a picture book. Henry rides in front, although he doesn't talk to the driver. He'd been so cheerful in the days leading up to their departure, when the life that he had chosen for his family stood ahead of them. Now that they are on their way he is silent, his elbow resting against the edge of the window, a loose fist pressed against his mouth, his gaze jumping from one passing object to another.

They step off the train at Tilbury to find the huge white boat towering over them, *Castel Felice* painted on the side in large gold letters. The dock swarms with people. Beside the gangplank a brass band plays bright tunes: songs from *Oliver* and *The Sound of Music*. The conductor – a jaunty little man in a blue suit, the silver buttons of his jacket fastened over a firm round belly – flaps and prods his baton, smiling and red-faced despite the drizzle. The instruments shine in the rain.

Charlotte never believed this moment would arrive. She always hoped, always felt sure, that something would occur to prevent it. They would not go. They could not go. It would not happen. Yet now the moment is before her; she begins to weep. She does not mean to but once she has begun she cannot stop. She wishes her mother were here. She wishes she had not, after all, forbidden her to see them off. Charlotte cannot help it: she sobs into her gloved palm, Lucie clinging to her free hand.

Henry holds May in his arms – the crowd pressing and jostling against them as they wait to board. He wishes his wife would not cry now, not in front of the children, for whom he wants this departure to be an uncomplicated, happy experience. If only Charlotte would not cry. There is the clacking of her bracelets as she wipes her face. The waft of her rose perfume.

Part of him wishes he could feel this sadness with her – that there was a place he, too, wished never to leave. He remembers this from a long time ago: a different boat pulling out from a different port. His mother crying. Crowds, smoke, the heat. Birds circling in the sky. In the heart of the country there were fields of marigolds. Elsewhere, high mountains of green camellia. He used to long for these things. But such memories are old and worn now, emptied of real power. For a moment he envies Charlotte's loss, then quickly pushes this feeling away.

For him, England has always been a land of fairytales: a world of pictures, of black and white sketches depicting pale, chubby children eating currant buns. A land of fairies and witches, hedgerows and secret gardens, goblins and magical woods. When he arrived here he was surprised to find it looked almost exactly as it did in the stories. The trees, the meadows, the little brick houses. He had not come to a real country but to a story come to life. Every day, then, he woke to a fantasy. And no matter how solid and cold and uncomfortable it was, he could never feel it was a country as such, could never quite believe that it had been formed from the same molten stuff that had made his birthplace. England was always secondary, always derivative, always an after-effect of a story. Perhaps this is why, now, he can decide to leave it.

He realises that the girls are staring silently at their mother. Mascara-blackened tears course down her cheeks. Again Charlotte wipes at her face with a sleeve, her eyes flitting away from the gaze of her family. Happiness is related to cheerfulness, Henry reasons, looking at his sad wife. Not the same, but near enough to be mistaken – for cheerfulness to be wrongly taken as a sign of happiness. Henry wishes the girls would look somewhere else – all of a sudden cheerfulness is imperative. To distract his children Henry mimics the happiness he no longer feels sure he can possess. He knows he ought to take Charlotte's hand but is afraid of touching her. He is afraid of the sadness he has caused. Instead he hoists May onto his shoulders and takes Lucie by the hand. He throws coins to the buskers, smiles, waves. May lifts her chubby arms above her head. She laughs and bounces.

The four of them board the *Castel Felice* and find a space on deck from where they can look out over the railings towards the shore and the crowd. Charlotte feels the engine begin to rumble beneath her, and sees the grimy ocean start to churn. Visitors are asked to leave the boat and the gangplank is pulled aboard. Thick coils of brown rope are lifted away from the pilings and a horn sounds before a jet of black smoke is released into the air. People ashore cry and wave, some run towards the ship, others turn away. There are whistles, hoots and calls. Paper streamers in bright shades of pink, blue and green are thrown down from the deck and strings of coloured flags sway between the masts. Passengers cast flowers into the crowd and bystanders toss their hats in the air, while a young woman in a polka-dot neck scarf stands weeping on the pier, pressing a pale handkerchief to a red mouth. Onboard, a small child in a grey coat and pink shoes jumps up and down in an attempt to see over the boat's railing, wanting to take a last look at the country she will soon hardly recall.

As the ship prepares to leave, Henry raises his arm, to everyone and no one in particular. It is hard to tell whether his loose wave is a gesture made in greeting or farewell, a hello that says, simultaneously, goodbye.

Charlotte stands beside him, looking out, wanting to remember the scene in every detail, knowing she will forget. The colours, the shapes, the round, white faces of her country's people. Over this the smells: fish, smoke, wet concrete, damp wool and dog. The low cloud keeping the odours close. There are the grey and brown brick shopfronts and behind these, out of sight, the green land – the place of meadow and field, oak and birch, aspen and yew.

She looks out and tries to remember all this for her children, so that she can tell them what it was like. She knows they too will forget, as one forgets, in winter, the brightness of summertime. Events are compressed, days forgotten. In the mind one jumps from one intensity to another, the hours in between elided and lost. It is the failure of life to stand out. As the ship pulls away the bright streamers begin to snap. One after another they tighten and break, the tail ends fluttering down into dark water. Red and yellow, blue and pink, until finally the ship is free. They sail down through the locks, out into the North Sea and south along the coastline. Night comes and snow falls, covering the shoulders of Henry's coat as he stands on deck, taking his last look at England, the white lights of Dover shining and blinking then burning out.

Part Two

LANDFALL

Perth, 1965

THEY SAIL SOUTH over the Atlantic and through the Mediterranean. When the boat docks in Port Said, people in dark robes climb on board with baskets of goods. There are smells that Henry does and does not recognise. Fish. Spices. It is night-time when they pass through the Suez Canal. Later there is Ceylon and the family leave the boat. They go to a market and Henry shows them the fruit he used to eat as a boy: mango, custard apple, persimmon. He bites the tough skin off a lychee and holds the fruit out to Charlotte. She opens her mouth, and as the fruit releases its flavour she thinks back over the many Christmases that she has wrapped an orange in tissue paper and placed it carefully in the bottom of her husband's stocking. All of a sudden an orange no longer seems exotic, but plain and sour. Henry buys a pair of sunglasses from another stall, then they take a taxi through the streets and get lost, making it back to the boat just before it sails. Not long after this they cross the equator; there is a party and the captain of the ship dresses up as King Neptune. He presents the children with a certificate proving their initiation into the Solemn Mysteries of the Ancient Order of the Deep, the document signed by the king and his servants. The girls are fed watermelon and ice cream, and entertained by a friendly steward in the playroom while Henry and Charlotte dance.

At night the cabins are unbearably hot; some have taken to sleeping on the deck. Early one morning another ship, returning to England, passes at a distance. The passengers call to one another, but the signs are not good – those on the returning ship wave in the direction of Europe, some swinging their arms in a cross above their heads as if to say stop, go no further. But then the ships move away from each other, Charlotte forgets the encounter and a few days later they see land.

Charlotte and Henry stand on deck, watching the new country come into view: a distant line of flat brown sand, a row of pine trees that look at first like a series of small dark triangles. As the ship moves closer they glimpse red-tiled roofs and white houses, dipping and wobbling in a sheen of heat. The country grows larger and people scramble to get a view. Charlotte glances up: the sun is a tiny white speck in the blue sky, but its power is monumental. Heat is everywhere, pressing down on her shoulders, throbbing beneath her skin, burning her face. Her cotton smock clings to the sweat on her back. A dry wind blows from the shore and the boat slows. She clutches her hat to her head. She can see no cars. She can see no people. What had she expected? An RAAF band playing, a welcome party with flowers?

They disembark and join the queue for the buses that are to take them to the migrant reception centre. The line is long and slow-moving. They shuffle, then stop. Then shuffle, and stop again. How long do they wait? Half an hour, an hour? It is hard to tell. Charlotte watches the sun lift itself up into the very centre of the sky. Her hands are red and swollen, her feet tight in her shoes. Small black flies swarm at their backs and faces. Charlotte flicks them away, only to look down and see the same insects clustered over Lucie's mouth so that her lips cannot be seen at all. There is no shade, no water. Charlotte feels herself growing faint. May begins to cry, her little face red as a pomegranate. Lucie needs to go to the toilet. The queue stops moving again and others around them start to grumble. From where she stands Charlotte sees the luggage lifted from the cargo hold in huge green nets, all the goods of their English lives hauled out like a sack of refuse. The ground tilts and sways. Charlotte grips Henry's hand.

Finally it is their turn; they step up onto the bus. It is old and dusty, with broken seats and windows that rattle in their frames. They've eaten nothing since breakfast and the children whimper as the vehicle makes its way through a country of sand. Cottages with wide verandahs litter the roadside. Geraniums and palm trees sprout from the dust. There are no people. They've seen no people. The bus bumps along.

Then it appears before them, although they don't know what it is at first: a metal shed with a hole in one end like a winter pen for animals. Everyone clambers out of the bus and they are told to make their way inside. From here they are to collect their luggage – Charlotte and Henry will then be free to go, but those travelling without sponsorship will have to catch another bus to the migrant hostel. Inside, the shed is dark and hot, and the small door lets in no air. Children and pregnant women faint, while around them other migrants push and scuffle, looking for their possessions. Luggage is strewn along the walls and people are crawling among the bags and trunks as they try to gather up their belongings. A large woman sits on the ground and weeps as she berates her husband. *What were you thinking? Why here? Would you look at this? Cattle!* A wiry girl in a Salvation Army uniform rushes about offering people tea in little paper cups too hot to hold, and a large, heavy-jowled, red-skinned man stands at the entrance to the shed and barks out names: *Barnes! Bertrand! Bunning!* Yes sir, yes sir, the respondents say, dashing forwards and climbing onto the next dusty old bus that is to drive them to the hostel in Swanbourne.

It is 105 degrees in the shade. Charlotte watches the bus fill up, glad she is not among that crowd; she's heard the stories, of families sharing a tin shed for months on end, of people just waiting until their two years are up and they can sail home again without having to repay their outward fare. These are the people who came without jobs. Not like her and Henry. There are rumours of contaminated water, infestations, insufficient food. Charlotte watches the bus lumber off then feels Henry pushing at her back, ushering her towards the taxi, his hand on her head as she ducks into the back seat. 'Seventeen Chester Road, Rose Cove, please,' he says, once everybody is in, and the driver nods.

It seems a long drive, from the water to the suburbs. Later it will feel no distance at all. But everything seems so strange at first – the wide streets, the cloudless sky, the way the leaves hang lank on the trees. She'd seen no real pictures, had no idea. 'Almost there now,' Henry says as the car makes its slow way. They pass wide brown lawns, and sun-bleached shopfronts – red letters now pink, yellow letters white. On either side of them the road disappears into sand.

'Almost there,' Henry says again, leaning his face out the window. He feels warm air against his cheek and breathes in, catching the smell of eucalyptus, cut grass. The air feels light in his lungs: dry and salty. The sky is high and liquid above the trees. They turn a corner, then Henry points and says something to the driver. The taxi slows, pulling up beside a white picket fence in the shade of a red flowering tree. 'This is it,' Henry calls, jubilant. He pays the driver, swings himself out of the car, then bends down and lifts the children from their seats. The driver takes the luggage from the boot as Henry and the children move towards the house. 'You coming, Charlotte?' he calls over his shoulder, his hand on the front gate.

'Yes, just a minute,' she says, stepping away from the taxi and slowly brushing down her dress. The taxi drives off and Charlotte watches Henry walk into the bright light of the garden then disappear around the side of the house.

⌒

Henry stands in the backyard and wipes his sweaty palms on his trousers; he is unsettled, but doesn't want Charlotte to know this. She didn't see the way the taxi driver looked him up and down just now. Nor did she hear what the Australian ship officer said to him the morning they docked at Ceylon: 'Well, sir, I expect you'll be leaving us here?' It makes him worry.

In the garden, the horizon stretches away on either side. One ought always to be thankful, he thinks, as he pushes his hands into his pockets. Now here he is, in the land of opportunity. Lucie runs in circles crying out with delight: it is a kind of space she's never seen before, while May blinks and stares – entranced by the tree shadows playing over the ground. He rocks back on his heels and looks to the sky – so big it makes him giddy.

'Poms, are you?' the taxi driver asked, his tone doubtful. 'Poor bloody prisoners of Mother England,' he said, checking the side mirror before turning back to inspect Henry more closely, an eyebrow raised.

Such interactions have been few, but the force of them never lessens. In London there was the landlord who told him across the door chain that the room had just been taken, and the secretary at the tennis club who inspected his driver's licence a little too closely when he went to fill out a membership form, looking at the photograph, then looking at Henry, then looking at the photograph again. And that encounter, years ago, when he and

Charlotte travelled to the north of India to visit Henry's mother. They were waiting for the Toy Train and his watch had stopped. 'Excuse me, chaps, but do you have the time?' he said to a couple of British tourists. They stared at him, mute, as if they had not expected him to speak English. Afterwards, when they thought he was out of earshot, he heard them laughing. *Chaps! Chaps!* they called to each other in jest: a British word they thought him unfit to use. Charlotte had blushed and pretended not to notice.

Henry realises that his hands are clenched into fists. He takes them out of his pockets, crouches down to the ground and pushes his fingers into the dirt. Sand, all sand. Yellow sand, grey sand, and what looks like rust but is really red sand, blown up against the side of the house. He wants to be grateful; he wants not to waste things. This is, after all, how he and Charlotte live. Everything used and reused and nothing unnecessary; plastic bags, heels of bread, the last spoonful of sugary milk at the bottom of the cereal bowl. There is nothing that can't be fixed or find a purpose. 'Come on, Charlotte!' he calls. 'Shake a leg!' He wants her near him. If she is near him, he thinks, it will be all right.

The house is made of weatherboard, painted pink with green awnings and surrounded by a long verandah. A tangled mass of wisteria and red bougainvillea flanks the verandah and shades the front windows. Bright green vines wrestle for space, clambering up the walls, over the gutters and into the chimney. From a distance she hears Henry calling her. *Charlotte? Are you coming? Come and see this.* Everything is wild and hot. Dry and wild. Hot and dry. But she does not want to be the thing that disappoints him. Then it will be my fault, she thinks, the failure will belong to me. *Charlotte?* he calls again. May wails in the distance. She will go into the garden for the children. He knows she will go for them. 'I'm coming, May,' she calls. 'Mummy's coming.'

She finds Henry standing in the middle of an old vegetable bed, now overtaken by sand and the brown runners of buffalo grass. He is digging the tip of his shoe into the ground, snapping off bits of leaf and sniffing them. She picks May up off the ground. 'Would you look at all this!' Henry exclaims, spreading out his arms. Lucie stands next to him, holding on to the cloth of his trousers. 'We'll plant tomatoes over there, along that fence,' he says, pointing. 'And lettuce near that tree, and—'

Charlotte doesn't hear the rest of his sentence. It doesn't matter, he is talking to the children anyway. She wanders over to the edge of the yard, looking for flowers. Henry's voice drifts towards her. *A bit of water is all the lawn needs.* He sounds ridiculous now; the grass looks like the mangy pelt of a dog, scratched and balding. Two ailing parsley plants on their way to seed and an overgrown, woody clump of rosemary are the only remaining vegetation. He'll see to it, he tells her, coming up behind and placing a hand on her shoulder.

Their shadows merge on the ground. 'How will the light fall?' Henry wonders aloud. 'Where will there be most shade?' These are the things he must find out. Charlotte can tell that he wants to keep her spirits up, to get her thinking about everything that can be done. True, it doesn't look like the picture he was sent, but they'll fix it. 'There's nothing that can't be changed,' Henry says. Charlotte is quiet. A breeze eddies in, carrying the smell of the sea and rustling the tall weeds. Silver gulls come on the back of it, their mewing calls first, then their darting shadows against the bright sky. They pass quickly over the iron roof, then rise up, coast above the high tips of the pines and head back to water. Charlotte goes inside.

It takes a moment for her eyes to adjust to the dimness, her focus swinging in and out as the walls and floor float into position. She's standing in the living room. There's the dark wooden floor, a high white ceiling with pressed metal flowers, then the hall, shadowy, running through to the back of the house, past the bedrooms and into the sun-filled kitchen. A gust of wind rattles the windows and comes up through the gaps in the floorboards. Thin air moves through the hall, lifting Charlotte's dress. She puts her hands against her thighs, pushing the fabric down. The house is hot; above her the roof creaks and pops in the sun. Except for the kitchen, the rooms are dark and stuffy, the air sharp with the stink of animal urine – mouse and cat. She moves through the house, opening the curtains. The first bedroom, the second, a haze of dust specks floating up on the bright shaft of white window light. She returns to the kitchen and looks out. Henry is there, in the backyard, swinging Lucie in wide circles. He holds her hands, lifts his elbows and turns round and round very fast, Lucie's feet coming off the ground as she swings out, loose, her face thrown up towards the sky, her hair fanning, eyes closed. Henry turns once, twice, three times, Lucie laughing and squealing then stumbling, giddy, over the brown grass.

Charlotte leans against the sink and closes her eyes. She listens to the sound of them. Her children's voices. So small and high. They are giggling, yelping. Their voices lift up and vanish into the trees. Charlotte feels a sharp tenderness, instant happiness at their happiness. Gratitude that Henry can make them so. She opens her eyes and he is there: being silly, pulling his jaw down in a funny monster face and stomping after the children, who wobble, trip and crawl across the yard. Drool. Red faces. Screeching. She laughs and the sound bounces off the closed window. She heaves it open, the frames stuck together slightly with glossy paint. She must trust him, she thinks, she must believe what he says. The garden air smells good: sweet, warm, thick with pollen. Henry hears the rattle of the window and turns round, smiling and waving, pausing in the game a moment. His big smile. Then he hunches his shoulders, lifts his hands into claws and chases after the children once more.

Their first evening in the house is the hottest she has known. All the windows are open but outside the dusk air is still. While the potatoes boil for dinner Charlotte sits in the green scratchy armchair sipping tea and feels the fabric beneath her thighs grow damp with sweat. Ants mass along the kitchen wall above the sink.

Henry sprays them and they disperse, only for another group to gather along the window ledge. Charlotte feels her whole body swollen with heat. Her legs, her feet in their strappy sandals. Her ankles are red with mosquito bites. She unclips her bra and pulls it off through the armhole of her shirt-dress, sweat dripping down from the fold beneath her breasts. The first throb of a headache is beginning. She rubs her forehead, her face slippery with sweat, and then pours more tea. What did her mother used to say? Ladies don't sweat or perspire – they glow. Her whole body is wet and sticky. Behind her knees, across the bridge of her nose, down her neck, all over the soft skin of her stomach. Further away there is the sound of flyscreen doors opening and snapping closed. Voices. Crickets. A bird flitting past. There is the smell of burning toast drifting across from next door and the sound of a breeze beginning to stir in the trees.

In the kitchen Henry fries sausages. They eat bangers and mash for dinner, and after the plates are cleared they all go down to the river. Charlotte looks out over the glassy, violet water stretching on for miles and imagines the silvery expanse of the damp fields she left behind. The river begins to glow as darkness falls on the land around it. The rushes and the she-oaks that cluster along the water's edge turn black as the sky shifts to orange then mauve. Beneath it, the river lies smooth as pearl and shines the colour of saffron; golds and pinks marble its silky length. Henry sees the river and in the back of his mind all the skies of the Indian plains come to life once more. The cinnamon and the gold and the pale, clear blue.

It happens like a chemical reaction: the sight of the new country immediately provoking a memory of the old. As though the two of them, he and Charlotte, can only see this new place through a veil of remembered ones – its differences noted, its similarities observed, the whole of it assessed and judged in light of where they have been before. Life builds on life. Only May and Lucie will ever see the river with anything like an original eye.

May looks out from on high, clinging fast to Henry's neck. Lucie wades forwards then lands on her bottom, splat in the water. Charlotte tugs off Lucie's wet trousers and lets the child waddle along the shore, the night breeze tickling her legs and belly. Henry takes Charlotte's hand and they follow behind, trailing their feet in the sand. Up ahead, two barrel-shaped women in armoured bathing suits march towards them, their feet clomping through the water, while in the distance Charlotte can make out the shape of a small boy and his father paddling in the white-flecked shallows. The air smells of fried meat and insect repellent, the residue of evening barbecues, of chops and mosquitoes, while the river gives off another smell, salty and vegetable, as the reeds and mangroves rot in the marsh. Further out a family of ducks sail across to the bushland on the other bank, leaving great sweeping lines in the still water, their bodies black against the sunset. Fish follow in their wake, a silver flash here and there as they break the surface and smack back into the wet.

—

Later, once the children have been put to bed, Charlotte sits out on the verandah listening to the drift of voices from next door. A mother and an adult daughter. They are eating a late dinner in the garden, the lilt of their conversation coming from the deep green. There is the sound of knives and forks on china. The mother's voice is old, warbling, slower than the daughter's talk, the two voices weaving together, the murmurs of the older listening woman mixed with the more varied melody of the younger woman telling the story. 'Considering his condition . . .' says the older voice. 'But life isn't like that,' replies the daughter. Around them dark settles. Mosquitoes nip at Charlotte's legs. She thinks of her own mother, alone in Highgate. Life isn't like what? she wonders. What is life like? They live together, Henry said, the mother and daughter. He said hello over the fence, when he was poking about in the garden. Mountainous clouds float overhead, close to the treetops. The women next door laugh. More tapping at plates. A long silence. She should go and introduce herself. But it is the wrong time of day – she is afraid of interrupting. Henry says he saw the older woman knitting in the sunshine. They have two cats that he spotted digging in the bare vegetable bed. Charlotte tucks her feet up under her dress. Across the way a screen door smacks shut. A light goes on. She hears plates knocked against the edge of a bin and scraped. Henry comes out, sits down in the chair next to her. They look at the yard.

'Have you had a bath?' he asks.

'Not yet.' Always this pleasure between them, sharing the bath, each washing the other's back, their wet, soapy bodies held close. Her mouth pressed to the wet curve of his neck. The taste of his skin. Sweat and clean water. Of course he knows she hasn't bathed. It is his way of asking if she'd like to. When did this ritual start? Just before she fell pregnant with Lucie, in the summer they spent digging over the garden at the cottage, the two of them filthy by the end of the day. 'I'll run the water,' he says.

When he calls for her, Charlotte comes in from the verandah, takes off her dress then sinks down into the tub. Henry gets in too, the water sloshing over onto the floor. Afterwards they make love in the dark, the bedroom window open, the late breeze moving over Charlotte's back as she rocks on top of him, his hands against her breasts. There is sand in the sheets, from the traces still caught between their toes, from the river. Sand on the floorboards of the house. Sand in their clothes. Go on, he'd said. Take off your shoes. The cold water. The silt. The smell of weeds and fish.

Through the open window comes the sound of crickets singing. She feels Henry's breath hot against her neck, the tightening of his arms around her. His mouth is open against her shoulder. His teeth at her skin. They are the same person then, she thinks. I am the same. 'I love you,' she says, the feeling inside her rising. In that moment it does not matter where they are, where they have come to. In that moment she does not know, cannot remember.

In the morning Henry reaches over and strokes her hair. Charlotte smiles. He thinks she has come back to him: that here she will be different, no longer the thin, sickly woman who paced the fields.

'Did the light wake you?' he asks.

'Yes,' she replies. 'It's so bright.'

There is the sound of wind rising and falling in the trees. A bird call. The distant horn of a train as it pulls out from the station. Henry gets up to make tea. He likes the quiet of the early morning, padding through the house while the children sleep. It is good, too, to commence the day with this act of service. It always feels like an ablution. Charlotte loves him for the tea and he loves her for her gratitude. Over time he has learned to make the tea exactly as she likes it. Very hot, but quite milky, yet strong at the same time.

He fills the kettle and sets it to boil on the stovetop. While he waits for the water to heat he steps out through the back door, into the garden. A thick mass of dry buffalo grass stretches towards the far edge, ending at a line of bright green banana trees. A warm breeze brushes his skin. Above him the leaves on the trees move up and down, around, side to side. The cicadas are inside the trees, shrieking, and every time the wind gusts they seem louder, closer. Behind the trees stands a wire fence with a red iron gate in the middle. A sandy path meanders away from the gate, leading down behind the backs of houses, through low-lying bushland and on towards the river. The sun rises this way, entering the yard over the high fence crowded with purple-flowering potato vine. The sea is in the other direction. Inside, the kettle begins to whistle and

Henry dashes in towards the stove, the flyscreen door banging shut behind him.

He warms the pot, stainless steel and dented on one side, then takes a tin from the pantry and measures out the tea leaves. One spoon, two spoons, three. He pours in the water, replaces the lid and eases the tea cosy over the handle and spout as though pulling a bonnet onto a baby. He brews the tea then places the pot, cups and milk jug on an enamel tray patterned with red and white roses. He shuffles towards the bedroom, sets the tray down on the bedside table, turns the pot three times clockwise and balances the silver tea strainer on the rim of the first cup. He lifts the pot and pours. A stream of amber liquid tumbles into the strainer where it pools and glints. Steam rises from the water's surface. Charlotte lifts herself up onto the pillows, leans over and turns on the radio.

TIME PASSES DIFFERENTLY in a new place; there are differences of wind and light that change the feeling of time. And there are things Charlotte must find out – the whereabouts of shops, libraries, parks – that change the feeling of space. Little things take a long time: finding marmalade in the grocery store, finding her way to the post office to send a letter home. Everything is hot and bright and far apart. She would ask for help, for directions, but has trouble understanding the answers, deciphering the mash of vowels. By accident she discovers Penguin books and Kellogg's cornflakes, Ajax laundry detergent and Imperial Leather soap: things she knows from home. When she finds these things she feels sudden comfort, sudden sadness – a mix of feeling a long way away and very close. Little things that are familiar but which rightly belong somewhere else. She buys these things and brings them back, and says to Henry, 'Look, I found things from home,' realising as she speaks that she still calls England home, and doesn't know what to call this new place that is, now, also home.

Months pass. The March mornings are beautiful – golden and full of bird calls. Charlotte lies in bed for as long as she can, sometimes bringing May in with her while Lucie sleeps. She lies there, listening, wanting to know what the birds are called and which song belongs to which bird. She has spotted a little bird with a stripe of fluorescent blue on its chest – a wren, perhaps – and a pink bird with a white crest. She will go to the library, she thinks, borrow a book on such things. She still has to carry a map so as to find the library. But she won't go today – their shipment of furniture and boxes has finally arrived and she must unpack. Already the bedroom is warm from the sun. 'It will be hot today, *a scorcher*,' Henry says, as he comes into the bedroom.

He's all freshly showered and shaven – a towel wrapped around his waist. There is a spattering of dark freckles over his shoulders, a fine mesh of hair across his chest. He rubs his jaw, checking for smoothness, and takes a clean shirt from the wardrobe. He's been up since dawn, revising an essay, and skips breakfast these days, preferring to get to work early. Because of the heat Henry wears shorts to work. They are navy blue, with a crease ironed down the front and back. Charlotte had never seen him wear shorts to work before, and she teases him; his legs are long, his knees knobbly. Henry is pulling up his socks now, smoothing back his hair. It is time for him to go. He opens the window so she can better hear the birds and then kisses her goodbye.

Charlotte pulls the covers to her chin and rolls over. She hears the front door close, then the car starting. She can't understand why he sits there, warming the engine, when it's already so hot outside. Around her the house is quiet, her children still asleep. It is not often that they sleep this long, through the brightness of the early morning. Charlotte wills them to stay this way: only when they are sleeping does she feel their consciousness detach from her own, her mind a free and drifting thing. In these moments the air about her seems full, radiant – time becomes untethered. There is no waiting, no urgency, no boredom. The wild swings between these states of being wear her down: this is what it is, she understands now, to care for a child. She thinks about the day ahead and feels tired, more tired, heavy in the limbs. The vigilance is exhausting: the things May will put in her mouth – a dead cockroach, a snail shell – and Lucie's stories that always demand a response. All this watching and talking.

There is a certain English dormouse, Charlotte remembers, which, upon ending its hibernation, comes out of its burrow and checks the air; if it deems the weather not good enough it retreats and sleeps for another year. How time passes differently for different creatures. Her days are long – the light makes them more so, the hours stretching on in either direction, the dawn too early, the dusk too late. Lucie turned two the other week. Charlotte baked a chocolate cake and they lit candles and sang. But Lucie didn't know what to do when it came to blowing the little flames out and sat there, hypnotised. After a long pause Henry huffed and puffed, making a show of it, and the flames were gone.

Henry releases the handbrake and reverses out of the drive. It's only seven fifteen, he should be settled at his desk by half past. He likes to be in before the other staff. Otherwise there are so many *hello*s and *good morning*s that by the time he puts pen to paper he's lost his train of thought. It makes him nervous, too, walking down the green corridor, with all the office doors half open. Did it mean they wanted him to say good morning, or not? Would it bother them if he did? Would it be rude if he walked past? No one, yet, has been exactly friendly. Officially welcoming, perhaps, but not friendly. It isn't the scene the brochures promised, with barbecues in the backyard and the neighbours dropping by with a casserole for dinner. And there had been that awkward introduction with his boss, Collins, when he stopped by the office on Henry's first day.

How was the move, Collins had asked, and are you settling in all right, hope you're comfortable. If there's anything I can do, and so on and so forth. Then the question: 'So, where did you say you're from?'

'England,' Henry replied.

'Yes, yes, of course,' said Collins, pausing. 'But where were you born?'

Henry didn't want to answer this question. His family had always been English, even in India. Especially in India. But Collins wouldn't understand this, and he couldn't lie. He waited a moment, staring at Collins as though he didn't understand the question, then opened his mouth. 'India,' he said, pushing his hands into his pockets and rocking back on his heels. 'I was born in India.'

'Oh?' Collins said. 'Yes, of course,' he repeated. 'I thought it must have been something like that. Very well then,' he said, backing out of the door. 'Have a good day.'

A week or so later, Collins came by again. 'Don't you have a place to go?' he quipped. 'Do you sleep under the desk?' Was he being funny? Henry wasn't sure. He must have looked quizzical, for Collins roared a big laugh and knocked Henry on the shoulder. It's true – Henry is always the first to arrive and the last to leave. He works hard, he wants to make an impression. It's also the case that he sometimes isn't in a hurry to go home of an evening – the radio always on when he just needs some silence, the children always tired and hungry. Little May hauling herself up to standing then falling backwards and banging her head, Charlotte picking her up and trying to soothe her while she stirs a pot of something, Lucie tugging at Charlotte's skirt. But after Collins's comment he has been more cautious. No need to draw attention. Now he leaves work at five like everyone else and sits down to dinner at six.

He flicks the indicator and turns left towards the highway. Three months. To think they've been here three months. He can't make sense of it. It feels like a year at least, at other times it feels only a matter of days.

Once Henry has gone, Charlotte gets up, pushes her feet into her slippers and goes to the bathroom to brush her teeth. As she bends over to run the water she slips sideways, lifting her arms and gripping the basin so as to steady herself. It is the fatigue, the run of nights with a teething baby. She had forgotten. How could she have forgotten? The way the solid world dissolves. Walls jump into her path, doorways narrow, sinks and counters shrink and pull backwards. Yesterday she dropped a plate and two cups, all of them shattering over the wooden floor. She remembers holding the crockery and then feeling her fingers let go. In between there was the quickest thought that moved ever so slowly through her mind: *I think the cup is slipping. I think I'm going to let go.* Now she shuffles to the kitchen, holding her hand to the wall to steady herself, and prepares breakfast: cereal, followed by toast and another pot of tea. She puts the placemats down, sets out the bowls and plates, knives and spoons. There is the milk bottle, the sugar, the butter dish, the cereal box. She takes the bread from the freezer and prises off three slices.

The crates and furniture sit in an awkward jumble in the hall and living room. Although she has been looking forward to the shipment, today unpacking is the last thing she wants to do. She opens the cardboard tabs on the cereal box and a flurry of tiny moths escape into her face. Charlotte leaps away, beating the air, but they are already gone – miniature, dusty, grey-brown things. They are not alone, the moths; the house, she has found, is infested with insects. Weevils crawl in the flour and spiders nest in the high corners of the rooms. Ants have found the sugar and the honey, and a few nights ago she woke in fright to the sound of Henry choking – he'd leaned over to take a sip of water from the glass on the nightstand and swallowed a cockroach that had been floating, drowned, on the surface. The next night she pulled back the sheets of May's cot to find a little beetle darting across the yellow cloth. Other nights she's squashed tiny brown spiders on the pillowcase, and last night in the dark she bruised her head as she flailed about trying to hit the mosquito that whined and circled around her ears.

Once she has laid the table, Charlotte wanders through the cool dark of the house towards the living room. Gentle morning light spills in through the front window and beyond this the grass withers. It is March, almost April, more than three months since their arrival, and in all that time there's been no rain. Nothing. Not even a passing shower. Although it's early the day is already heating up. She can tell by the look of the sun, thick and honey-coloured, a white haze shining along the edge of everything it touches. She ties the cord of her dressing-gown and steps out onto the front lawn. Henry waters with the hose in the morning, he waters in the evening, and still the ground dries up and returns, slowly, to sand. The buffalo grass in the back survives somehow, but everything else struggles. Flowers are scorched and sit shrunken on the ends of dry stems. The sun burns brown circles in the front lawn. Henry hoses these spots, trying to coax green life back into them. But everywhere the sand is showing through. A high, dry wind blows in from the desert. 'No, it's not dying,' he says, talking of the grass. 'Just in need of a little care.' So hopeful. Always so full of hope. It is what she admires in him, most of the time. Until she sees that the thing that makes him great also makes him foolish; in such moments his hope seems silly to her, naive, unwarranted. She knows she shouldn't think like this and that it is only because she's tired, but over and over again these two ideas battle for primacy: he is good and he is a fool. He is a fool for bringing us out here, she thinks, yet he did it because he thought it would be best for everyone. He is only capable, it seems, of wanting the best for everyone.

Henry parks the car and makes his way to his office. It is a small square room on the ground floor. It has dark green carpet, a high ceiling and a single window facing east across the playing field towards the river. He'd not have guessed the room's modesty from the outward appearance of the building: a tall, wide, sandstone structure that shines white and gold in the sun.

He settles himself and pours a cup of coffee from his thermos. A bulging manila folder rests on his lap and he flicks through its contents: pages and pages of notes that he took on board the ship. They have become the basis of first semesters' lectures and maybe they'll be something more, a book perhaps. There is the shadow of something larger hiding in that forest of words – if he can just find his way through, clear a path. He checks his watch. There's still a good hour before the lecture is due to begin. Second year, Swinburne and Hardy. Although he's starting to wonder if the students even read the poems. It makes him nervous, the way their gaze slips up and sideways, so that they seem to be staring at a region just above his brow, or towards his ear. Then he rushes, speaks too quickly and loses his way. They give him such blank looks it seems they don't know what a poem is. He thinks about this. What is a poem? If he asked them, could they answer? It is a reasonable question. A good question. A difficult question that appears simple.

Today he'll talk about Hardy's elegies. *But what are they about?* his students will ask. They want the love story. How he hates this question, understanding, now, in the shade of his office that poetry is among the few things that can survive this question. If the poem is very good it is very hard to say what it is about. It is this and it is not that. It seems like one thing and then, after a while, not so much, one's understanding always shifting with the images and the sounds. He'll add something on Tennyson, perhaps, something on rhyme. Something about that very question, about poems being one of the few things that cannot be summarised, or that can survive such an evil with something left over, something else. Something remaining. A trouble. A pleasure. A little extra.

On the oval, a game of cricket starts up. An early crowd cheers and boys call one to another. There is the thwack of leather on willow. It gives Henry the pleasant feeling of being in company

77

even when he is not. Summer is over, but it's still ghastly hot and he's glad to be working at his desk in the cool, dark room while the boys are on the bright green. It is right this way – the vicarious pleasure is real. He looks up and into the shimmering air outside: there is green grass, dark river water overset with glinting sun. Then he turns back to his notes. He writes quickly, the words scrawling themselves across the page, humming through his mind so fast he hardly hears them but merely channels them through the tip of his pencil.

When the time comes to shuffle his papers and slip them into his briefcase he's blunted several pencils and covered ten pages. His hand hurts. His eyes are tired. He thinks of Charlotte then, as he picks up his bag and begins to walk down the corridor towards the lecture theatre. What is she doing? He feels a little pang of homesickness, of longing. He wants just to be near her, to hear her clattering about in the kitchen or calling to the children in the yard. The din of their family life. He thinks perhaps he'll start off the lecture by reciting the poems they used to read to each other. He always thinks of these poems as having a kind of talismanic power. Were they happy poems or sad? He is never sure; they are sad poems that once made them both happy and now, for some reason, make him feel a little sad. He pushes the thought away; he is almost there now – he can hear the hum of the students, talking, laughing. Then the door clicks open and the voices die down.

⌣

After breakfast Charlotte takes a box of linen outside, thinking it a fine day for airing. She plunges in her hands and lifts out an embroidered cushion, sniffing it to see whether it still smells of England, of damp mustiness sweetened by the smell of toast and fried onion. She thinks she catches it for a moment, but then it's gone. Charlotte holds the cushion out before her and shakes it, bright dust floating up and out. Then she takes the extra bedding, the quilts and feather duvets, and pegs them on the line. From the corner of her eye she can see Lucie and May playing in the square of dirt reserved for winter crops. Lucie is fast on her feet now. She fetches and carries and digs. Tomatoes and beans grow on either side of the children; behind them stand the tall, spindly lettuces, too bitter now to eat. It's not much past ten but the sun is already hot, the children playing under its butter-yellow light, their chubby naked bodies turning grey with dust, and their wide-brimmed hats – pink and lilac – flopping down over their eyes so that they live in their own private, shady circles, unaware of their mother in the distance. Lucie soon tires of digging and finds the small red watering can buried among the pumpkin leaves. There is still water in it, so she sets about making little muddy puddles. May remains where she is, sifting the dirt with her fingers and popping handfuls in her mouth.

Charlotte shakes out the blankets next, her gaze drifting away from her children and into the trees. The sun is still rising, its bright core hidden behind a net of leaves. In the margin around the sun the sky is white and parched of colour. The leaves flicker in and out of this radiance, each one coated in light. The branches wave up, then down, then side to side, arching and dipping in the breeze. It reminds her of an underwater landscape, the strange plants pushed one way then another, their limbs floating and sinking at different times, moved by an invisible undertow. Breezes come and go. They meet in the trees and eddy out again. The branches sway and flap very slowly and when the breeze passes they fall back to their former shape.

She can feel sweat trickling down the backs of her thighs. She wipes the perspiration from her top lip and brushes her damp hands over her skirt. The face of her watch flashes as she places the cushions and pillows on chairs and on the grass for airing; it is hours still, she notices, before the children will lie down for their nap. If only it were sooner – she feels so heavy, so very tired. She feels she lacks the endurance necessary for an ordinary day. Charlotte rubs the back of her neck. Henry will have finished his lecture by now. For a moment she envies him – moving about in the world, unaccompanied.

Lucie calls to her. 'More water? More water, Mummy?' The watering can is empty.

'In a minute, sweetheart,' Charlotte replies. 'Do some digging.' She turns her back to her child and shakes out the rug from the bottom of the box.

'Now? Water now?' Lucie cries.

'Soon. I'm busy, see?' says Charlotte, hoisting the rug over the washing line. If she can just delay for long enough Lucie will find something else to do and forget about the watering can. I don't mind filling it up once, Charlotte thinks, but it is never once – it is five, ten, twelve times, bending over and standing up and bending over. It should not be so difficult. It should be a joy. I should know how to make it a joy. Today, though, the repulsion overwhelms – this need to be alone, away from the children. She is so tired, and it is so hot, so terribly hot now.

'Mummy?' Lucie calls again, her voice plaintive.

'Yes, darling?'

'More water?' Her voice rises and cracks.

'When I've finished here.' Charlotte knows she does not have long. 'Just wait,' she says, her voice tightening. She knows it'll only be a few minutes before Lucie begins to cry. She should go now and get it done with. If I just fill it once, she thinks. It takes no time to fill the can, no time at all, and it makes Lucie so happy, the splash of the water, the tiny streams that trickle out of the spout, the dirt that the silvery water turns to dark mud. Just once, she tells herself. But she doesn't want to do it once. She doesn't want to do it at all. The child must learn to wait and she must teach her, Charlotte thinks irritably, picking up a stick from the grass and testing it against her thigh for strength. Then she lifts the stick and swings, striking the carpet. Behind her Lucie begins to cry, but Charlotte does not go to her. She doesn't want her daughter to think her fickle and changeable. '*Mummy!*' Lucie wails as Charlotte beats the carpet. '*Mummy!*' Charlotte swings the stick and hits again: once, twice, three times.

'Not long now!' Charlotte calls, lifting the stick. 'Not long—' she says again, bringing the stick – whump – against the carpet.

'Finish now!' Lucie calls. 'Nooooow!' Her cries ripple out across the yard and into the street. Charlotte catches her daughter's gaze then looks away. *'Now! Now! Now!'* Lucie screams, as the dull thwunk, thwunk of the stick continues, its pace increasing. Lucie's separate cries blur into one long, loose-ended wail.

As Charlotte works, she feels the labour give rise to a certain glory. The girls will not come near her while she strikes at the carpet. She is alone, free. *This* second is hers, goes the stick. And *this* one, and *this* one and *this*. 'No, I cannot come now!' she yells at Lucie. 'No, not yet!' There is only one stream of time and somehow it has to be divided into her time and the children's time. She knows the waters cannot be parted like this, she knows it is useless, struggling to keep the minutes to herself. But that is all she has; there is the brightness of the outside world and then the starved, dark space of her own consciousness. It used to be wider and deeper, voluminous and rich. This moment is hers, thwack, and this one, thwack, and this one, thwack, thwack, the stick whistling through the air. She feels them, these severed moments, piling up like sandbags to hold back a deluge. The children will break through any second now.

There's a flash of colour as Lucie steps forwards. She stands to the side, her face a mottled grey and red, streaked by the clear lines of tears. As Charlotte keeps on – thwack, thwack – Lucie screams, a wobbling, grating sound, half cry, half yell. Dust has stopped rising from the carpet. Charlotte sees this and knows that the job is done, knows that she keeps on now only to spite her child, only to prove that she will not bend to her. It is wrong. She understands this even as she continues. Lucie's breath quivers and hiccups as she steps closer again, her chin held up towards her mother.

Charlotte stops and lets the stick hang at her side. She turns to Lucie and shame washes through her like acid. She feels her grip weaken. The stick drops to the grass; she is a selfish woman, she thinks. Lucie should turn away and be cross with her. It would be proof, she thinks, that she is not fit for this after all. It would be a blessing, to have the truth made plain. But instead of turning away, Lucie dives at her, clutching at her legs and pressing her face into Charlotte's thighs, into the rough fabric of her mother's skirt. Charlotte sways like a tall tree struck by the wind, then bends down over Lucie's small body, slips her hands under her daughter's arms and hauls her up. Lucie twists her legs around her mother's waist and buries her hot wet face in the curve of Charlotte's neck. Her little hands pat her mother's back as though she is the one in need of comfort.

'There there, there there,' Charlotte says, stroking Lucie's head. 'Mummy's here now, Mummy's here.' She presses her face to her child's sun-warmed hair. She feels Lucie's belly expand and shrink with deep, trembling breaths. She smells her long, fuzzy hair, sweet like wax and biscuits and fresh hay. Loose strands cling to Charlotte's cheek. She is always surprised by the relief she feels when her child is close, by the strange peace of feeling themselves joined, one creature once more. It is the struggle to be separate that pains them. Now their single, tall, bulging shadow moves slowly over the grass as they walk towards May, who remains in the dirt, cooing excitedly at her mother's approach: she bobs up and down then throws herself forwards into a crawl. Lucie continues to pat Charlotte's back. Tears prickle in Charlotte's eyes; she must be good to them, she must be better. They are so small, Charlotte thinks, holding one child and looking down at the other. Tiny. In her mind they seem so large, simply because they take up the whole of it.

'Come here,' she says, bending down and pulling May towards her. 'Shall we go for a walk?' she says. 'Shall we walk down to the river?'

Over dinner Henry talks about his lecture and the plans for his book, his mouth full, fork waving in the air. Something about Richards. About the brilliance of his idea, that literature is of the body, that the response to literature is of the nervous system. Delicious, he says, spearing another chunk of meat. *Bloody delicious*. He tries out new words: bloody, mate, love. It is not him, though. He does not really know these words. They are sounds only. They are ideas, the jarring unbroken codes of a people. He swallows and carries on, speaking as himself again. Something about the surge and resurgence of an image in Hardy, not seen so much as felt, the image rising, sharpening, as if it were lifting up out of the blood, a shape out of the dark. Something about the transformation of one thing into another. Rain into seed. She loves this talk of his, the prattle of loose thought, the random leaps. He stops to think, chewing his food carefully. The thing about poems, he says, reaching out and taking a sip of beer – is that they can be so sad, so difficult, and yet the sound can make them into something lovely, something pleasurable, even if they are not about that lovely thing. Anyway, he says, he's been thinking about that.

'And your day?' he asks, wiping his forehead then his mouth with the cloth napkin. The weather is still hot. 'How was your day?'

She describes the trees, the midday light on the surface of the river. But it is hard to describe. The day is hard to describe. The silent happy children and the unexpected plunges into panic: spilled food, accidents, pains that arise with no outward sign. The beating of the carpet. It is not coherent, her day, the experience of it not captured by saying what she did. What did she do? 'Yes, we went to the river,' she says. On the way home they stopped at the shop to pick up a magazine and the ingredients for dinner. As they walked home she thought about how she might surprise Henry, how she might please him with fancy meals, with the recipes she cut out from the *Women's Weekly*. Potato salad with condensed milk and citrus served in the emptied halves of an orange. Beef Olives, Chicken Dijon. Sponge Sandwich and Butterscotch Tartlets. 'Then we tidied up,' she says, 'and we cooked dinner.' This royal we: a mother and her children. How easy the day seems in summary. How unequal to the event. Like a poem, she thinks. 'Fine,' she says in conclusion. 'My day was fine.' She is tired of these questions. Who did she see today? What did she do? It makes her anxious.

As if each day must be accounted for. As if she were always failing at some task he has set for her.

'I'm only trying to help,' Henry says, scraping at the last of the gravy on his plate. 'Collins mentioned his wife goes to some Sunday painting group.'

'And is that what you think I am – a weekend hobbyist?'

'I didn't mean that.'

'No, of course not.' But as she speaks she realises that this is exactly her fear, exactly her doubt. Has she already become this? Her paints and easel are still packed somewhere in the shed. She keeps a sketchbook in the kitchen drawer. She doesn't know what to paint. It is a strange feeling, as if the world has stopped resonating, as if she's lost her feeling for beauty. She tried sketching a tree the other day and it ended up looking like a scarecrow, all gangly arms and scruff. 'Never mind,' she says.

Later that evening Henry finds her leaning over the kitchen sink and weeping. She is halfway through the washing-up, the children asleep. 'What's this?' he asks, placing his hands softly on her waist. 'What happened?'

'Nothing,' she says, wiping her nose on her sleeve. 'Nothing's happened. That's just it. You go to work and until you come home again nothing happens.' Nothing real, it seems. Nothing lasting. She's tried gardening but the heat makes it unbearable. She would paint, if only she knew what. She goes to the park. She stands in the bush. She waits for the day to end. She cooks dinner. Once a week they go to the library. There is nothing here that is hers.

'You should make friends with the neighbours,' he suggests. Wasn't that what the book said? A memoir written by a fellow migrant. *I went to work while my wife got on with the local ladies.* 'Or go to a playgroup,' Henry says. But he knows it is not what he's meant to say.

'I miss home,' says Charlotte.

Henry drops his head. She's being nostalgic, he reasons. Things will improve. He will see that they do. 'Nothing is perfect,' he says softly. 'Give it time.' She turns towards him. He reaches his arms around her shoulders and pulls her face to his chest. 'There now,' he says. She sobs quietly, and when she lifts her face away the buttons of Henry's shirt leave small red welts in her cheek.

A stray cat has taken to visiting and now meows at the door. Charlotte slips out of Henry's arms and fetches the cat some milk. Henry picks up his gardening shoes and busies himself unknotting the laces. He wants to find the snails that are eating the seedlings. He doesn't know what else to say to her, what to do, so thinks it best to go outside and leave her be. 'I'm going to lie down,' says Charlotte, and Henry nods.

She spreads out on the pink chenille bedcover, her shoes still on and her feet hanging off the end of the mattress. She lies there staring at the strangely patterned wallpaper – row upon row of yellow and orange daisies – until the flowers blur into one long stripe of colour.

Some time later Henry comes in. Henry, her husband. She is still intrigued by the force of that title. When they were first married she used to blush every time she said it. My husband will get the bags. My husband will fix the bill. Their intimacy made public, official. To be a husband and a wife. To have become archetypes. To feel touched by something ancient although they were, are, still young. She lies there with her eyes closed; there is the meaty smell of his sweat and the smell of dirt. Charlotte hears him sit down on the slipper chair beside the bed. He hates the colour of it. Turquoise green, the silk stained by spilled tea. The top of the chair thick with the smell of her perfume where her neck rests. She will change it for him. The colour. He likes things matching. Likes things cheerful. Pink, perhaps, to match the bedspread. She hears him folding and refolding the newspaper, then hears the paper slip to the floor. She opens her eyes, rolls over. Henry bends down to pick up the paper and she sees the thinning circle of hair just back from the crown of his head. In the photographs, his father had lost much of his hair by the time he was Henry's age. She reaches out and puts her fingers to this shiny patch of skin. Warm, softer than she expected. Fuzzed like the head of a baby. Henry sits up and takes her hand in his, running his thumb back and forth across her knuckles. The pad of his thumb rough from the garden.

That night she dreams of England. She dreams of the fens in springtime: the grasses covered in dew, trails of mist rising with the pale sun, the grass and the vapour aglow. She even dreams the smell of it, the sweet rot of leaf mould and mud. She dreams of the cottage, the narrow stairwell, the creak and bang of the kitchen door; she dreams of the kitchen windows, the bluish winter light outside, the concrete courtyard, the yellowing willow in the yard behind. She dreams of tea-coloured sky, low cloud, green light through tree leaves. She dreams of wind. The ancient wind in the ancient fields. The dreams are so vivid that when she wakes in the dawn she does not know where she is. It takes a moment to remember and even then she can't recall the geography of her new house. When she thinks of the new bathroom she sees the bathroom of the cottage. When she imagines the living room she sees the living room of the cottage. These days she dreams of England more than she dreams of her dead father. A heart attack, seventeen years ago. There was a time when she spoke to him in her dreams. Long midnight conversations, so clear that she was sad to wake and realise they had not been true, real. Now he is reduced to myth. A man who lived and died a long time ago. She remembers his face, the side of his face, the stubble on the side of his face when he bent to kiss her cheek. She remembers his voice, how he said her name, how he looked when he was tired. His slow-booted footsteps on the wooden floor. But there is little else that comes to mind. The memory of him, so diminished. Now she waits for the memories of England to fade in the same way.

In the morning she opens the flyscreen door, stands on the verandah and calls out. The feeling of the dream is still with her. She sees Henry moving amid the trees. She wants to be rid of the dream, she thinks, watching as Henry and the leaves shift in different directions. Green, white, white-green. Wind fluttering the leaves. The birds wake him at daybreak and so he goes out to the garden. She can see his bright shirt moving behind the branches, his arms deep in the foliage, checking for signs of disease, for leaf curl and black spot. Perhaps he didn't hear her. She calls again, her voice carrying. *Henry, He-nry.* There is always the new hope of morning. Today she has made him eggs for breakfast. Eggs and fried bread. She wants, like him, to believe that her homesickness will pass. It is such a strange feeling. She does not feel sad so much as unearthed, un-real. Un-existent. But there is always more hope in the morning. The hope of change and betterment. Of something new. By evening she'll have given up and will want to go back, will do anything to go back. For a moment, she thinks she catches the sound of a blackbird. The call is soft, scarcely audible through the din of cicadas. It is easier when Henry is here, she thinks. It is easier when he is near her. As if his continuing presence were proof of her own. A stronger gust of wind lifts her skirt and the bird stops. The air is cool, from elsewhere, the clouds higher up in the sky today. They must call this autumn, she thinks. The morning smells of damp eucalypt and fresh-mown grass. 'Coming,' Henry calls.

LATER THAT DAY she does as Henry suggests and takes the girls to the local playgroup by the river.

'Come on, darling, go play with the other children,' Charlotte says to Lucie. The child shakes her head and stares, clinging to her mother's leg. There is a piano at the far end of the hall, a fat woman sitting at it, belting out tunes: 'Baa Baa Black Sheep', 'Ring a Ring o' Roses', 'Incy Wincy Spider'. The children are meant to join in and sing along, but nobody pays the music any attention and it becomes just another booming, clanking noise in the general cacophony of boys making engine sounds or banging drums made from old biscuit tins, and babies crying and small girls whining for their mothers, who now sit in three neat lines along the edge of the hall, sipping scalding tea from tiny china cups and shuffling uncomfortably on the small wooden school chairs. Some talk over the noise.

'And which is yours?'

'How many did you say?'

'Lovely weather,' says the woman beside Charlotte. But for the most part the women do not look at each other. They watch their children, and every now and then cast a nervous glance at an adult face, smile quickly, then look away. They are all unused to the company of grown-ups. They spend their days talking to small children in the strange language that small children understand. Charlotte remembers how, after Lucie was born, she spent hour upon hour lying on the bed with the baby and making gooing noises. It was a surprise to see Henry at the end of the day. She remembers looking at his head and thinking, *My, what a big face you have.* How foolishly large adults seemed then, how odd-looking they became – almost monstrous – with their sprouting tufts of hair and yellowed eyes and slabs of flesh and creases.

Next to her, three women lean in towards one another, gossiping. Two friends confiding in the third. The first woman says, 'She looked like a prostitute, didn't she, love?' All three guffaw.

Then the second woman. 'She was dressed like that to pick the kid up and she goes to me, "Does little Bertie want to come and play? We've got a new tarantula."'

'She must have been joking—' says the third woman.

'No!' The first again now. 'She tells us, "Don't worry, it's in a glass case and everything."'

'Then we saw her, didn't we,' continues the second, 'later that afternoon, getting her shopping out of the boot, still wearing those silver stilettos, with those boobs. She looked like a prostitute, didn't she?'

'I just have to look at those shoes and I get a nosebleed.'

'She used to be a hairdresser.'

'You'd never know from the look of her.'

'Looks like she's got a cat on her head.'

A small child in bright red trousers runs up to Charlotte. 'I'm a boy,' he says. 'My name's Michael.' Then he runs off again and disappears into the throng of toddlers. She realises that she doesn't know how to make friends. She came to the playgroup to make friends, but now that she is here she doesn't know what to say, what to do. Who is she now? There must be something she can tell them. The mothers who know each other talk about their children. They exchange facts concerning the hours their children sleep, what they will or won't eat, and swap advice on remedies for colds or stomach ache. Or they gossip, cruelly, like this, about the women who don't fit in. Charlotte doesn't want to talk about her girls. She knows no one is really interested in hearing about them and that the other women share anecdotes as a way of boasting about their offspring, not because they are genuinely interested in other people's children. Besides, when she speaks people look at her uncertainly. They pause in conversation, then say, 'You're not from around here, are you?' And Charlotte explains, her exclusion immediate, her status as an outsider everlasting. 'Are you English, or just educated Australians?'

asked the man from the nursery when he came to deliver three poplar saplings for Henry to plant by the back fence.

Across the room a boy slips on a toy truck and crashes down hard on his face. There is an awful silence as his mother gathers the limp, quiet child into her arms, then the air cracks open with a loud, breathless wail like the one you wait for when a child first slithers into the world.

'Is there blood?'

'He won't let me look.'

'I'll fetch ice.'

The child starts to roar. Charlotte hears the way his voice catches against the soft wet membrane of his throat. In the meantime the fat pianist begins telling a story and the other children gather around on the cold wooden floor. Two teddy bears travel on a boat to a desert island. In the bottom of the boat they find a map with an 'X' marking the place of buried treasure. They follow the map past a volcano, past a very tall tree, past a swamp, and find the treasure buried on a far beach. The bears dig and dig until out of the hole comes a jewelled box. 'What do you think is in it?' the fat woman asks.

'Gold!' cries one boy, leaping up and down with his hand in the air.

'Alligators!' says another.

'Lollies!' yells a girl whose face is laced with the white crust of dried snot.

'Hairclips!' calls a skinny child decked out in a pink party dress.

Charlotte is watching this when a woman comes up to her and holds out a hand. 'I'm Carol,' she says. 'I've seen you before. I think we live on the same street.'

The two women walk home by the river. It is windy there and the brown water rushes back and forth in long muscled ridges. The water throbs and the sun is sucked into its depths. They stop at one of the small jetties and peer in. Carol has two small boys who jump and yelp and tackle each other like demented puppies. They climb the wooden railings of the jetty and look down. The colour changes as the water deepens: tea-gold in the shallows, brown, then greeny-black far below. Purple-hued jellyfish hover close to shore, and the sand is littered with their flat, transparent bodies. The women walk along the narrow beach, and Lucie pokes the dead jellyfish with a stick then crouches to stroke them with the palm of her hand. Charlotte bends down with May and listens to the small waves hissing at the ground.

Around them the boys run and squeal, leaping from sand to rock to sand until one of them stubs a toe and cries, so Carol hoists him onto her back and carries him. It is quieter then. The women talk a little, of places they've visited, the difficulty of gardening in this heat, whether or not there are to be more children. Carol's husband works in real estate, away often at weekends. All those open houses and auctions. She doesn't mind, she says. She's learning the piano and he doesn't always like to hear her practise.

'Do you play anything else?' Charlotte asks.

'Just the radio,' Carol says. The two women laugh. 'But I'm good at that.'

Charlotte tells Carol about her painting. Or what used to be her painting. She should at least find the paints, get the box out of the shed. They walk further, then stop for the children, walk a little more then stop again. The path snakes its way through river grass and dips beneath the tall limbs of the gums. Charlotte thought the trees terribly ugly when she arrived, with their asymmetrical branches and scraggly clutches of dull, tough leaves. But she sees, now, that they are beginning to change – how she sees them is beginning to change. Lucie scratches at the base of their trunks, gathering thin white shells. Charlotte crouches down to help her and sees the trees from below. Their marbled skin circles the trunk and spirals upwards, round and round, higher and higher, moving from the roots out to the tips of the branches as though they were something much more than trees, something much stranger, as though the trees were the final manifestation of a force erupting from deep inside the earth, and the limbs, the branches, all twisted and wrung, mangled in fierce torsion, are the accidental shape taken on by a molten substance when it sprang up into colder air and froze. They seem not trees as she knows them but the residue of something ancient and explosive and long gone. Carol tells her the names of things: river red gum, banksia, swishbush and swamp paperbark. Charlotte tries to remember so that later she can tell Henry.

It is heading into afternoon by the time they reach Charlotte's house, and she invites Carol in for tea. 'No,' Carol says, 'I'd love to but can't. I have people coming over for dinner.' Then she says, quickly, 'Would you and Henry like to come? Please do. Please.'

Carol lives at the far end of the long street, over the hill and close to the sea. They drive there, the children in the back. A white bungalow, leadlight windows. The front garden full of frangipani. Who else is there? Another married couple, Sarah and James. Sarah with the arched, bony nose. James with the jowls. And an old friend, Nicholas. 'You two should meet,' says Carol, ushering Charlotte and this man together. Seven in total. Three couples, plus Nicholas. Four children, all combined. The children play on the floor in the living room with an overflowing basket of toys and a wooden train track. There is chicken for the adults, a platter of green beans, carrots, roast potatoes. There is red wine. Later there will be trifle with custard and cream, decorated with blanched almonds and slices of kiwifruit.

Carol talks about her boys, the things she does not understand about boys. The smell of the toilet. ('They cannot aim! Adam, I said, please teach them to aim!') Other things that Charlotte does not understand either, because she does not have boys. 'Like wild little animals!' Carol says, laughing, as if this is both the thing that alarms her and the thing she loves. The talk shifts, dips, rises. People want Henry to tell stories about his childhood in India, and he obliges, giving a dry history of his family. All nod, feigning interest, although hoping for something more exotic. The monkeys. The silks. The ancient ruins.

'We're taking a cruise soon,' says Sarah. 'Port Said, Athens, Venice – all over really.' Some *Women's Weekly* thing, she says. 'It was a promotion a few months back – the one with the cover picture of the poodle in the yellow life jacket.'

In the garden, crickets hold the beat of night. From the table the guests can hear the surf. Huge waves, high tide. Water smashing down on the sand. Charlotte sits next to Nicholas. Conversations have started up on either side of them and he leans forwards to hear her better. He wears a pale blue shirt open at the neck and a pair of dark-framed glasses. They are fancy glasses – the frames are shiny, and shaped to suit his face. She wonders what kind of car he drives – something dark and glossy to match his glasses, although she doesn't know why she thinks this because she doesn't generally care for cars or for the relationship between men and cars. There are brown flecks in the blue of his eyes. He moves slowly, Charlotte notices, when cutting his meat, for example, or lifting a glass to his mouth.

She says something then that amuses him and is surprised by his laugh, deep and soft. He looks at her, she realises, more with his left eye than with his right: a slight tilt of the face, left side forwards. He holds her gaze when he laughs, encouraging her.

In the background she can hear Henry. 'The second rule,' he says, 'is that life isn't like that because—' She knows his rules by heart. There are five of them: keep your chin up; better the devil you know; don't fix what isn't broken; waste not, want not; and the last one, which seemed to cancel out the ones before it, nothing ventured, nothing gained. He calls them rules, but they are not rules exactly, more a hodge-podge of proverbs that he randomly adheres to and expects others to adopt.

She hears Sarah then: 'My mother said the woman would have been very beautiful when she was younger. I didn't know what she meant. How could she tell? The woman was old.'

'You swim, don't you? You used to swim,' says Adam, Carol's husband.

'Used to,' Sarah replies.

'Do you miss it – England, I mean?' Carol asks Charlotte.

Henry hears this and cuts in before Charlotte can reply. 'We hated the weather. Awful weather,' he says, meeting Charlotte's eye as if in challenge. He does not like her to contradict him, and this – the weather – has become the official reason for their leaving. 'The winters, the summers. Just awful.'

Charlotte can't decide if he sounds ungrateful – if he sounds like he's whingeing – or if it is a sign of burgeoning patriotism towards his new country. She stares at her plate; she will neither confirm nor deny his claim.

Carol nods, sympathetic, then changes the subject. 'Tell her,' she calls to Nicholas across the table. 'He's a great patron,' she says to Charlotte. 'Quite a collector. You two must talk.'

The table is soon cleared and the party migrates towards the living room, to the turntable and the sofas. Henry stands in the corner, talking to Adam. He thinks Charlotte is beside him. He can feel the warmth of her hand there, on his arm. She has such hot hands, and they sweat terribly when she's nervous. He can feel her damp palm pressing into his shirt. He and Adam are talking house prices, land, whether Henry will or will not buy property. 'We'd like to, wouldn't we, Charlotte. We've been thinking—' He turns his head towards her, but she isn't where he thinks she is. 'Oh,' he says, 'she was right here, she—' Then he hears her laugh, high and light and unmistakable. It is like clear water falling into a deep pool. She's standing by the fireplace talking to Nicholas.

She fiddles with her earring and flicks loose hair back from her face. Henry sees Nicholas lean closer. Charlotte is flushed, her eyes bright. She is stunning to look at. The sharp cheekbones and the big eyes – her skin so fine that when she throws back her head and laughs he can see the delicate blue ribbing of her throat. He wants, instinctively, to put his hand to it. The frame of her body is small, bird-like, but she holds herself so straight that she seems regal. She reaches out and puts her hand on Nicholas's arm. He touches the gold locket that hangs on a chain at her neck. They are drawing attention: Carol is looking their way. Henry wants to put an end to the flirtation and take Charlotte home, but cannot do so without making a scene.

'You should come for lunch,' Nicholas says. 'There are views of the ocean, and the cool of the living room is like the shade beneath a giant birch tree.'

He smiles at her as though he's known her for a long time, and she can't help but smile back. He has a wide face, and dark hair worn a little long. It is not a neat face, but it is handsome, the nose slightly off-centre, the eyes large and deep-set. When he talks his left eyebrow lifts and when he laughs it tends to twitch. The asymmetry of his features makes them seem in constant motion even when they are still.

'You're from London?' she asks, catching the lilt in his voice.

'Yes, I am, although that was a long time ago. And you?' he asks, tipping his head back and finishing his drink. 'What are you doing here?' He shrugs his shoulders as he says this and casts a quick glance about the room. 'Please. I want to know,' he says.

Charlotte stares into her empty glass. 'It was my husband's idea,' she says.

'And how are you finding it?' Nicholas asks.

'It's not quite what I expected.'

'No, I'd think not. How long have you been here?'

'Three, four months.'

'A drop in the ocean.'

'Long enough.'

'So what will you do?'

'I don't know. I'm a painter – or was, it feels now.'

Nicholas cocks his head to the side. For a moment she forgets what she's saying, distracted by the way he looks at her. She's never seen a man listen like this before, as though he were waiting to give her something, or waiting for her to ask him for something, to make a request or beg a favour, anything, anything at all that might mean he could be of service. He smiles as he listens, but with lips closed and eyebrows slightly raised. He nods. 'Yes, yes – of course, of course,' he says to things he might not understand, to things he perhaps has no experience of. He seems certain that if she says this is what such a thing is like, then it surely must be. He makes her feel that he believes her completely, trusts her every word.

In the car on the way home Henry is silent. The children are asleep in the back. Charlotte thinks of the week ahead. She accepted Nicholas's invitation to come to his house for tea. *Why not tomorrow?* he asked. *What are you doing tomorrow? Well, nothing, nothing in particular.* He was a psychologist. *I used to work at the hospital, but now I run a small private practice from home. A few patients a few days a week. Yes, I do collect*, he said. *No, I don't paint. Not anymore. But your painting*, he said. *Tell me about that.*

'So,' Henry says, interrupting her thoughts, 'what were you two chatting about so happily?'

'Nothing much.'

'It looked like something.'

'You don't like him, do you.'

'I don't know him enough to form such a strong opinion.'

'I like him.'

'Obviously. I could have done without the embarrassment, that's all.'

'The embarrassment?'

'You, disappearing just when Adam was talking to us.'

'He was talking to you.'

'You could have waited. Instead we had to witness your flirting.'

'I wasn't flirting.'

'Well, whatever it was—'

'And if you really want to know, we were talking about England.'

Henry tightens his grip on the steering wheel. Charlotte turns her face away and stares out the window. A dark flat expanse of sandy country slips away into the night. Low trees lean in towards the road.

'I want to go back,' she says. 'I want to go home. I'm not saying this on a whim. Three months is long enough. We've had our holiday. You know—'

Henry lowers his voice to a stern whisper, the way one might speak to a child who's finally outworn all patience. '*You* know,' he says slowly, 'that is not going to happen.'

'Because you will not let it happen,' Charlotte shoots back.

'Because it *can't* happen.'

'You say that,' Charlotte says, turning to face Henry, 'but people go back all the time. I've seen them queuing up on the docks. We saw them, you and I, on the boat, the other boat that passed us, with the people calling out. I should have listened. I should have listened to my mother. I should have—'

'You and your damned mother!' Henry spits. 'We are *here*. This *is* our home now. *No one* is going back!'

Charlotte pushes her fist against her mouth and starts to cry, her shoulders trembling in the dark.

Henry eases the car down the driveway, and as soon as he has pulled on the handbrake Charlotte gets out and runs inside. Henry stays where he is, his hands holding the wheel. He cannot pretend he's sorry for coming out here. He's not. He's glad for it, most of the time, and even if they're yet to make friends and he doesn't always like the heat he is forever relieved to be out of the cold. It is so good to be warm. It sounds insignificant but it is not; it's so good, it is such a relief, not to be cold and damp all the time. It's impossible to think of going back. She must know this. It's not fair of her to ask for something she knows he cannot give.

The light in the living room comes on and Charlotte appears on the verandah carrying a jug of water. She bends down and tends the pots of petunias. They struggle terribly in the heat, their petals wither, but still she tries, watering them to the point of drowning. Why these flowers? He keeps meaning to ask. There seems some element of decorum involved – the way she *must* have petunias – as if it is yet another English rule that he doesn't understand. But perhaps the petunias are just for memories' sake – the good ones, the happy ones. Flowerpots on a sunny doorstep. He has fond memories too: the memory of her old laughter, loud and bright. What had he said that was so funny? 'You do make me laugh,' she'd told him. Then, more quietly, 'You do make me happy.' She had reached across the table and stroked his fingers, the back of his hand, then the length of his forearm from elbow to wrist. He remembers her looking down at the table while she did this. He remembers her mouth moving but forgets all sound, remembers their faces leaning in towards one another, the light disappearing. He remembers what came later – the tiny child in her arms, a warm, pink, wrinkled creature. How it opened its little black diamond of a mouth, its eyes still closed, and wobbled its head around to find her breast.

Charlotte is showering when she hears Henry come inside. There is the smack of the screen door, then a little while after this, the sound of him singing. He will have carried the girls in to bed, humming to soothe them, and now he is out in the kitchen warbling a tune from *The Sound of Music* – making an effort to appear happy only because she seems very sad.

Henry knocks on the bathroom door. 'Do you want me to wash your back?' he asks. He comes in and Charlotte turns, offering her body. He takes the bar of soap and lathers her down with warm, slow hands.

Yes, she will let him wash her back – she will not forgive him, but she will let him wash her back. It is habit, after all. Once upon a time such things seemed trivial. But lately she has discovered that within the intricacies of these repeated actions lies the old order, preserved. Habit is the only thing that can travel from one side of the world to the other and remain intact. He makes her morning cup of tea. She brings him his dinner. She lets him wash her back because he's always washed her back, because such gestures involve a complex system of kindness and gratitude, assumed even when not deserved. And because the refusal of one act of kindness would throw all such acts into doubt. Besides, she knows that after any altercation Henry likes to pretend that there is really nothing wrong. They were angry. Now they will act as if they were not.

She feels her insides sink, her heart a dark cave, a tiny bird fluttering wildly inside it. There is a speck of light in the distance but the bird cannot find it. She will keep doing what she does not want to do. 'It is not fair,' she says to him. 'It is not reasonable. I feel like I have no choice.' Henry's warm hands move over her shoulders, up and down her neck. He doesn't reply, so she twists away and his hands slip off her body.

'What do you want me to do?' Henry asks.

'You know what I want.'

'Please, can we not have this conversation again?'

Charlotte turns off the taps and steps out into Henry's arms, the towel held open for her. Everything will be all right if only they carry on doing the things they've always done. The strange time that she must endure will disappear in the common time of habit. He wraps the towel around her and holds her to him. She feels his heart beat against her cheek. She pulls back a little and he holds her tighter. 'You're tired,' he says. 'You'll feel better after a good night's rest.'

—

But Charlotte cannot sleep. At three in the morning she gets up and goes to the kitchen. She flicks the light switch and cockroaches dart across the floor to disappear beneath the oven. She makes a pot of tea, takes her sketchbook from the small drawer next to the cutlery and sits down at the kitchen table. The work, she thinks, will calm her, the feeling of the lead against the grain of the paper, the nervy movement of her hand, shaping, scratching. The physical pleasure of this is great, sometimes greater than any visual delight.

Outside, birds gurgle and whistle in the bushes. Strange birds, the way they hop about on the grass as if lame. She's heard them at night on other occasions and opened her eyes, thinking it must be nearly morning, but they sing all through the dark, it seems. Two whistles and a gurgling trill that are somehow made at the same time. How many notes at once was that? More than two, perhaps five. It sounds like three birds, and sometimes seven or more singing together, depending on whether you concentrate on the whistle or the trill. She pours a cup of tea and looks over what she's done since they arrived: a few sketches of the children, a vase of flowers. A sleeping cat. They are all true to the world but that is not what she wants. It is another world, the one she's lost, that she wants to capture now. The pencil moves quickly over the paper, shading in clouds, drawing the sightlines of fields, working from memory. Here is the church, and here is the steeple. Here are the hedges and the apples and the long line of ancient pears, tall and gnarled. Here is the road and the bridge and the hill and the kissing gate and the blackberries and the hole in the rotting fence, the willow and the low cloud, the hill touching the cloud, the shapes of the clouds, always the strange vertical reach of them, the sky tilting ever downwards, the field below it, and the small boy standing in the wind, his father beside him, the two of them holding the string of a high-flying kite.

She and Henry are both children of England, but as she grows older it seems as though England has become her child, a bundle of life that she wants always to have within arm's reach. She thinks of her mother's words the last time they saw each other. 'We don't know what will happen,' she had said. 'That's all, we don't know.'

Iris had caught the train from London and together they took a daytrip to Ely. Charlotte drove. Her mother gazed out the passenger window watching the flat black fields skitter past. The mud came right up to the roadside: the dark mud of the farmland and then the grey mud that seeped up through the yellowing grass growing on the verge. A light rain began to fall and for a while Charlotte didn't turn on the windscreen wipers but let the grey haze of water slowly obscure the view, so that all they could see was the road snaking out in front.

'I'll miss you, you know,' said her mother.

'I know,' replied Charlotte.

'It won't be the same.'

'It will be okay.'

'But not the same.'

The weather worsened and the clouds sank closer to the ground, leaving just a thin strip of white daylight above the dark horizon.

Iris tapped at the window with her knuckles. 'No doubt you'll be glad to see the back of this.'

'Of what?'

'This muck and cold.'

'No,' Charlotte said. 'No, I won't actually.'

'Henry must think you mad.'

'Yes, I think he does,' Charlotte said. Iris folded her hands in her lap and hummed a little song. 'What's that?' asked Charlotte; there was something familiar about it but she couldn't say what.

'You don't remember? I used to sing it to you when you were a girl. Funny, how things come back to you.' Iris kept on humming.

'You'll see me again soon, I promise,' said Charlotte.

'Now, darling, let's not be silly about this.'

'I mean it.'

'I'm sure you do, but that doesn't mean it will happen. Life goes on. Your life will go on. You're young.'

Charlotte sighed. 'I don't feel it. Not anymore.' Iris reached across and patted her daughter's leg. Then she turned away again to stare out the window. Charlotte watched the road, slippery with water and ice.

'You will again,' Iris said. 'I'm only saying this because I *am* old. We don't know what will happen, that's all I'm saying, we don't know.'

They drove on, the tyres hissing. Charlotte flicked the indicator and they turned into the village. 'I'll miss you too,' she said.

They parked near the cathedral and strolled under the dripping trees until the wind picked up, turning the rain on an angle and pushing it beneath their umbrellas. By the time they reached the tearoom their coats and shoes were wet through. They took a seat in the corner and ate scones piled with jam and cream and shared a large pot of tea. Her mother's hair was wet from the rain and lay plastered about her face. She made a great effort with her hair and this was, now, rather an embarrassment, the silvery white curls lost to the weather. 'I should get a towel,' Charlotte said. 'I'm sure they could give you one. You don't want to catch a chill.'

'Humbug,' said her mother. 'It's just a bit of water.'

Charlotte concentrated on pulling apart a warm scone. She was not accustomed to seeing her mother without curls. It was one of Iris's little rules that she did not let anyone into the house, nor did she ever leave the house, until her hair was washed, set and dried. She thought the curls deflected attention from her wrinkles and made her appear taller, the fluffy hairdo adding an inch or two to her shrinking frame. She was very particular about such things: her soft glossy hair and her matching neck-scarfs and earrings – yellow today, Charlotte noticed. Charlotte realised now how well the curls disguised her mother's age. Without them the bones stood out, like some curious rock formation exposed to the elements, the high forehead and the sharp cheekbones loosely draped in powdered skin.

Iris glanced nervously about the room, her painted eyebrows, too pink and too arched, lending her a look of constant fright. Charlotte turned away. It was not fair, that the weather could embarrass a woman like this. But it was true, her mother was frail, older than her years.

'I suppose it's too late to change your mind?' Iris said, picking up her teacup.

'Yes,' Charlotte replied. 'Everything's done.' She pulled at the string of beads on her neck, running her finger and thumb along the loop. 'Strange to think we go in just a few days. I never would have thought . . . I never thought . . .'

She wanted to say that she had considered letting Henry go alone, that she would stay if she could, that she didn't want to go, that it was his decision. That she'd never really said yes, or if she had she'd never meant to. She opened her mouth to tell her mother this, but something stopped her.

There was a time when she told her mother everything, but while the desire to confess was still there, it now felt as though any mention of her own feelings would be a betrayal of Henry. It was not just that some of those feelings would be about her private quarrels with Henry, and so sharing them would mean speaking badly of him. No, the betrayal would not be a simple one to do with secrets but a deeper betrayal, for now that she was married it was Henry who was the rightful receptacle of those feelings, and her mother had no claim to them. Besides, Henry might be right, their new life might be something wonderful. There was that possibility.

'I'll write,' she said.

'Yes,' said Iris, holding her napkin to her mouth and wiping a streak of cream from her top lip. 'Yes, you do that.'

CHARLOTTE IS STILL sleeping when Henry leaves for his office early the next morning. He readies himself quietly, careful not to disturb – he heard her moving about in the night. Such restlessness troubles him; it is too much like the time before, that old life when she was as good as lost to the fields.

He pushes the thought away: there is a busy day ahead. He has essays to mark, an article to finish and a new book of poems he must start in on. Once settled at his desk he drinks his coffee and organises his papers. But his mind won't stick to the tasks at hand. Instead the scene in the car comes back to him, over and over: *Because you will not let it happen*, she said. *Because it can't happen*, he corrected her. For Charlotte's sake he will act as if the argument has not bothered him, although in truth her request has left him unnerved. Surely, he thinks, surely she understands the impossibility. She must. They can't go back now – they couldn't afford it; it would mean they'd have to repay their full fares out, as well as the return. And even if they had the money, he wouldn't want to go. It would be a failure on all fronts. Yet for her to be unhappy like this?

He sits with his shoulders hunched over the desk, papers spread around him. Beyond the window the sky is high and clear, pale and bright. He spends a lot of time looking at the sky. He does so, at first, in order to better think about his work, then to better think about Charlotte, then he looks at the sky to clear his mind, to stop thinking about these things altogether. A new feeling troubles him, as if the centre of his life were somehow slipping away. Hours pass, unproductive, until eventually he rouses himself. What is the point of this, he thinks. He stands up, shuffles his papers into his briefcase and leaves for home.

Back at the house he finds Charlotte in the kitchen, the children playing on the floor in the doorway. He steps across the mess of toys and kisses her on the cheek. She tilts her face towards him without pausing her work, making it clear she is busy. Henry would normally take a cold drink from the fridge and sit down, but today he fusses about trying to be helpful although really just getting in the way – refolding the tea towel on the rack, sweeping the crumbs from around the toaster into the palm of his hand. There is a bill on the counter and he slits the envelope open with a butter knife.

'I've been thinking,' he says slowly, inspecting the piece of paper without reading it, 'perhaps we'd be better off in a city, out of the suburbs.' His voice is soft, his tone casual – he wants, more than anything, to appease. 'Somewhere else,' he continues, 'not here perhaps. Perhaps we'd be better off in South Africa. It's an option, you know. The jacaranda trees in Cape Town are meant to be lovely, one of the most beautiful cities in the world, I've heard – high up on the mountain. Or we could get an acreage, if you'd prefer, just out of the city. Maybe this isn't the place, maybe you're right—'

Charlotte is pouring batter into a tin, the *Golden Wattle Cookery Book* open to a recipe for sponge cake. 'What?' she says. She looks up at him, her voice loaded with disbelief. 'Henry, you'd be subject to Apartheid.'

'Oh,' he says, his gaze sinking down and landing somewhere to the left of her feet, the toes of her brown house shoes dusted with flour. 'Oh, of – of course,' he stammers. He'd returned home hopeful, pleased with this new idea. It had come to him while he was driving, looking out over the tawny grasslands. The surprise now is not so much that he hadn't thought of his own predicament, but that she does. For the first time he understands that in her eyes he is, or could be, that thing: a person others would call coloured. 'Of course,' he says again, his stomach lurching. 'How did I not think of that?' His eyes dart across to Charlotte, but she is busy pushing the cake into the oven. She slams the door closed and turns to the sink. He wants her to say something else. He wants her to absolve him of this embarrassing blunder. Instead she seems to be pretending that he is not there. Henry hovers in the doorway a minute longer, then he moves to the sideboard, takes the placemats from the drawer and sets them out for dinner.

During the meal Henry is silent, and as soon as it is finished the children are whisked off for their bath. He pours a drink then, and sits down to the television news. There is the trumpet call of the evening broadcast, followed by the first bulletin, the presenter's voice drowned out by the racket coming from the bathroom, the water too hot then too cold then not deep enough, Charlotte's stern voice pitted against Lucie's wails. Henry feels a rush of shame. It was a genuine suggestion but now he must pretend it was not. Worse, perhaps, is that his own error of self-judgement has been revealed; she knows what Henry, until tonight, did not know or did not wish to admit to himself. In marriage one wants to be equal. Such a desire might not be conventional, but it is what Henry wants. Yet now he feels lesser somehow, foolish and lowly. Fraudulent. Misplaced, even to her. As if Charlotte has known all along how the world must see him and for his sake has pretended otherwise.

His attention drifts back to the set; the picture is fuzzy. He gets up from his chair and wiggles the antennae then sits back down again. It doesn't really matter, he isn't especially interested in the picture, more irritated by the flickering of the screen. It is the peace and quiet that he likes, Charlotte and the children leaving him alone in the belief that when he sits down to the evening news he is doing something noble – *Don't bother your father now* – keeping up with the events of the world for their collective benefit. 'You are an intelligent man,' Charlotte said over dinner. 'Really, how could you not think?' Her voice was steady – a parent reprimanding then absolving a wayward child. But he only suggested it for her sake, to help her and make things better. His attention drifts in and out. Sometimes, when the children are being bathed he has a little doze as the news rolls on, and this, too, is a failure to be accommodated, with Charlotte coming up behind him and stroking his head. 'Poor darling,' she'd say, 'you've been working too hard again.'

By now the news has passed and the presenter introduces the weather. The cardboard map of the country comes into view, with the weatherman standing to the left of it and pointing with his wooden rod. There are numbers stuck on the map indicating today's temperatures, and wavy lines to show low- and high-pressure zones. He's never understood these details – the way air moves up and down, in and out. Many times he's marvelled at a bird rising higher and higher on an invisible current and supposes this must be part of it, but maybe not.

In the background he can hear the bathwater gurgling fast down the plughole. Charlotte struggles to get them in then struggles to get them out – pulling the plug is the only way, playing on the fear that they'll get sucked down and end up somewhere else: China, she used to say, but now it would be England. Whatever place happens to be on the other side of the world. Upside down, back to front. Topsy-turvy.

The picture on the television flickers and jumps. This time he gives the set a good thump and the picture steadies. There's only a few minutes left, the presenter now tracing the wavy lines to indicate how the weather will change or not, depending; more heat, no rain. Henry stares blankly, not really listening but taking in the shape of the country, so large and roughly symmetrical. An island with a centre, a centre that is an interior. There is something consoling about this image – how it seems geometrically stable, as if it were of the right proportions to function as a raft, a landmass capable of floating amid all the surrounding water. A place of safety. Dry, and buoyant. A line comes to him: No man is an island. *No man is an island entire of itself.* But that is the fear, isn't it? The fear and the desire. And there he was, being exactly that in suggesting South Africa, showing his ignorance. Self-enclosed, rootless, dislocated from the main. A person painted with the tar brush – a nigger, for want of a better word, because nobody knew what else to call an English Indian man in Australia. He's heard of others not so unlike himself being excluded from the bowling club and the RSL, having stones thrown through their windows. Aliens, they were called, in formal parlance. He hadn't really meant it, the South Africa idea, she must know that. It was just a thought, that was all, just another foolish thought.

Henry switches off the set and sits back in his chair. The house is quiet: Charlotte is putting the girls to bed. He can hear, ever so faintly, the lilt of her voice as she sings to them. He closes his eyes and listens, Charlotte's voice mixing with the sound of a bird call coming from the night garden. The bird makes a hollow, hooting song, like that of an owl, but it is perhaps not an owl.

—

From where Charlotte sits she hears it too, the bird call carrying through the house. She stops singing then and listens, the bird hoot-hooting while May drifts off to sleep. She imagines, just for a moment, that it is the sound of a ghost. But come now, she thinks, there is no such thing – this is what she tells the children – and wishes only that she knew the name of the creature so as to dispel the inexplicable rush of fear. May whimpers and Charlotte is pleased to move closer to her, finding comfort in the comfort she gives. For the bird ignites a familiar, troubled feeling, the feeling she often has at night, when the children are asleep and Henry has nodded off in his chair and she is left to wander through the house switching off the lights. She feels, then, not just that she is surrounded by a country unfamiliar, but as if the whole known world has disintegrated into the salty, black air that floats around the house.

The next day is Saturday and Henry is up early, digging in the garden. The ground is tough, full of rock and root. He has no stomach for company and works hard; the sky is still pale, the sun not fully risen, but already he has sweated through his shirt. Almost there now, he thinks. Just this last corner to clear. After this he will double-dig the new beds, plant out the cucumbers in mounds. The carrots have come out looking strange: stubby and knotted, with extra roots shooting off the sides like tentacles. He has put them in a bucket and will give them to Charlotte for scrubbing. He'll have to talk to her then – they haven't said a word since dinner last night. Henry can count on one hand the times they've gone to bed without talking. It's never any good, he can't sleep on a fight. Is it a fight? He's not sure anymore – it feels as though they've reached a stalemate and he doesn't know, now, who should be sorry for what. If only she would paint again, he thinks. If she could find her way back to this. Then maybe they could forget all the rest of it.

He places his boot on the top edge of the pitchfork and presses his weight down on it. The prongs move deeper. He wriggles and levers and pulls the fork out, then drives it in again, wrestling once more with the mangle of stones and weed roots and the spindly suckers of palm trees. It is good, this. It is what he needs, what he's always wanted – to be outside, in the sun, in the air. He straightens up and rests a moment. The sun is higher. The air hot and dry. He can hear Charlotte calling to the girls. His shirt clings to his back. He closes his eyes, to better feel the sun, and knows what it is, this place, its unexpected hold on him – how it reminds him of his old life in Delhi – the flat land, the pulsing, throbbing heat, the sky. If only he had never left it. If his sister hadn't died and he hadn't been sent away to that school in the hills. That was the beginning of the end, for although he was still in India, Shimla was where his life in England really started, in that mountain fog that the British flocked to, breathing it in and savouring a memory of home, the damp air carrying the faint smell of old pea soup, vegetable and foetid. He tries to unravel the logic of his life: if he'd never been sent to the hills, if independence hadn't come.

He gives a few more good heaves with the pitchfork, applying his weight to the knot of palm roots and levering the handle back and forth. When the root is exposed he bends down, grabs it in both hands and pulls. He heaves and yanks and grunts and bit by bit the root separates itself from the dirt. Henry pulls harder, and harder, and harder still – he'll get it this time, dammit, he'll get this, he'll damn well— Then the thing snaps and Henry is thrown backwards. He lies there, blinking slowly. The breeze moves over his face. The blue sky swarms above. There's not even a cloud to look at. Trees move a little at the edge of his vision. A bird calls. A child can be heard; their voice higher, then lower, then higher again as they jump up and down on a trampoline. A dog yaps in a nearby yard.

The world is drenched in light. Then, for a moment, it falls dark as Charlotte's shadow steals across his vision. She is making her way towards the washing line. Henry stands and brushes himself down; her shadow is the only dark spot in the glaring landscape, the black bend of her shoulders and the curve of her hat wobbling over the lawn.

At the opposite end of the yard Charlotte cranks the line lower. She hauls the white sheet onto the wire. The sun is too bright, shining on the white cotton, so she has to peg the sheet with eyes half closed. The bottom of it trails on the ground. She ducks behind and pulls the hem down over the other side of the wire to lift the sheet out of the sand.

Henry watches her bend down to gather up a wet towel. She wears an A-line skirt, a split running up from the knee. It is the skirt she often wears when doing housework, and the seam at the top of the split has torn open and been mended many times. It must have recently torn again and not been fixed, for the split is long and ragged, running halfway up her thigh. As she bends over, Henry glimpses a flank of white skin. He imagines it warm, a little sticky with heat, soft. He'd like to touch it. He'd like to come up behind her and put his hand inside her skirt. Run his palm along the length of her leg. To say, Leave the children to play. Come inside with me.

Henry slips away into the front yard. Charlotte does not notice him return, so when he steps through the wet washing she starts in fright. 'Here,' he says, passing her a posy of new roses, wrapped hastily in a sheet of newspaper. Charlotte shields her eyes with one hand and takes the flowers with the other. The scent sweeps over her. Black Prince, Wild Edric. Henry reaches for her head and pulls her gently towards him. Her hair feels warm to the touch. 'I've been thinking,' he says. 'Why don't you paint me?'

Charlotte lifts her face to him, uncertain, the roses held to her nose. 'Just let me put these in water,' she says.

All that day the air hums with the sound of lawnmowers. Now the window is open to the night and the sweet green scent of cut grass drifts through the kitchen. Charlotte pushes the dining table against the wall to create room for her easel and positions a chair next to the sideboard, a brass lamp lighting the space. 'Make yourself comfortable,' she says, and Henry fidgets, crossing and recrossing his legs, putting his hands on the armrests, then taking them off and folding them in his lap. Charlotte lines up the canvas and takes her sticks of charcoal from their tin.

'It's a bit difficult,' he says, 'when I know that I'll get uncomfortable one way or another.'

'Remember,' she says, 'that you'll have to keep your legs in the same position for each sitting – it affects the slope of your shoulders.'

'Yes, yes,' Henry replies, crossing his legs the other way.

The self-portrait asks: *Is this who I am?* And almost in the same moment the painting replies: *Yes. I am this question.* Meanwhile, the portrait says, *Look. This is who I have become*, and the best ask yet another question: *Who do you see, who do you think this is?* It is the question of the self, for the self, one that brings a little tremor to the eyes of the sitter, and which makes them appear nervous when they are trying to look strong, sure, brave or wealthy. Henry holds a blue hardcover book in his hand, his index finger wedged into its depths to mark his spot. 'Can I read?' he asks, waving the book in the air.

'No, better not, it will disturb the angle of your head. Besides,' she says, shifting the easel further into the corner, 'I need to see your eyes.' He takes his final position and Charlotte crouches down to run a piece of chalk around the feet of the chair legs.

After a while he begins to notice the sounds outside: the crickets chirping in the grass, the frogs out by the water. They must have been there all the time. Strange, that he did not hear them at first. Lucie heard these sounds as she fell asleep. 'What's the night singing, Daddy?' she asked, as he tucked her in. 'What's the night singing?' Every question always posed twice. Once for her. Once for the person with the answer. They are not the sounds he fell asleep to as a boy – the caw, caw of the peacock and the rumble of trains. And they are not the night sounds of England – the wind moaning around the house, the squeak of rusty bikes passing by in the summer twilight, their riders whistling. Lucie's first memories will be of an entirely different place. And how right that seems – whatever Charlotte says about tradition and history – how right that our experience should evolve and that our children's experience should move in ever wider circles than our own. 'My children,' wrote Hawthorne, 'shall strike their roots into unaccustomed earth.' Henry wants his daughters to have something like this, something different from what he'd had. Something better.

The breeze moves at the back of his neck, and for the first time he feels a coolness, almost a thinness in the current of the night. First signs of water have begun to appear as silver dew on the lawn in the early mornings. Sweet white blossoms burst open on silver trees. Weeds have begun to sprout in the dirt and even the seedlings that Henry was sure had been killed off by the heat are coming back to life – the tomatoes and silverbeet, lettuce and pumpkin. There has been nothing but sand, and yet out of it come miraculous bright green shoots, small and thirsty.

He stares down at the floor; through the cracks of the boards he can see the dirt cave beneath the house. When he looks up Charlotte is staring at him and swaying as she considers his face from one angle then another. Her gaze jumps back and forwards over the surface of Henry's body. Every now and then she makes a mark or scratches out a set of lines, but most of the time she waltzes back and forth, then side to side, measuring his face with her thumb held to the vertical stick of charcoal. It is not what he expected. He thought he'd sit down and she'd set to work with the paints, throwing an occasional glance in his direction. Henry hears the clock, tick – tick – tick. Then he doesn't hear it at all. Then it comes again, louder than ever. Tick – tock – tock – tick. It is as though time passes only intermittently. The clock on the wall is one of three clocks given to them as wedding gifts, this one a wooden cuckoo clock with white numerals and a yellow bird that peeps out at every hour. The other two clocks remain wrapped in paper and stowed in the bottom of a packing box. They hadn't asked for such things. They already had sufficient; Charlotte had the grandfather clock, and they had the wind-up alarm clocks on either side of the bed. Not to mention their watches. Charlotte doesn't like them – clocks in general, and the given ones in particular – and shipped them over only due to some peculiar superstition that it is poor form and a breeder of misfortune to discard such presents. The gifts were given, after all, to celebrate the longevity of love.

Half an hour passes. An hour. Henry's left foot grows numb, then his right buttock begins to ache. His bladder presses against the waistband of his trousers. These dull pains flare then recede, flare and recede, and each time the space between them grows shorter, the intervals of peace smaller and smaller, until each different sporadic pain becomes constant and the three or four small agonies coalesce into one and become fierce, the different parts of his body united by the strange blaze of total discomfort.

Henry is taken aback when he looks at the canvas. After all that, there is hardly anything to see: a few lines, a mark where his eyes will be. The rough outline of a head. It will take a long time, he realises, much longer than he thought. 'Months, weeks, I don't know, it's hard to tell,' Charlotte says. 'Tomorrow?' she asks. 'We'll keep going tomorrow.'

EVERY NIGHT FOR the next three weeks Henry sits for his portrait. The chalk lines that mark the chair's place begin to fade. Before each sitting Charlotte gets down on hands and knees to find the marks and line the chair up exactly. She'll have him staring straight ahead, she thinks, into the face of the viewer, his big dark eyes like tunnels. She wants to create that odd moment when it is hard to tell whether those eyes are looking at you, or whether you are looking into them – a certain opacity, a certain depth – the deep wild eyes of an animal, like the horses with which her career began. Horses in the fields. Horses drinking water from troughs covered with ice. Old dappled horses in their stables. She liked the shape of them, the wide neat planes of their faces. What would she call this one? *Man by the Window. Man Sitting. Portrait of Henry. Portrait of a*

Husband. It was like naming a baby: the title fitted for a while, then didn't, the creation outgrowing her meagre definition.

'Could you turn to the left a fraction? And tilt your face down a bit? There. Good,' Charlotte says, hovering before him and pulling on her cigarette – a habit reserved for when she's painting. She stands back, staring at the canvas, then squints as she sucks down more smoke. She breathes out, opens her eyes wide and steps forwards with the brush.

'Watching you at work makes me think I ought to write a book about painting, about the use of museums and galleries in novels, perhaps. Something like that,' says Henry. 'Characters in galleries.'

'Oh?' replies Charlotte, distracted.

'Yes, James and George Eliot. Rome.' It is nice, this time together. There's something new and quiet about it that he likes, that helps him think, the feeling of her concentration in the air. It seems infectious.

Charlotte peers at him, makes a few sweeping gestures with her brush, then steps out from behind the canvas. 'Yes, I suppose so. That could be interesting,' she says. He finds it hard to tell when she is listening and when she isn't, whether she is open to conversation or not. 'And now?' she asks. 'Have you finished the chapter on Hardy?'

Henry lets out a small groan. 'I'm tired of it. I don't know how to finish it. People walked out today, you know.'

Charlotte is standing with her back against the wall, watching him talk. Watching, always watching. She looks down to her palette and mixes a shade of beige. She wants the texture of flesh, the illusion of candour. 'What do you mean?'

'The students. Some walked out of the lecture this morning. They slip out when they think I'm not looking, but I hear the door. Everyone hears the door.' It had been a horrid day. Out of nowhere he has started suffering memory lapses in the middle of his lectures, the last four ruined by this forgetfulness. Today he was determined to get it right; he memorised and repeated and memorised. He carried handwritten pages, and notes on little rectangles of ruled paper.

When he stepped onto the stage he knew the lecture off by heart, all the twists and turns of argument, the unfolding of ideas like a shining, rising marble staircase. He took the first step up, reached the landing, moved higher. The faces were below him, bright-eyed, listening. He talked. They listened. He took another step, talked on, and when he looked up he could see the top; he could see where he was going, where he was to end up, the sun streaming down. For a moment he was distracted by the beauty, light overwhelmed him, and before he realised what was happening the steps had fallen away and he was left floating in the light of huge, confused, crazy ideas. Dust motes coasted on the air. He saw them rise slowly towards the closed window and thought of Lucie watching them float up and up on a sunbeam and trying to catch them in her dimpled little hands. 'Mummy smells of strawberry,' she said as she banged her palms together, causing a spray of gold dust to fan out. 'What is it?' Lucie asked. 'What is the floating?'

He didn't know where he was supposed to go next. He stared at the fluorescent light, at the little black dots of dead flies caught in the white tube. He looked out into the rows of seats, at the young, wide-open faces, watching him, waiting. He opened his mouth, sucked in the cold air, then started again. Anywhere. Somewhere. He didn't know. He kept going, head down, eyes on the brown linoleum, his shiny shoes pacing the floor, trying to find the small turn he had missed.

Charlotte sighs. 'Don't say it,' Henry warns. 'Don't make excuses for them. It's me. I forgot where I was up to and bungled the lot, not just a bit, the whole of it. It's not coincidence. That's how my thoughts are now, I don't know why. It's how the book is. Or whatever you want to call it. A complete mess.' He wants her to console him but she works away in silence, the brushstrokes scratching and wobbling the canvas. Charlotte mutters something to herself then comes towards Henry, peers hard and leaps back, ducking behind the painting. She glances at him, then back at the canvas, then glances away again.

'Do you remember when we took Lucie to the National Gallery,' Henry asks, 'and people stopped to stare at her like she was part of the exhibition?'

'Yes,' says Charlotte, pausing and holding the brush in midair. 'I remember just being so happy to be out of the house and looking at colours. You know, I haven't done that since we've been here.'

'What?' asks Henry.

'Craved the sight of colour. Like I used to, in winter, when it was all grey and just the little dots of primroses could send me into giddy bouts of joy.'

'I remember the Constable room,' says Henry. 'I keep thinking of Henry James sending his characters wandering off around the Constables. Of course that's not where they were, not where he put them, but I can't change the image in my mind. For some reason that's where Isabel always is when she meets Osmond again, in London, looking at Constable's clouds.'

'We finally got to those rooms and then had to rush out because Lucie started screaming. We went there for those paintings. Then we never saw them. Maybe that's why,' says Charlotte.

She wipes her brush on her apron, the same one that she made scones in just that afternoon. Then she fusses about, looking for a tube of sienna. She is beginning work on his eyes. 'Could you lift your chin half an inch or so? And left?' she asks.

Henry fixes his vision on her. He thinks if he stares hard with wide, lifted eyes, he might channel some intensity into the painting. Over the past weeks he has begun to care about the future of this image. He wants it to succeed. He wants it to succeed while knowing the risks – that he might appear ugly, or old, or mean. But she seems happier now. She seems better than before. She is always happier when she works.

'She told me she wanted to go home today,' Charlotte says.

'Who?' replies Henry.

'Lucie. She said, "I want to go home now."'

'What did you say?'

'What do you think? I told her we were home, that this is home.'

'And?'

'She gave me this dreadful look – so fierce, so confused – then turned and ran out into the garden. It was horrible. She knew I'd lied.'

'But you didn't,' says Henry.

'I feel like I did.'

'I thought she would have forgotten.'

'Me too. I was afraid she would, and now I almost wish she had.' Charlotte's hair has come loose and long wisps fall across her eyes. She lifts the back of her hand to her forehead and pushes the hair away.

'She'll get used to it,' Henry reasons, looking to the floor. Paint is spattered across the floorboards and there are small tracks between the kitchen and easel from a blob of pigment stuck to the sole of Charlotte's shoe.

'Will she?' asks Charlotte.

She works on in silence for another half-hour or so, until she looks up and sees that Henry has nodded off in the chair. She puts down her brush and touches him gently on the face. He startles, 'Sorry, I didn't mean to.'

'Never mind. You go to bed,' she says. 'I'll clean up and come in later.'

She puts the paints away, washes the brushes, pushes the easel to one side and then takes the kitchen scraps out to the compost. She shakes the plastic container, dislodging the wet globs of tea leaves and potato peel. The garden is lit up by the upstairs lights of the neighbours' house. Charlotte has still not said hello, although she has heard them calling each other's names: Delilah, Doris. Doris is the younger one. She can see her now, the shadowy outline of her body visible behind the lace curtains and thin blind. The woman sits on the edge of the bed in her nightie, the slope of fabric loose across her large breasts. She sits there very still, all alone, and after a few minutes reaches over and switches off the light. In the morning the blind will go up – although the lace curtain is always drawn – and she'll be heard, downstairs, calling to the cat, the door open, her voice drifting through the trees, up and down the street. The sound of dry cat biscuits rattling on a tin plate, a fork tapping on the edge of a can.

A few days later there is a knock at the door. Henry is at work and the children are finally asleep after lunch. Charlotte has just set up the canvas and taken out her brushes when she hears the knock, and opens the door to find Nicholas standing there, holding a box of apples. Charlotte apologises – she hasn't visited as she promised, and realises this just now. There had been the car trip home, the argument and then the work on the painting.

He waves her apology away. 'Never you mind,' he says, holding out the box. 'I just came by to bring you these. They're from the garden, and one can only eat so many. You'd do me a favour taking them. The whole place stinks of rotting fruit.'

Charlotte lifts the box from his hands. Thanks him. 'Won't you come in?' she asks.

'No, no, I couldn't.'

'Please,' she says.

He follows her inside. All about is the mess of paints and jars. 'I *am* interrupting,' he says. Charlotte shakes her head and tells him she was just packing up, that she needs some tea. He slips his hands into his pockets and swings round from the hips, looking about. The photographs on the wall. The vase of wilting flowers on the dresser. The fallen petals. Piles of papers and books pressed open, facedown. He swivels, and sees the painting. 'Yours?' he asks. Charlotte holds out her hands, palms up, showing the paint stains on her fingers. He steps forwards, peering at the canvas. She comes to stand behind him.

'How incredibly wonderful,' he says softly.

'You think so?'

'Absolutely.'

'I'm not sure if I've got the eyes quite right, that left one espe-cially,' she says, walking forwards and standing next to him.

'Does anyone really care about getting it right?'

'I don't mean identical so much as—'

'Yes. Yes, of course.'

'—the life of it.' They stand for a moment, looking. She can hear Nicholas breathing, the air coming fast in and out of his nose.

'But there is the likeness,' he says, 'of an unexpected kind – what you were just saying. The atmosphere of a man, so to speak.' He is quiet then. She wants to believe him.

'Will you stay for tea?' she asks.

They sit on the verandah and watch pigeons peck at the crumbs left over from the children's sandwiches. Charlotte likes his chattiness, the gentle banter that is meant only to put her at ease: how he struggles with a coastal garden, his admiration of Henry's vegetable beds, how he loves to swim far out to sea and float there on his back.

'Have you ever?' he asks.

'No, no, nothing like.'

'The sky here. That is the thing.'

He is wearing corduroy trousers and a white shirt with sweat marks growing at the pits and back. He tips his head to get at the dregs of his sweet tea. From deep in the house comes the sound of a child's cry. Lucie waking. They both hear it. He puts the cup carefully back on the saucer and stands. 'I'll leave you—' he says.

'No, please stay.'

AUTUMN SLIPS QUICKLY into winter; the change is faster than any they've known before and it seems that there are only two seasons here instead of four: just hot and dry or cold and wet. There are no gradations, no signs of slow change. One afternoon a biting wind blows in from the south and by nightfall they have the fire burning in the living room. Lucie sits on the hearthrug and brushes her doll's hair. May chews on the leg of her crocheted monkey. The wind pesters; the old walls creak, the windows rattle, the air whistles in and out of the chimney. Cold gusts blow up through the gaps between the floorboards. Come midnight the wind drops and the house fills with a strange quiet. Charlotte is still up working on the painting, Henry seated before her, wishing he could have gone to bed hours ago, or got on with his own work – marking, an essay to finish, the next round of lectures.

Charlotte knows she is making slow progress; she is struggling with the movement of the thing, how best to give a sense of the muscles working, how to animate a still face. The nose has appeared, and the shadow above the top lip, but she is thinking too much, losing the connection between eye and hand. She thinks of how Nicholas stared at the painting, how he admired it. She wonders if he was telling the truth, or if he just wanted to please her, and if so, why. At this rate it could still be many months until the painting is finished. Rain starts to fall, she hears it on the tin roof. They are both tired. Charlotte has a cold. The girls have been unwell. Henry is busy and keeps to himself more and more these days. He is distracted when he walks in the door of an evening, surprised by the sight of the children. It is as if he forgets about them during the day.

Tonight she has painted and repainted the blue of his shirt. There is something wrong with the colour but she can't determine what. The colour she put down previously no longer matches the shade she sees on his body. It must be her eyes. Or the light. The fatigue perhaps. The brush feels heavy in her hand, her feet ache, and she is distracted by the knowledge of all the chores left undone. Carol came over in the afternoon with the boys. She brought cake, and while she and Charlotte sat talking in the kitchen the boys ran amuck – books were pulled from the shelves, the linen press was used as a hiding place, the taps at the bathroom sink were left running and the water overflowed onto the floor. Charlotte was late with dinner, trying to clean up. Now she has washed the plates and cutlery but left the saucepans until morning. There have been days during the past week when so many dirty dishes accumulated that she resorted to piling them on the kitchen floor or stacking them, filthy, in the unused oven, out of sight. Tonight she burned the sago pudding while changing May's nappy, and the pot, full of black sticky mess, soaks in the sink. The washing has been done only to be abandoned in a basket by the back door. By morning it will smell musty and have to be rinsed again. The dustbin is overflowing and toys lie scattered over the floor.

'How much longer, do you think?' Henry asks.

'Until we take a rest?' He isn't wearing his watch.

'No, until it's finished.' He knows, as soon as the words slip out, that it isn't a question he is meant to ask.

'Do you want to stop?' asks Charlotte, coming out from behind the canvas.

'I was just wondering.'

'And if it is too much longer?'

'I didn't mean that.'

'You mean you think I'm working too slowly.'

'No, I know that you—'

'That I'm going as fast as I can?'

'Look, you're unwell, we're both tired, I didn't mean—'

'It will take its own time,' Charlotte says, interrupting him. 'I've told you.' She turns away and fishes in the jar for a smaller brush. The smoke from the burnt pudding has drifted through the house, and everything smells of it. Henry is right. She is taking too long. She is taking up his time.

'What I meant—' Henry begins, but Charlotte cuts him off.

'I know what you mean,' she says. 'It's over. Don't trouble yourself. I understand.' She drops the palette on the table, marches into the bathroom and closes the door. Henry gets up to follow her but Charlotte clicks the lock. She sits on the toilet seat and cries.

'Now there, it's not so bad,' Henry says, his voice muffled through the wood. 'I didn't mean anything. Come out and we can talk.'

But there is nothing to say, she hasn't the energy to say anything, and she knows now that their coming here was due to the simple fact that she didn't have the strength to refuse him. *Fine, fine I'll go.* But she hadn't really meant yes. She was exhausted, and preoccupied with Lucie and the coming child. She was, quite literally, not herself then, but a woman dispersed among her children. The thought is there now, at the edge of her mind; the truth scurries from attention, from the swinging arc of the mind, the hunting light looking for it now. The thought is fleeting, only half understood, so simple it can't quite be believed. She was too tired, that's all. She hadn't the energy to say *No, I am not going. No, I am staying.* To say *Fine, you go.* And now she knows this. It makes the portrait seem paltry, a minor act of compensation, and in this moment she knows that she must make plans. Secret plans. Fantastical plans, even. She will paint and sell the paintings and keep the money in an old cake tin. She will keep the cake tin in the bottom of her wardrobe, beneath the jumpers, and she will save every cent until she has enough to send them all home. Henry can't argue, surely, if she has the money. He can't stop her. How long will it take to save so much? Years, years upon years. But it will happen eventually: she and her children at home amid the foxgloves and hollyhocks. Then she'll keep her apples wrapped in paper in a box in the cool of the cellar. She'll wake to hear cuckoos in the summer morning. She'll make jam from rosehips and hedge plums. She'll not mind the cold, she thinks, remembering the pleasure of gathering sticks and logs from the woodland in the autumn dusk. How she and Henry used to go fossicking in the evenings, creeping through the darkening patch of wood, moving over the damp earth, through the birch and oaks, dragging whole fallen branches back along the path to the house, great thick pieces of lichen-covered trees, her belly huge with Lucie then, the evening air shading to mauve, the smell of other people's fires burning, and above them the rooks coming in to roost.

'Come on, Charlotte,' he says, still talking to her through the door. 'Don't be like this.' She is tired, he thinks to himself. She is unwell. She will come out soon and they will carry on. But does he want to? The effort of sitting still, in the same position, night after night, was more than he'd imagined. He sat there on the hard wooden chair and dreamed of lying on a featherbed. Of lying on a beach. Of lying down and being fed cherries and grapes, fruits dangling into his mouth from a stalk. If only he could sit there and read. *Portrait of a Reader*, she could call it.

'No,' she'd said. 'I need your eyes.'

'Couldn't I read until you get to my eyes? Or once you've finished them?'

'*Henry*,' she'd said, as though he were a small, silly child.

Charlotte fills the basin with hot water and scrubs the skin of her hands with the nail brush. The water burns but the brown paint sticks to her cuticles. The painting is the only thing she has for herself, he must know this – how she endures the chores of the day so as to have these hours, this task. And without it? What will she be then? She is a fool, she thinks, as she scrubs her skin pink. She is a fool for thinking she could live this way, to think she could hurry it along, to think she could redeem the situation with a painting. Her plan is unreal, ridiculous even. Henry would laugh. She splashes water on her face and rubs hard with the small damp handtowel.

Henry knocks on the door again. 'Charlotte?' he says. 'Charlotte – come out of there now.'

Next morning she wakes early, carries the canvas out to the garage and covers it with an old blanket. It is still dark outside and the air smells of smoke. Inside, the fire has died down to black. She clutches her dressing-gown against her chest and crouches, poking and prodding the embers. Burnt wood breaks up into splinters and ash floats out into the living room. She pokes some more, finds the small red centre of the log and blows.

Henry lies in bed. He is awake but keeps his eyes closed, listening to Charlotte tend the fire. He knows he ought to get up but it is too cold; the walls are icy to the touch and freezing air seeps in between the floorboards. He thinks of his book, the hypothetical book, not yet in existence, the book that will be, eventually, new essays on Hardy.

Charlotte puts a cup of tea down at his bedside, the soft grey glow of daylight slipping in behind her. She switches on the bedside lamp and goes to the wardrobe for her clothes.

'What are you doing?' Henry asks.

'Going into town.'

'So early?'

'Once the girls are dressed and fed.'

The children hear their mother's voice and come into the bedroom. Charlotte opens the curtains. A film of condensation covers the lower half of the window and Lucie clambers onto a chair to run her finger across the silvery wet glass – *through the mist*, she says. Her finger squeaks as she draws. She draws eyes, a bird, a long banana with caterpillar legs. There is the phlegmy sound of her breathing, in and out through her mouth, chest rattling. When she speaks her voice sounds wet and bubbly: *Look, look whad I dwawed*. Little strips of bright world appear through the sketch, small finger-widths of world, the frangipani with its leaves almost gone, the calico cat on the tin roof of the shed. She presses her nose to the cold glass. Fine white light comes sidelong into the room, illuminating her silhouette: the bright haze of her hair, all knot and curl, the fluff and pill along the sleeves of her blue jumper where her little arms rub back and forth, back and forth all day long. On the ground below her, May chews on a lemony biscuit – yes, it is good, she nods. Sweet crumbs dot the crown of her head and float in the wisps of her fringe. She holds the small biscuit in both hands as if it were a sandwich. Then she lifts one hand to brush her hair away from her face and leaves a dusting of crumbs, yellow against her creamy forehead.

The river path leads, eventually, to Nicholas's house. Charlotte sits in the conservatory sipping tea while he waters the geraniums, the room a bright tangle of flowers, wild blue, trailing purple, common brick-red and white. 'Welcome to the jungle,' he says. The glass wall overlooks the front garden and the sea, and from where she sits the horizon is a high, flat wall of watery blue. In the garden the children play, teasing Nicholas's dog, a labrador called Gretta. Henry does not know she is here.

Water drips through the bottom of the pots and onto the ground. She tells Nicholas about the portrait, about her and Henry arguing, then feels guilty for doing so and tries to make up for it by telling him more – about her plan that feels, now, in the light of day, rather embarrassing. No, he says, not at all. He seems, perhaps, even excited by it. They sit at a low glass-topped table and the flowers engulf them in a wide green arc, arranged behind and around Nicholas as he sits back on a cane lounge. Charlotte sits across from him, perched on the edge of a low rocking chair. The glass door is open to the breeze and the geraniums bob up and down, nodding their bright heads. She watches the girls dance around outside; they pull Gretta's tail and stroke her ears and the dog grins and drools and rolls over.

'And then I just keep thinking,' she says, 'how much easier it would be if I didn't do this. If I didn't paint. I think of quitting altogether but as soon as I do I'm overcome by this terrible empti-ness. I think of stopping, and then I think, but what would I do?'

'What would you do?' he asks, leaning forwards.

'I don't know. Nothing. I'd do nothing. I could do nothing. I'd have to reinvent myself, but when I think about that, it would be like trying to become no one, to become someone else, someone not me.'

'And then?'

'Then I think, well, I can't stop. Because it's the only way I know how to live. It's the only way I know how to try. I don't know. It's a continuity. The thing that makes me feel continuity. Of life. Myself. It feels like I would just be nothing if I stopped. It would be an erasure.' Her gaze drifts back outside. Lucie strokes Gretta's pink belly. Charlotte has said too much and feels herself shrink back. She puts her teacup down and stares at the bright patch of sea in the distance, the grey outline of a cargo ship balanced on the horizon.

'Maybe it's the hope that gives you the sense of continuity, not the painting itself. Maybe – maybe the painting doesn't matter as much as you think,' he says, reaching over and picking a few dead flowers off the geranium closest to him.

'Don't say that,' she replies.

'No. Of course not,' he says, looking down and stretching his legs out before him. The tips of his brown shoes shine in the sun.

'But perhaps, perhaps that's part of it,' she says. 'I don't know. I blame things, and then I feel awful for it. I blame the place, the weather, the country. I blame Henry. I wish everything wouldn't always come back to that.' She picks up her teacup again. 'I shouldn't tell you this,' she says. Nicholas blushes and Charlotte realises that what she first took for arrogance is simply nerves. He is more beautiful than she first thought, too. His eyes seem to brighten when he looks at her. She has the urge to touch him, just for a moment. What would that be like? This clever man bristling with talk. What is he doing here? And why her?

'No. But it is difficult,' Nicholas says.

'Painting?'

'Marriage.'

'Yes, people say that, don't they.' Charlotte closes her eyes.

She stays there all day. They talk and drink more tea. They go out into the garden. Everything that moves seems alive. The shadow of the tree branches on the grass. The dappled light on the dark lower boughs of the tree. There are soft circles of light that widen then shrink as the leaves above lift and open in the breeze. Then comes a quick gust of wind, and the flickering of light makes it seem as if the trees are shivering.

They sit beneath the plum that in the strange weather has not lost its foliage, and in the green shade her legs look terribly white. Around them are mandarin trees, lemon and orange. Some leaves curl and hold the light. Others droop, letting the light slip and fall. Strings of spider web glitter between the branches. Birds sing further out, the sound higher up, floating above the human voices. What she wants, she realises, is a witness to her life. Someone who can affirm what is true. She is thinking of the doubt that has grown between her and Henry, how neither of them believes the other's story, the other's version of historical truth. Why they moved, why they must or must not stay. Who they moved for. There is something impoverishing about this mutual mistrust, this mutual suspicion – something mean, and they do not know how to rise above it. Yet both are nostalgic for the same thing: the good life, or at least the fantasy of it.

She does not remember travelling home. She remembers moving, but does not know how. Was it the bus, or a taxi, or did someone drive her? She remembers images: the light moving between the trees, the sight of water, then no water, then water again. There is the memory, further back, of children wading, of the sky through dark branches, of the sun pushing its way through dense canopy. At lunchtime she and Nicholas had packed a picnic and they all walked down to the sea. There were green apples, ham sandwiches, tea from a thermos. Seagulls squawked in the air above. Then everything seemed terribly bright, too bright; something flashed at the corners of her eyes.

She feels a coolness against her skin now as a cold flannel is pressed to her forehead.

Then it is removed, dipped in water – the sound of ice against the edge of a bowl – and replaced, the cloth again cool and damp on her face. Henry is beside her, stroking her arm; the room is dark, the window is dark. 'You have a migraine. It was the midday sun,' he says. 'The brightness of it.' The same thing used to happen to his mother in Delhi. He sits beside the bed and tells Charlotte these stories: of the heat, the gold haze of the sky, the birds of prey drifting above the city. He tells her of his mother, vanishing for days into her darkened room, attended to by whispering servants bearing heavy silver trays that never held more than a fine porcelain cup filled with beef tea. Charlotte reaches out and takes hold of Henry's hand. 'What happened today?' he asks, but she just closes her eyes. 'There now,' he says, stroking her arm. 'Sleep now,' he says. Now, she thinks, now, now, now.

When she wakes it is just after two in the morning. She slips out of bed and goes to the garage. The migraine feels like a black hole into which the day has vanished. The afternoon seems to have occurred so long ago, and in her mind's eye it appears smaller because of this: Nicholas, the scene in the conservatory, the trip home, the cool water on her forehead – all this has shrunk in her memory, so distant, so small in her mind, like a miniature; the room is small, the people are small, as if she is peering at the scene from a great height.

She switches on the light and squints against the bare bulb. Her head is tender and her body feels light, as though she's emerged from days of fever. She drags the painting from its place behind the boxes and pulls the blanket away. Then she sets to work, filling in the mouth, broadening the forehead, blocking in the blue of his shirt. All painting is done from memory, she reasons. Even when Henry sits before her, she turns away from him every time she makes a mark, holding the image of his face in her mind and matching it to the image on the canvas.

Henry gets up in the night for a glass of water and sees the light on in the garage. *What happened today?* She still has not answered. The water is cool and tastes of river. He has been dreaming – they were on their way to Africa. He wanted to take Charlotte on safari. He thought there was nothing much to the dream, but as he looks out across the dark yard the memory of it comes back to him. 'There are lions and tigers and bears,' he'd said to her – *lions and tigers and bears!* He held out a guidebook, on the front was a photograph of an elephant and a leopard. 'I don't want to die at the hands of a wild animal,' Charlotte said.

'Wild animals don't have hands.'

'I don't want to be chased, eaten, squashed in a stampede, lost in the jungle—'

She pretends she is not afraid of things, but Henry knows she is – she is afraid of insects, spiders, snakes, very large dogs and very small dogs, mice, heights, swimming over seaweed. 'You will be happy there,' he said.

'How can you predict the future?'

'Because I am getting older and once you are my age you have been into the future many times.'

He knows she is out there painting. Is it still the portrait? Something happened today. He feels afraid of this.

With the winter nights, rats have come to nest in the roof. In the dark, when the house is quiet he hears them – they scratch and make strange clicking, hissing noises that must be their speech. They are there now. Above him in the kitchen. The sound makes him shiver. He hears one gnawing low down at the wall near the oven, trying to make a hole. He stamps then, to frighten it. The scratching stops a moment, then starts again. He puts his glass on the draining rack and goes back to bed. He tries to stay awake for Charlotte's return, so as to ask her what she's doing, but she doesn't come to bed, and when he wakes again it is light and Charlotte has already dressed in fresh clothes and set out the bowls and plates for breakfast.

A FEW DAYS later the phone rings. The children are taking their morning nap and Charlotte gets up quickly to answer the call, not wanting the sound to wake them. The book she is reading slips off her lap.

'Gretta is sad,' Nicholas says. His voice surprises her – she had forgotten she'd given him her number. 'I think she misses the children,' he continues. 'I thought I might take her for a walk by the river over your way. Would you join me?'

'I'd love to,' she says, 'but the girls are sleeping.' She looks down at her yellowed copy of *Mrs Dalloway* lying on the floor. There is a chair in the kitchen that is always in sunlight and she's been sitting there, reading. This is one of her most treasured moments of the day, the house quiet, still. Today she has been reading the opening pages of the book over and over again; Clarissa setting out for flowers. *What a lark! What a plunge!* It makes her think of Lucie as a baby, riding on Henry's shoulders as they walked down Oxford Street in London in the spring – Lucie's hair lifting in the breeze and her chubby arms waving in delight above her head, the child laughing, chortling, thrilled by the height and the crowds, Henry holding fast to her legs.

'Couldn't you come when they wake?'

'Well, yes, I suppose. But dinner—'

'Oh, come on, the rain has stopped and it's a beautiful day.'

Something always surprises her. Today he seems taller than she first thought. When he tilts his head towards Gretta his soft hair falls forwards over his eyes. Gretta licks and jumps at the children, leaping one way then the other and eventually falling over sideways in excitement. Three brown ducks skid across the smooth river and Gretta lunges after them, thundering into the water. Nicholas throws the ball further out, past the ducks, and Gretta swims to fetch it, forgetting about the hunt. The sky has grown overcast, a white circle of sun just visible through the film of cloud.

Gretta comes back with the ball. Nicholas picks it up and throws it out across the grass then wipes his hands on the front of his trousers. Dog slobber and mud. His hands remind her of her father's hands, thick and veined, the white skin gathering a reddish tinge.

Again and again the ball vanishes into the distance, Gretta and the children racing after it.

Charlotte is starting to like the path by the river, perhaps even love it a little. Yet she feels somehow troubled by this, as if it is a betrayal of sorts, something to be suspicious of. As if this flicker of affection is not part of her real feelings, or at least not as strong as her real feelings, and thus shouldn't be permitted – as if this new sentiment were trespassing in some way.

It would make life easier to feel this – to feel real affection for this new place. It would make Henry happy. But she is afraid – without clear reason – that it would necessarily lessen her feelings for home. As if there were only so much affection, so much loyalty, to be portioned out. It is the same kind of fear, she realises, that she felt when pregnant with May. Would she have enough love for a second child? Would it mean giving up some of the love for her first? How mad that seems now – the foolishness of not seeing, not knowing, that such love simply doubles, triples, quadruples as required. Unless one refuses, of course – unless one resists.

At some point they leave the river and walk beneath the pines. Beneath the trees it is always dark. Small wedges of light shine down through the spaces between the needles.

'And the portrait?' Nicholas asks.

'Yes,' she says, dropping her voice as if sharing a secret, 'it is almost finished.'

He nods as if this news satisfies him. 'And how do you know when it's finished?' he asks. She likes the way he begins his questions as if picking up in the middle of a long chain of thoughts: and, and, and.

'I suppose,' she says, 'when it is no longer changeable, for better or worse.'

They have become friends. Or conspirators. Something, anyway, that Charlotte does not quite understand. They walk further into the trees.

'There was a man once who became a priest because I didn't marry him,' says Charlotte.

'Was he terribly ugly?' Nicholas laughs.

'No, not at all. I just didn't know he wanted to marry me.'

'He didn't ask you?'

'Apparently he was going to, but then he heard I was engaged to Henry.'

'What makes you think of this?'

'I don't know – walking here with you, thinking about the other lives we all might have led. Other lives and other places.'

The path turns uphill and the trees thin. Overhead, clouds break apart and windy light ripples the long grass. The yellow blooms of dandelions nod at the ground. They talk about Duccio's flat panels of face, Bacon's smears. Lucie runs ahead then comes back and takes hold of Charlotte's hand. She tugs at Charlotte, pulls her round. As she does so she begins to sing – *Ring a ring o' rosies, a pocket full of posies*. The light high voice of a child. Charlotte joins her, the two of them singing together, their outstretched arms and interlocked hands forming a rough diamond. Charlotte looks down at her child, the top of her hair brown, the long ends blonde, even white, lightened by the sun. And below this the small dress decorated with a pattern of violets, its skirt fanning out over the grass. *A-tishoo! A-tishoo! We all fall down!* Nicholas claps as Charlotte and Lucie land on the ground. The last wild frangipani leaves sway up above, the branches wobbling, making light appear and disappear through the shifting triangles of green. The sky seems far away, the sun close. Nearby a boy flies a yellow kite. The kite is arrow-shaped, with a long rainbow tassel for a tail. The boy holds the line tight while the kite noses the high air, dipping and tugging – the wind strong. It looks alive up there, an animal trying to escape its invisible tether, eager to follow the pull and blow.

They part company at River Drive. Nicholas reaches out and takes Charlotte's hand. He holds it too gently, and for a moment too long. She feels his palm against hers, soft and dry. There is ink under the nails of his right hand. They stand at the corner of the street, the sun in Charlotte's eyes. 'See you soon, I hope,' he says. Behind him is the copse of pines they have just walked through, the trees dark against the bright white sky.

While Charlotte is out walking, Henry arrives at work to find his office locked. His books are boxed up and his name on the door replaced by another. The secretary points the way to his new office, a poky little room at the end of a brick alley in the far corner of the courtyard. It is smaller than the last, and its narrow, dirty window looks out onto another brick wall. He pushes at the window but it will not open. Some new professor has moved into Henry's old office. Someone American. Young and already famous, so the rumours go.

While Henry is unpacking his books there is a knock at the door. It's Collins. 'I'm sorry about all this,' he says, waving an arm in the direction of Henry's files and papers now spread across the floor. 'It was a last-minute thing. We'll have you back in the other room for next year.'

'It's quite all right,' says Henry. 'I understand.' Of course he understands. It is clear to him that they both understand everything. He pushes a book into place on the shelf.

'Actually,' Collins says, glancing down, 'I came by on another matter.'

'Oh?'

'I'm afraid there's been a change of plan. A change of numbers. That new course you planned – on Yeats. We might have to postpone it. There's just not the numbers.'

'But I thought—'

'Yes, there was interest. But it clashes with the course on Donne, and I'm afraid the numbers there were greater, and it's been running for a long time, that one. Be a terrible shame to stop it now. It's almost a tradition in these parts.'

'What about something else, something new? Something to catch their interest.'

'Their interest?' Collins asks, confused.

'Something modern.'

'It would have to be discussed. But I suppose if they're all reading it anyway – Plath and Larkin and all that – well, why study it? Anyway, let's raise it at the next meeting.'

'Yes, I see.'

'Next year, though, we'll have you back in your old room and you can run Yeats then. Although it would be good to teach a poet whose name the students know how to pronounce. Anyway, Donne doesn't run first semester.'

'Yes, of course,' says Henry, picking up another book from the box. 'Yes, I understand. Thank you.'

'Good then,' Collins says. He makes to leave but then turns back. 'By the way, I'm thinking of writing something on Hardy. The elegies, actually. Incredible poems, aren't they? Don't know why I'd never thought of it before. I'd appreciate a chat when you've got time: pick your brain and so on. Anyway,' he knocks a light fist on the doorframe, 'I'll be in touch.'

Henry is left standing, book in hand, as Collins's footsteps fade down the alley. Collins is a Medievalist. What is he thinking, taking up the Victorians? He's moving in on Henry's territory, that's what. Crowding him out.

Australia is a land that offers a vision of the world as it was at creation, a country of new beginnings. It is where one comes when one needs to feel close to the original ferment of the earth. That is the story, is it not? Great men have become part of this place in one way or another and Henry has made it his business to know of these things. Two of Charles Dickens's sons came out to make their lives here; both Joseph Conrad and Thackeray walked around Sydney Harbour; Alfred Marshall built up his economic theories based on money made through the labour of convicts and Aboriginals. It is not a bad place. But it is not quite what Henry thought it would be. It is not the free place he was promised. There is freedom looking up into the sky, and when he tends the vegetable garden, or plays with his children, but not everywhere. He should have seen it coming. 'Where did you say you're from?' Something like that. Of course it was *something* like that.

Once more no one knows quite who, or what, he is meant to be. He experienced this in England, but it is worse here – with his Queen's English and his strange-coloured skin. Just last week he noticed a small article in the newspaper about migrants going home. 'I miss the BBC,' one woman was reported to have said. And sure enough, everybody likes his voice because it reminds them of England or of the voice they'd like for themselves. The voice of the homeland. The voice of the clever and the worldly. But his voice and his appearance do not fit. Not here. Perhaps not anywhere.

He can not have been what they were expecting. A British citizen, according to the British Nationality and Aliens Act of 1914, which deemed all people of the colonies and dominions British subjects. Had his parents known of the changes that were coming? Was that why they hurried Henry out of India? By 1948 the Nationality Act had been forever altered, and under this new legislation it was quite possible he'd never have made it into England, and certainly not Australia. Under this act he'd never pass as white, not officially, not on paper. Could he prove the British ancestry on his paternal side? The stories were all there but he'd never seen the documents. As it happens, he is deemed a White Australian by default. Because he is legally British, and British in dress, custom and family ways. Yes, they ate roast on Sundays. Yes, they went to church. Yes, they were members of the tennis club. Because he is British he travelled on an assisted passage to this mythical country. Utopia – that is how he described it to Charlotte. They didn't interview him for the job. They had no idea what he looked like. He was coming from England, that was what they knew. And now what? He's been moved to a poky little office, his course has been cut, and Collins is preparing to stake his claim. It is over, that is what he thinks. I am done.

His hands tremble as he fastens the buttons on his coat. The buttons are large and covered in cloth and the holes are a little too small. He will go home and see his children. That is all he wants these days, the company of his family. It will not be long now. Just a short drive and he'll be home. Will they have eaten lunch? Will they all sit down together? And little Lucie, what will she tell him about her adventures? He never imagined he'd be impatient to talk to a two-year-old, but as he drops his notebook into his briefcase and turns to leave he knows that is all he wants, all he needs.

CHARLOTTE ARRIVES HOME from their walk to find Henry's car parked in the drive. She pushes open the front door and calls out, she and the children tumbling inside, all talking at once. They fall quiet at the sight of Henry sprawled on the sofa fast asleep, one arm flung over his head, a leg dropping off the side of the cushion, his mouth hanging open. Charlotte crouches down next to him. He snores once and his eyeballs flicker beneath their thin lids. The children look on. This, Charlotte thinks, is what he might look like when he is dead – the bluish tinge beneath his sunken eyes, the dark hollows of his temples. And his jowls, the way they fall back towards his ears, pulling the skin of his cheeks tight and exaggerating the fine bone-work beneath. Charlotte leans over, watching him breathe; he takes shallow gulps of air through his open mouth, thin lips just covering his small, tightly packed teeth. Looking at it like this – open and still, the lips stretched taut – his mouth seems not a mouth but a black and shallow hole in the lower half of his face.

Just then Henry startles and wakes, his eyes opening straight onto Charlotte. He blinks and the black circles of his pupils shrink, pulling her into focus. 'Oh—' he says. 'It's you.' He sounds relieved, pleased, perhaps a little surprised, as if she has come back to him, as if he's lately become accustomed to seeing her as someone else. She leans forwards and kisses him on the cheek then goes outside to fetch the washing. The breeze has looped the tablecloth over the line and made a tangle of it. Charlotte gives the cloth a few good tugs and pulls it free, bundling the washing against her stomach and carrying it to the house. She feels the air shift around her; a change is coming.

Inside, Lucie wants to read Henry a book – she has in her hand a copy of *The Tale of Mrs Tiggy-Winkle* by Beatrix Potter and is already telling him the story. 'And they find a door, a mountain, and is a key, I think? And spikes. There. See? Can I touch spikes? They are not spiky.' She is referring to the illustration of the hedgehog's head, tucked up beneath a cotton handkerchief. It is like listening to someone recount a dream, Henry thinks, the connections grand and infeasible and incomplete. Lately she has taken to reading to her dolls. What did he hear her say? *Once upon a time and long long ago and again and again and again.*

In the kitchen the phone rings. Charlotte answers. He hears her voice lifting and she laughs. It must be Carol. They call each other often these days and can chat for hours. Henry doesn't know what women find to talk about for so long. It suits him though: right now he really doesn't feel like talking. Normally it is Charlotte who checks the mail, but because he came home early he was at the gate when the postman arrived. He knew the paper straight away – rough and cream-coloured. A letter from India. He read it in the kitchen then put the letter away and lay down on the sofa where Charlotte later found him. It was too much: the scene with Collins, then this news.

It had been a poor monsoon, the letter from the nursing home said. So much rain and fog and dampness. His mother hadn't handled it well. There'd been the flu, then a chest infection and now she was refusing to eat. 'I write only to inform you,' the director said. His mind jumps from one difficulty to another. He'll have to think about it. He doesn't want to go – he thought he'd left that place forever. And Collins? It's clear the man is out to make him obsolete. Henry pulls Lucie up onto his lap. 'Read! Read!' she says.

'Once upon a time,' begins Henry, 'there was a little girl called Lucie, who lived at a farm called Little-Town. She was a good little girl – only she was always losing her pocket handkerchiefs!'

Lucie giggles; she likes the book because of the pictures, and because she and the girl in the story share the same name. She strokes the picture of the tabby cat. 'Nice pussy, nice pussy,' she says. Henry relaxes. He likes the feeling of his child against him. He twists a strand of Lucie's hair around his finger. He's worked so hard. And now? He could let it all go. His mother would never stand for such a thing. She didn't send him to England so that he could capitulate. But now, now she might never know. What is the point, really, of a life spent in the hope of becoming a footnote in someone else's work? There is something oddly seductive, he thinks, about the prospect of giving up. He could let Collins have what he wants and be done with it.

Lucie turns the pages, wanting to look at all the pictures. While she does so he drifts off into memories of India, to thoughts of that high, wide Indian sky racing across the plains. He hasn't remembered India for a long time, not properly, not deeply. He's thought about Australia, and he's remembered England, and he's thought of how good it is to be in Australia and not England. But this experience is new. He does not know, in fact, if he has ever remembered these things before – they are so vivid, so surprising, like first memories, even though he knows they are not, cannot be first memories. The gardener sweeping the lawn, gathering the fallen neem leaves into a small pile then wrapping them in newspaper. The green, green grass beneath the yellow leaves, soft as carpet. The gold embroidery on his mother's day bed glowing in the sunlight – carefully stitched pictures of doves and elephants, children dancing in a ring. His father taking him by rail trolley to the tennis club in the summer. The slingshot that Henry wore around his neck and loaded with plum stones. The parrots, the pigeons, the green butterflies and the black ones with turquoise specks, the bats flying over at dusk.

Birds flying in separate directions. And Henry charging about, far below, firing fruit stones and pebbles into the air. Rarely did he hit anything – a lame pigeon perhaps, unable to take flight. But England cured him of his outdoor ways. That, and the awful sadness of leaving his mother behind. He realises, now that he is older, that he knew her for such a small portion of his life, just one decade of childhood. To think of sending his own children away at such an age.

Lucie pulls at his shirt. She wants him to read again. But his voice betrays his wandering attention and Lucie jumps off his lap and goes in search of Charlotte.

How long has it been, he wonders, since he's seen his mother? Seven years, more? He and Charlotte visited her shortly after their engagement and she hardly recognised him. It was his fault. He shouldn't have left her there. He should have brought her out to England after his father died in '54. But he couldn't force her, and she wouldn't go.

Her great and foolish dream was that the British would return to India and she would find her place again in the strange seam that ran between the two cultures. If the British were there, she could aspire to be one of them. If they were not, she was as good as lost in a foreign country. Now she lives on the dark fringe of the hills, belonging to no one.

Outside it begins to rain. Light at first, then heavy, torrential. Rain lashes the garden, wind lashes the rain. He hears the back door open then sees Charlotte braving the weather, her thin body folded over behind an umbrella that she carries like a shield in front of her, fending off the downpour to get to the vegetable patch, where she tugs three lettuces free of their moorings in the mud. She will make lettuce soup because that is what they have in this climate: summer vegetables in wintertime.

The next day Nicholas comes over while Henry is at work. Charlotte takes him to the garage and shows him the finished portrait. She knows no one should see it before Henry has and yet there they are, she and Nicholas, looking at the picture together. 'This painting,' he says, 'is a marvel.' The slight disturbance of balance across the face, the blurring of shadow over the cheeks. She has done something that he has never seen before. It is so beautiful, so strange, real and yet not real. True somehow. 'Do you know,' he says aloud, 'do you know how good this is?'

He takes off his glasses and inspects the surface of the painting. Charlotte hasn't seen him without his glasses before. It is like the removal of a disguise – his face is lovely this way, she realises. Brighter.

'No,' she says, 'I'm not sure. It's not—'

'Of course it is.'

She must show this work, he says. She must do more. The world should see this, he tells her grandly. His tone makes her nervous. *World*; the word echoes slightly in her head. As if there were such a thing; her life here has become so small. For a moment she thinks she could love him – does love him – simply because he wants this for her. She hasn't fallen in love for a long time and the feeling frightens her: a nervous rush in her stomach, the need to touch him. 'Now you're being silly,' she says, flapping a hand at him, although the thought thrills her; she wants to believe him. She wants them to believe in this together. They stand in silence, looking.

She shows him other paintings as well – the canvases shipped from England. There are still lifes, landscapes, the painting of the storm coming over the fens. 'This,' says Nicholas, pausing at the storm canvas. 'This is the one. May I?' he asks, picking it up and holding it at arm's length. They look at the bruised English sky together. Then he puts the painting down and leans it against the wall so as to get a better perspective. 'Wonderful,' he says under his breath. 'Just wonderful.

'I'd like to buy it,' he says. 'Really I would.'

'No,' says Charlotte. 'I can't.'

'I think you can,' he says. 'I think about nine hundred dollars should do it.'

'No. No, I'm not sure. Besides, that's far too much.'

'I think you'll find that it's exactly enough.'

'For what?'

'The cost of a ticket to London. You and the children.'

'But why?'

'You know very well why. Because it's time for you to go home.'

She hadn't forgotten about the plan so much as pushed the thought away, as if it might somehow jinx the painting. During the day, when she is at home with the children, such a plan seems fanciful, ridiculous. A kind of gross ambition. Yet then, at night, when the girls are asleep and she's out in the garage working away again – then the plan returns, but differently. Then it seems exciting, the obvious thing. A night vision. It hadn't seemed possible to carry this dream into daylight, and yet here he is, standing beside her and making this suggestion, offering this thing that she's told herself, sternly, she must not hope for. Not ever. Not really.

'So,' Nicholas says, 'will you let me?'

THAT EVENING SHE watches Henry tend the roses. He has cured them of rust and mite and now they flourish and grow up past his waist. There is a breeze and the flowers sway. Henry is tall, his long arms reaching over to check the buds. In his blue shirt he is the same colour as the dusk. She watches him fade.

Later that night, over dinner, Henry says to her, 'Where is the painting?'

'What painting?'

'I had to find something in the garage this afternoon and I noticed the storm painting is gone. I'd seen it. Now it's not there.'

Charlotte meets his eyes. 'I sold it,' she says.

'What?'

'I sold it.'

'To whom?'

Charlotte is quiet, her eyes lowered to her plate. She twists her wedding band round and round her finger.

'Surely not,' Henry says. He knows she has befriended Nicholas; he doesn't approve, but he knows. 'After all I . . . after you—' He bites his tongue. It is an accident and the pain is fierce. He snaps forwards, holding his mouth, his face wrinkling.

Charlotte tells him what happened – that Nicholas came to the house and saw the paintings and offered her money. 'Enough money, in fact, to go home.'

When Henry speaks there is blood at the corner of his lips. He spits his words. 'How dare you, how dare – if you imagine I'm going to . . . A man, that man, here!'

'He's a friend,' says Charlotte.

'He's not a friend, he's a cad. He's a—'

'Henry, stop it.'

'*Me?* That's what I should be saying to you. So what, he wanders around, stays for tea, *buys your painting*. How dare he think—'

'Stop it, Henry!' Charlotte yells. The girls stare. May begins to wail.

Lucie kicks in her highchair. '*Sdop! Sdop!*' she cries.

'When will you accept this?' Henry says. 'We don't need to go back. It is an insult and the man means it to be. He's not interested in the damned painting. Fine, keep the money, but don't think I'm letting you go anywhere.' He shakes his head. 'The gall,' he says quietly. 'The gall.'

'It was mine,' Charlotte says, looking down at her plate. 'It's a painting. I sell paintings.'

'Well, what did he pay?' he asks, sawing into a piece of meat. Charlotte stands and clears the other plates from the table. 'Tell me, Charlotte!' he calls after her. 'Tell me, damn it!'

Charlotte disappears into the bedroom and Henry puts the girls to bed. He is an anxious father, always worried about colds and chills, and as a precaution covers the children with extra blankets, leaving them to sweat and thrash about in the night. By morning the spot where Lucie's plait meets her skull is damp and matted.

'Turn around,' Charlotte says, 'and let me get this mess out. You let me brush your hair,' she tells her, 'and I promise a trip to the park.'

She sits on the edge of the bed and grips the child between her thighs. The elastic is tangled up in tight loops of hair. Charlotte tugs at it and Lucie's head jerks backwards. 'Ow!' she cries. '*Ooow*. You're hurting! You're hurting!'

Charlotte hears the faint sound of hair snapping as the elastic begins to come free. 'I'm not hurting. Just stay still and it will be done.'

But Lucie only squirms, pushing at her mother's legs. 'Let go!' she cries, her little voice breaking up into tears. 'Let me go!'

'If I let you go now there's no trip to the park.'

'No!'

'No what?'

'Don't brush my hair! Please don't brush my hair!'

'And no park?'

'Yes, park!'

'Then stay still and let me do your hair!' Charlotte tugs hard, removing the elastic, and with quick fingers rips the plait apart as if unwinding a rough rope.

Lucie begins to sob, then scream, as Charlotte takes the brush in her hand and hacks away at the knots. She hits her mother's legs and squirms and wails, but Charlotte's thighs hold her fast. 'Nooo! You're hurting me! You're hurting!'

Charlotte brushes faster. It looks like it hasn't been brushed in weeks. Surely not, though. Surely she brushed their hair yesterday morning. 'I'm sorry,' she says to Lucie. 'I'm sorry, but it has to be done.'

'No, it doesn't have to be done!'

'Do you want me to cut it then? Because if I can't brush it I'll have to cut it.'

'Cut it! Cut it!' Lucie wails, her head wobbling back and forward as the brush works in and out of her hair. She is crying so hard now that she begins to cough and retch.

Charlotte sees the glint of her sewing scissors on her dressing table and just then hears the squeak of Henry's study door. She grips Lucie's hair in one hand and lunges for the scissors. Then in one swift motion she swoops back and drives the scissors into the matted root of the plait. They are small scissors and the knot is thick and wide. She has to saw at it, opening and closing the blades, the cutting making a rough, scratchy sound. Just as she is about through, Henry steps into the room. There. It is done. Lucie runs to Henry and hurls herself against his legs.

Charlotte stands up, a bunch of pale baby hair in one hand and her little blue-handled sewing scissors in the other. 'Your princess,' she says and drops the hair on the floor. Then she pushes past Henry and leaves the room.

Henry gathers Lucie into his arms and lies down on the bed with her, rocking her until she falls asleep, still whimpering. He loses track of how long he lies there. When finally he eases himself off the bed the first thing he does is get down on his knees to gather up every last piece of hair and put it in his pocket.

For days they do not speak. He knows Charlotte did it to punish him, and that it had nothing to do with Lucie. He will never forget the scene he came upon in the bedroom. His blubbering, inconsolable child, and her mother, rising up from the bed with the trophy of hair in her fist. How she held it out to him.

Over the next week, Henry stays out of Charlotte's way. He leaves for work early and when he comes home he keeps to the garden, busying himself with the orange tree. Charlotte watches him from the kitchen window – the stepladder, his grey gardening slacks visible only from the knee down, his torso and head sunk in leaves. He has found an infestation of stink bugs and is killing them. The air around the tree reeks: a mix of turpentine, acid, petrol. Who knows when the insects came, but they have descended, grown fat and black without his noticing and now swarm over the leaves, curling them, sucking the juice from the fruit, waving their orange antennae above their beady orange eyes. Henry holds a bucket of water and picks off the bugs one by one then drops them in, trying to drown them. He keeps his white golfing hat pulled down low towards the bridge of his nose, and when he spots a bug, he ducks his face, pinches it off the leaf and drops it in the bucket. 'Get back!' he shouts if Lucie or May venture near him, their faces upturned. The stink juice spray can blind. He seems to like this fact – it means no one can come near. He is safe here, hidden. He can kill and kill and kill. It is somehow satisfying. When the bugs are too high to reach he takes the pruning shears, lops off the tall branches and chops straight through the insect. The girls stand on the verandah, watching. Henry brings them a leaf, holds it out and points to the neat rows of tiny bright green spheres all clustered together. 'Eggs,' he says, then drops the leaf on the ground and stamps on it.

Every evening he thinks he's got them all, and every morning there are more. They do not drown in the water like he hopes. Instead they writhe and crawl over one another, trying to get out. The bucket is a black swell of wet beetle legs waving and sliding, wings lifting and falling. He goes to the garage to look for a bottle of poison. Then he laces the bucket with arsenic, digs a hole, tips the dark mass inside and covers it up.

～

It is Saturday evening when he dumps the insects into the hole. When he comes inside Charlotte can smell the bugs on him. The smell is in his hair. On his shirt collar. Inside the red creases of his knuckles. At dinnertime he saws at his meat and chews his food to liquid. It sounds like someone squelching through mud – the wet slap of tongue on teeth. He chews with his mouth open: sucking and cupping and pulverising the steak and potato. She waits for him to finish and finally swallow, reminded of a man she once knew who insisted that the radio be left on during dinner so that he didn't have to listen to his wife eat. She and Henry have nothing to say. Perhaps he chews this way because it acquits him of the expectation of speech. She pushes her hands beneath her thighs, leans forwards. The food on her plate is untouched. Henry takes another mouthful and begins chewing again.

WITH SEMESTER OVER, Henry stays home; he shuts himself up in his study and works on his book. Charlotte retreats to Carol's house and tells her – of the visits with Nicholas, the offer, the plan she had half abandoned because she thought it would never come to anything. They sit on the verandah and talk. Then for a long time they do not talk and instead watch the trees, the distant, eastward line of tall pines. They are thin trees, narrowly branched, more branch at the top than the bottom. Ivy, bright green, grows thick along the trunks. Behind the trees are spindly gums, their tops standing taller than the pines, and behind the gums lies a stretch of blue mountain. The children play at the bottom of the garden. Every now and then there is the blur of a running child, a call and squeal. Carol pours more tea and says that one of them needs to make peace. That is her phrase, *make peace*. 'Oh, Charlotte,' she says. 'Oh dear.' Afternoon light shines softly from behind the trees, making their trunks appear black, and when the wind gusts the trees sway differently. The pines tilt one way then another, stiff at the hips, while the gums swing and bend, back and forth, elastic, wild, leaves flailing. As the trees move, the mountains behind them become more and then less visible. Blue then not blue. Blue then not blue. Hills, Carol says, not mountains.

At dinner Henry sends the children into fits of giggles, pulling faces and teasing. Charlotte eats quietly. He makes a special effort to be gentle with them, kind, full of life. He bends his body towards them, dips his head, his eyes soften and shine. His hands move in and out towards the children's faces, pinching their red cheeks, then tickling their bellies. He makes them chortle, pretending to steal their dinner then lifting his eyebrows and opening his mouth wide in mock dismay when they eat the spoonful of potato he coveted for himself.

It makes Charlotte feel bereft, this purposeful display of happiness. This loving father. So alive to the present moment, so lighthearted, so eager to jump and swing and put on silly voices. So childlike. There he is now, chewing his dinner then opening his mouth and showing its mashed-up contents, the girls shrieking with joy.

She thinks of Nicholas. She hasn't seen him since she sold him the painting, two, coming on for three weeks. It feels like a deliberate silence, a silence that is meant to say to her: Go. Go now. And why doesn't she? There is still a little light outside and from where she sits she can see the rainy garden through the window. It grows wild now. The silverbeet droops in huge arcs, each leaf wide enough to wrap a baby in, the white stems standing taller than the children. The lettuces have grown three times the size of a human head. Red poppies bloom madly, nasturtiums matt the spare ground and thick swathes of grass shoot up in a hedge of bright spiky shrubbery. It rains and rains. Wet trees hiss and drag across the tin roof. She watches Henry, but instead of meeting her eyes he looks at the children and it becomes clear, after a while, that he will not look at her, so she drops her gaze to her hands, opening and closing her fists in her lap, picking at the dirt under her nails. She finds it hard to tell whether he is angry at her or afraid. Is it easier to love a child, she wonders, than it is to love a wife?

A knot forms in her throat, but she cannot cry in front of the children – she cannot cry in front of Henry. 'What's wrong?' he asks eventually, looking at Lucie, and Lucie thinks the question is meant for her.

'*What?*' she asks.

'Not you,' Henry says.

And Charlotte says, 'I'm fine,' understanding the question was meant for her, and Henry says, 'No, you're obviously not fine,' and she says, 'It's nothing.'

'Yes, it is obviously something.'

'It doesn't matter. Really. I have a headache,' she tells him. As if he needs to ask. 'Would you mind putting them to bed?' she says. He looks at her with blank confusion, then blinks twice. Charlotte carries her plate to the sink. 'They can go without a bath tonight,' she says, then steps into the dark bedroom and closes the door.

Later that night Charlotte is woken by Henry gently shaking her shoulder. 'Come,' he says. 'Come for a walk with me.'

'I'm sleeping,' she replies.

'Please.' There is something in his voice. Something she hasn't heard for a long time. 'I have your jacket,' he says, his voice sad, gentle. He stands beside the bed, holding the jacket open, then helps her arms into the sleeves. There is no sound of rain.

They walk along the path until it meets the river. Black water stretches out into black sky, and the cool air smells of wild frangipani and orange blossom. It reminds him of the smell of the estate after monsoon rains: sweet and damp and grassy. That time, that country – had any of it been real? It seems impossible that it might still exist, or that such a place could exist alongside this one, now. He tries to explain this to Charlotte. 'I've been thinking about it,' he says. 'I can't stop thinking about it.'

She nods in the dark but says nothing. Henry takes her hand in his. 'It's like a little bright circle in my past that is not linked to my life now, not really, and yet I feel it inside me, that place. I always thought life would be governed by some deep sense of continuum.

Now there are too many parts. Too many places. Too many things that happened in too many places. And the children—'

'What about the children?' Charlotte asks, defensive.

'I think it is them, having them, being around them, hearing them when I am trying to work, hearing you with them, all of that – it makes me think of the time when I was a child.'

They walk on, past the jetty and down towards the bridge. Henry says quietly, 'I don't remember it as well as I think I should – childhood, I mean. I don't remember much, really, just bits here and there.' They come to a narrow crescent of sand and stand still. Small waves lap at the shore. Henry eases his feet out of his shoes and pulls off his socks. The sand is cold. The water colder.

'What are you doing, Henry?' She means wading out into the rising tide, his trousers rolled to the knees, and is about to warn him – *You'll catch your death* – when he replies, misunderstanding her question.

'I don't know, Charlotte. I don't know what I'm doing. I should be finishing this damned book but it's going nowhere. I don't know why. I write and write and then throw most of the stuff away. I think too much, but about the wrong things. I feel like I've lost something but I don't know what it is. Maybe it's you. Maybe it's us. Is that what I've lost?' He kicks gently at the water, moonlight rippling over the broken surface. 'If only life would feel like a poem,' he says. 'If life felt, always, the way a poem can make life feel. Stronger, more vivid, more important than it felt before. If I could make life be that perfect thing.' His voice is quiet, the words mumbled as if talking to himself. 'I don't know. I don't expect you to answer me. But when I think of my past it seems made up of so many bits and pieces, and this wasn't how it was meant to be, it wasn't, and now we are here – finally – and all I do is think of there.' He turns back to face her a moment.

'Where?'

'India, the hills, the house in Delhi. My mother.'

Charlotte sighs and shuts her eyes. For a moment she felt a great balloon of hope pushing up beneath her ribs; she thought he was talking about England, that they might go home, all of them, after all. Without all this arguing. Without fighting for it. But of course not. She knows now that leaving a place you love isn't the worst thing; it is arriving in the second place and having to live as if the first place has disappeared. This is the tragedy – given enough time you come to doubt the place you knew before. That first life, once real, truly does disappear. Unspoken of, it becomes forgotten.

And so her memories condense, smaller, but brighter than before. They are images now, rather than stories, the connections between the images breaking down. The frozen duck pond on the way home. The bulrushes covered in hoarfrost. The westward path making a sharp turn south, through a stretch of woodland. Then grey sky, and a slip of late sun yellowing the far hill. She is on her bicycle, it is blustery and cold. Squirrels dart through the undergrowth. Birds swoop and dive in the wind. Her freezing hands grip the handlebars, her knuckles red and chapped.

'I had a letter about her,' Henry says. 'I'm sorry I didn't tell you. We weren't talking. I should have told you anyway. I thought you wouldn't care.'

'About who?'

'My mother. She's ill.'

'How ill?'

'Very.'

A copse of she-oaks surrounds the sand, and as a breeze blows in off the water the trees let out a high, whispery moan. Charlotte purses her lips and says nothing. Moonlight falls through the gaps between the trees and hits the white river shells, making them glow in the night. She watches Henry walk further out into the water, his head down and his hands pushed deep into his coat pockets. She feels all the tender feelings she's ever had for him rise up inside her. She thinks again of the old path home and how they used to ride down it, very fast, side by side, the wind behind them. She thinks of the hill where they used to walk, the spot at the bottom where you turn and vanish behind the hedgerows. She thinks of the worn grey track still snaking around the perimeter of the village, sandy and cracked in summer, wet in the autumn, coated in ice throughout winter. Her mind is overtaken by fleeting images of these very particular, very small sections of what seem, now, like lost and only imaginary places. The fields of broad-bean flowers, the seedy, sharp smell of them, the mud and weeds, then the rise of grass, the birds looking for grubs, the dawn fox creeping forwards, she and Henry out early, startling the red animal to a run.

'I thought I might go back,' he says. 'Just for a couple of weeks. You could come if you want. You and the girls.'

'Really, Henry.'

'No. I didn't think so.'

When they return home the house is dark and quiet. The children have not stirred, both sleeping with their arms tossed up over their heads. Charlotte stands at the entrance to their room, and leans against the doorframe. Henry comes up behind her, kisses her neck and pulls the door gently closed. Then he leads her back to the bedroom, feeling for her skin beneath her heavy jumper. They make love in the dark. Afterwards Henry rolls Charlotte onto her stomach and kisses her back. She has a dark birthmark high on the outside edge of her thigh, roughly a hand's length down from the curve of her bottom. Its colour is something between aubergine and chocolate. Henry can feel it under his palm – a thick, smooth coin of skin. He runs his fingers down the warm meat of her leg then puts his tongue to the mark. His fingers stray into her pubic hair, then away, down the inside edge of her other leg. He touches her from behind then slips inside her once more.

Thunder wakes her late in the night. She dreams she is hearing fireworks, until the weather moves overhead and the crack of the storm makes the house shake. It passes slowly – the thunder, then the rain. 'Henry,' she whispers. 'Are you awake?'

'Yes,' he says, rolling towards her. He puts his hand out, trying to find her face in the dark. His palm opens against her nose, his fingers stroking her forehead and coming down towards her mouth. He feels her lips move beneath his hand.

'You should go,' she whispers. 'If you want to, you should.'

Part Three

HOMECOMINGS

1965–1966

HENRY LEAVES TWO days later. He kisses the girls goodnight and slips out once they are sleeping. Charlotte helps him with his bags then watches from the verandah as the taxi drives away, the tail-lights disappearing in the trees. That night she sleeps with the children and in the morning meets Carol, and the group of them walk down to the river. At the water's edge a giant gum has turned grey and lost its leaves. 'What happened to it?' asks Lucie.

'It has grown old,' Charlotte replies.

'What is old?'

Charlotte thinks for a moment then says, 'Days and days and days.'

Lucie stands watching the tree then stumbles up to it and touches its smooth trunk, quickly, as though it were scalding hot, then a second time, slowly. 'I'm stroking it,' she says. 'I'm stroking the tree.'

They arrive home to find a dead worm curled up on the garden path, its body baked hard by the sun. 'What is dead?' Lucie asks. Several answers flash through Charlotte's mind but they are all inadequate. Instead she cheats, distracting her child with the blooming flowers, the torrent of red geraniums over the side of the hanging basket – *Let's pick some for the table.* But the next day Lucie finds the worm curled in the same place. Is the worm still dead? Yes, the worm is still dead. The sun is out and the grass is shining with the remains of night rain. Lucie crouches down to touch the wet grass beside the worm. 'Who makes the rain?' she asks.

—

Henry flies in to Delhi late at night and takes a taxi, the city dense with sirens and horns and headlights. The car plaits its way through the streets, tailgating a motorbike, buzzing up to race a truck then overtaking a bus from the inside lane. Henry grips the cloth of his trousers with his sweaty hands. Further ahead an amber traffic light turns red. The driver pushes his foot to the brake and the car skids to a stop. A beggar comes up and puts his hand to the window just as the lights change again and the car takes off, roaring across three lanes of oncoming traffic to make the exit. Horns. Lights. One horn: *hurry up.* Two horns: *I'm passing.*

Henry sits in the back and gazes out the window. He paid for the airfare with the money from the trust fund his father left him. He'd not told Charlotte about the fare. He'd said his mother was covering the costs, but he knew she didn't have any money to give and now feels his guts twist up with the lie. There's not much left of his father's money, he reasons, not enough to make a difference to them now. It paid for Charlotte's new shoes before they sailed out, and for the new bikes they'd bought on arrival. They were going to save the rest to put towards schooling, be sensible. Or he could have been kinder and given it to her, helped her go home. And now he is here. Of all places. Along the roadside is everything his mother wanted him to forget: the men sleeping on benches and on the ground and on the footpaths; the man defecating by the bridge – not squatting but just standing with knees a little bent, the shit falling out; the stone and cloth shacks by the highway and the thin mangy dogs; a truck piled full of corpses, the pale soles of their dark feet sticking out through wooden railings.

'Where have you come from?' the driver asks.

For a moment Henry can't remember the right answer. 'Australia,' he replies, looking up. The driver is silent. They've not got far to travel and Henry is glad for it.

The driver punches the horn as he speeds past a rickshaw then eyes Henry in the rear-vision mirror as if doubting what Henry said. 'And where are you going?'

The power is out when he arrives at his lodgings. Everything is dark. The attendant lights a lantern and walks him around the side of the house towards his room. It all looks very different to how he remembers it, when the guesthouse was their family home. The attendant places Henry's suitcase at the foot of the bed. Would this have been his mother's room? He is jet-lagged and his sense of the house is confused. Which way had the attendant brought him? By the fish pond, he guesses, close to the front gate, which would mean he is in one of the outer rooms and that the room where his mother once slept would be through the adjoining wall. Of course no one knows who he is now. After his sister died his father stayed on in Calcutta, while Henry and his mother moved here, to be with his mother's family. It was a fine new house then, built by his mother's father, with rooms for everyone and a wide green garden glittering with orange and blue dragonflies. Everyone hoped that his mother would recover here; she would be well cared for and would not have to look out every single day over the places where her daughter had played. But it never happened, and soon enough Henry was packed off to school in the hills. By 1947, when India became independent, Henry was already in England and the house was sold to a wealthy developer who turned the building into a guesthouse. The family had dispersed.

Henry switches on the fan to disguise the sound of traffic. Mosquitoes bump against the high ceiling then swoop down towards his arms. He knows that his is an accidental return, an accidental journey – like all his journeys, he thinks, created by the rough chances of the time. Charlotte must understand this. She must forgive him this. The ideas have not come of their own accord. It has always been someone else who suggested it, some other set of circumstances that made it possible. His geography has been determined by forces outside himself: the war, India's push towards independence, Australia's own fear of invasion. They shouldn't have taken him – they did not really want him. Neither England nor Australia, nor India for that matter. He could see it in the glare of the taxi driver's eye: he is too fair, but not fair enough; his English is good, but a little clipped, something you see as well as hear, something that makes him seem, just for a moment, like one of them – the way his lower jaw moves out when he speaks, pushing his chin forwards and bending his bottom lip down away from his teeth. He wonders what it would be like to belong somewhere and never doubt it. To not be constantly pestered by the knowledge of your own foreignness. He knows that his mother felt this herself, and sent him off to England in the hope that he might avoid this same experience, that he might come to feel himself part of a country, a rightful member of a place. But family has a way of passing down its fate. How he envies Charlotte her feelings for England, her sense of kinship.

He takes his breakfast early, while the sun is low behind the trees. His bags sit by his feet and the lanky black and white dog sniffs them over while Henry butters his toast. Two elderly ladies sit at the far end of the table, each picking at a basket of stuff in her lap. He thinks it some kind of intricate needlework at first, then realises that the two are slowly working their morning pills out of their packets and lining them up next to their plates piled with rice and vegetables. Beside him sit an older man and a younger woman. The man is touching sixty perhaps, the woman thirty-five.

But he can never tell with women, something that always amuses Charlotte. 'How old do you think she is?' she'd ask, meaning the woman at the grocery store, or a lady at a party, or the librarian, or the woman with six whining children.

'I don't know.'

'Well, go on, have a guess.'

'No, really, I don't know.'

Five wooden bird houses hang from the branches of the neem tree that shades the breakfast table. The day is still but the little wooden houses swing gently on their ropes as lorikeets and squirrels wrestle for seed. Henry glances again at the woman and man sitting next to him. At first he assumed them to be strangers. They do not seem to notice one another's presence; they are sitting across from each other but have turned away so that they are facing in opposite directions. The man has taken an early swim in the green pool and now sits at the table in his bathers, staring into the hazy distance of the garden. The woman sits angled slightly to the left as if to signal to the man that she is not open to conversation, her head buried in the newspaper. For a long time they do not speak, then the man says something without turning towards her – Henry doesn't catch what it is – and the woman replies, just as briefly, without looking up from her reading. They are not strangers then, Henry thinks. Strangers look one another in the eye when they speak. They might be father and daughter were it not for the difference in appearance: the man thin and gingery, the woman round and dark. Perhaps they are a couple? Old couples ask questions and give answers, all without noticing the person they are talking to. But she looks too young for them to be married, and they are too unenthusiastic – too uninterested in each other – to be travelling as friends or lovers. They could be siblings, Henry thinks, if not for their age. Siblings and old couples can be quite similar, really, both cool with years of residual irritations and rivalries. But perhaps he has the woman's age wrong and they are husband and wife after all? Do he and Charlotte look like that? Will they soon? How sad it must sometimes feel, but happy too, he imagines, and peaceful, the accumulation of years a kind of comfort in itself. He pictures his own parents ploughing on through the decades, breakfasting on the verandah every morning. They were always very calm. He never asked if they were happy. Now he realises that of course they were not. Henry stands and goes in search of more tea; there was a man about just a moment ago, carrying a silver pot.

Later, once he's finished his breakfast, he calls for the porter, who takes his bags and stacks them in the boot of the white Ambassador. Henry climbs into the back seat, and as the driver closes the door the cuff of his blue shirt slips back from his wrist, revealing a single red prayer string. Henry has seen men with inches of wishes tied to their wrists, and now this. Such frugality. If he made only one wish, what would it be?

At half past seven the train pulls out of Delhi station. His seat is by the window, and although he tries not to look he can't help it.

He sees it all: the miles and miles of slums, the dwellings made of scraps of sacking and plastic or cardboard, the roofs pinned down by bricks, the pigs and children digging in the pyramids of rubbish, the women washing in greenish water or cooking over damp fires fuelled with refuse, the rags of clothes hanging on decaying brick walls, the buffalo and goats wandering through the mud and slime. No one else in the carriage is looking. They have seen it too many times and for too long to bother noticing it anymore. Henry has forgotten these things. He must have seen these sights as a child, seen them without judgement or understanding; he would simply have seen children and animals, women washing.

Henry leans his head back and closes his eyes. When he opens them again the train is speeding through rice paddies spotted with small grass huts. The flat plains of green stretch out in every direction. Rain begins to fall, spattering the windows. Soon the green of the rice fields gives way to trees – thin, silver-limbed eucalypts.

The train starts to climb and the eucalypts are replaced by acacia, then conifer and deodar. The bright green of the hillside is coloured with pink hibiscus and waves of yellow lantana. Fog collects below as the train moves higher and higher, vine-covered branches leaning out over the deep valley that is soon sunk in cloud. Monkeys perch in the forks of the trees, watching as the train passes, then they run across the vines and jump down, out of sight. They are so much bigger than he remembers – these creatures as fat and tall as dogs.

Opposite Henry sit a husband and wife, fast asleep, their toes turned inwards. The woman's chin collapses on her chest, the man's cheek presses against the window. Henry slides his own window open and breathes in the high, cool air. It smells of diesel and freshly wet earth. The air is cold and dark beneath the trees and they speed now through tunnel after tunnel, black tunnels glistening with water, yet when they emerge the train still seems to move beneath the earth, with high slopes of wet grass and moss-covered rocks rising up beside the carriages. Henry presses his face to the gap of the window and looks up – the spires of conifers tower straight above the train, their uppermost branches lost in the bright fog, their lower ones black with water, the railway tracks running along beneath their roots.

CHARLOTTE WAKES TO a freezing dawn and opens the curtains: what day is it? Henry has been gone for a long time. It feels like a long time. Has it been four days? Five? He called once from Delhi but she's heard nothing since and without his coming and going the days are undifferentiated, full of chores and accidents – spillages, injuries, fits of wild crying.

She hadn't realised how much she looked forwards to him returning home in the evenings – how his presence soothes her. She wants, more than anything, just to lean against him now and rest her head on his chest. Since he's been gone, May has suffered from nightmares, crying out in the dark and then refusing to be left alone; Charlotte spent much of the previous night sleeping on the floor beside May's bed. Now she is tired and sore. She sets the children up at the kitchen table with paper and coloured pencils and goes about preparing breakfast.

At the edge of the garden, crows gather in the pine tree. They cluster along its branches, wing to wing, and caw. They cry all at once but not in unison, some cries ending as others begin, each bird's single, repeated caw linked into the next, rising and lowering, lowering and rising, like a volley of sirens wailing through the cold air. Then all of a sudden the sound stops. For several minutes there is just the wind in the trees. The green triangle of the pine stands dark against the bright cloud. Then one bird swoops down off a branch, circles the tree, lands and caws again. The others join in and the sky around the tree grows rough with sound.

The children eat buttered toast for breakfast and later, Charlotte bakes scones. The girls want to help. May sits in her highchair while Lucie stands on a stool at the bench and spoons lumps of butter into a measuring cup. White flour falls like fine ash. It covers the floor, the table, the bench. It is in the children's hair. It is trapped in the fine down covering Charlotte's arms and scattered over the toes of her shoe. She tugs the fridge open to get the milk and the magnetic letters on the door fall off, into the flour, landing wrong side up. Through the window she can see the hibiscus and hydrangea bushes bowing down under the weight of water. Each day now it rains. Spring should be here. It is time. A breeze comes and mountainous clouds move quickly across the sky. The days are long and strange. Each day she goes down to the river and thinks of Henry. She didn't like India, when they visited. What she remembers most is eating kulfi and reading *Anna Karenina* while they waited out the monsoon rains. She remembers the feel of the book – a heavy, green, cloth-bound copy, the pages warped by damp.

'I'll write,' promised Henry, the morning he left.

He is a long way away now, on a green mountain in the north. He walks slowly uphill, his feet slipping on the moss. He thinks of Charlotte, imagines her doing what he knows she does: cooking, pushing the pram, drinking tea from the floral Wedgwood cup. Now, as he walks, he phrases and rephrases a letter. *I always thought that we. Do you remember. The weather is.* He has been writing the letter in his head since he boarded the train at Delhi. That must be more than twelve hours ago now, four or five days since the taxi drove him away from the house in Australia. There were lengthy delays with the train and the change in Kalka. Then the creeping Toy Train up the mountain. He forgot what a long journey it was. He is in Shimla now, finally, and walking towards his mother. A steep road narrows to a steep path. He watches his feet, placing them on the grass or in the mud but not on the slippery wet green stone. He feels he has been climbing for a long time now, first the road, then the path, but when he lifts his head he is surprised to find he is almost there, the tall white building visible up ahead and glowing amid the jungle. The house is built into the rock of the hillside, the original owner a marine engineer who ordered another level be constructed every time he came home on leave. It now rises five storeys. Long ferns curl around the walls, jasmine clambers over the windows, pine trees and bright vines carpet the hill behind.

'It's urgent,' he says to the secretary stationed at the entrance and asks to be shown to her room. 'You wrote to me. I've travelled for days.'

'Yes, yes,' replies the secretary, a tiny young man from the south. He wobbles his head as he speaks, as if he might really be saying, 'No, no.' 'I will call the director,' he says, and disappears into the dark house.

Half an hour passes before the director arrives, the gold trimmings of her sari glistening in the dim hall. She is a short woman who holds her head high as she walks, chin lifted, never looking at the ground. 'Mr Blackwood? Thank you so much for coming,' she says, holding out her hand. 'I am Mrs Ghosh. Please. Follow me.'

'I'd like to see my mother now if I could.'

'Yes, sir. Just some paperwork first.'

'If I could just—'

Mrs Ghosh stands at the open door of her office and holds out her arm, ushering him into the chair beside the desk.

The place is rancid, the air thick with the smell of mould, cat piss, wet dog and mice. Grey-green butterflies of mildew grace the windows and pattern the walls. The worst-affected areas have been covered up with white paint, but the shadow of mould remains visible beneath. 'It is just the season,' explains the director. 'You wait, in a couple of weeks it will all be gone, everything sunny and bright.' Henry nods as his eyes skirt the office. The walls are cracked and the paint flakes off onto the floor. Water seeps through at the bottom of the wall and makes a dirty puddle on the carpet. 'In November,' continues the director, thumbing a pile of damp, wrinkled papers, 'in November we have one of our best seasons. Sunny, cool. Just a few days now, you'll see.'

'November,' Henry says, 'is almost two months away.'

'Oh no, not so long,' she replies. 'Ah, here it is,' she says, pulling out a string-bound folder. 'Your mother's records.' She licks her thumb and turns the pages. 'Ah, yes,' she says, pushing her large black-framed glasses up to the bridge of her nose. Henry fidgets.

'I know you are in a hurry, sir. But you must not be. She will not know if it is now or later, if it is you or not you. I must warn you, that is all. Your mother has suffered a multitude of small strokes,' she says, checking the paper in front of her. 'That, combined with the dementia, well, it is not good. Not good, I am afraid. She hangs on, you know – I wish I had known her as a young woman, she must have been very strong, very wilful. Perhaps she is waiting for you, I don't know. It can't be long now. I must say this. But I see from your face that I do not need to. Here, come with me, I'll show you the way.'

It is a terrible place, dark and cold, the walls wet and foul-smelling, the paint bubbling up where the damp comes through. He feels shame creep over him. Nobody in India leaves their parents to wither in a home. He should have made her move to England before it was too late and she was too ill to leave. It isn't all his fault, he reasons: there were no other siblings, there's no other family, and Henry has his own life. That, his mother must know, is what she prepared him for. And why here? At least she might have been better cared for down in the plains. The disrespect would be no different, but she might have been better cared for. At least in the cities there are more people who've been abandoned. And the sheer number gives them a certain fiscal value – something that his mother, cooped up in this tiny private establishment, has no chance of benefitting from. He's heard the British still help to fund one of the homes in Delhi, and there is another place, west of Calcutta. But there has never been any arguing with his mother. The hills are the only place for her. They remind her, she says, of what India used to be. No, she told him when he tried to encourage her to come to England years ago. No, she could never leave. 'There's nothing worse than the life of a migrant,' she said. 'You lose everything. Everything.' Now, the two of them, Henry and his mother, have become like each other in so many ways, alone in the world and forgotten by it. Or so it seems, so it feels.

Beneath the sheet her body is just a few small bumps, her head sunk in a mound of pillows. A mouldering wicker chair is placed beside the bed. Its feet scrape over the cold stone floor as Henry drops his weight into it. His mother's hands are folded on her stomach. Henry reaches out and takes her right hand in his. Her eyeballs flicker behind their shut lids but her fingers do not move. The bed is pushed up beside a large window. There is a view of the mountain, wet and dripping and covered in green – the bright green of the ferns and the darker green of the deodar trees. He strokes the top of her hand while two yellow butterflies weave a path through the woodland. Her skin is thin and comes together in pleats like the cooled surface of warm milk. Henry leans forwards and rests his head on the bed, the covers damp to the touch. He can see, through the opening of the pillowslip, that the cushion behind her head is completely black with mould. He pulls away and feels the chill rising up through the thin soles of his shoes.

On the wall above her bed is a framed picture of the Queen. It is a poor black and white reproduction that looks like it has been cut from the newspaper and is now yellowing under the glass. Other objects of reverence are placed about the room. On a shelf by the window stands a set of silver teaspoons with English place names and some funny little pictures decorating their handles, all displayed in a velvet case. Beside this are two porcelain animal figurines – a robin and a Staffordshire puppy. And next to the bed stands a plastic figure of Jesus, the details of his face worn clean away by his mother's devotions, her thumb working sandalwood over his brow, day after day after day. Henry has seen little brass figurines in shrines that have been rendered featureless out of love, their faces smoothed to a shine – the Seven Wives, and Krishna – but never before Jesus. The plastic statuette looks defaced rather than worshipped, and the ghostly image startles him even though it should not – after all, he had seen her do this over and over again when he was a child: put her hands together in prayer, then touch the figurine's tiny white forehead.

—

He doesn't know for how many hours he sits there. By the time he leaves for his hotel the rain has begun. It falls fast and heavy, the warm bullets of water breaking down through the trees. The valley is white with cloud and the steep road quickly turns into a brown river. Henry's small blue umbrella bobs through the grey haze as he picks his way among the rocks and dirt and rubbish that litter the edge of the tarmac. His feet squelch in wet shoes. Others pass him on their way up, men and women in sandals with their trousers rolled to the knee. Their eyes meet his briefly then slide away.

Back in his room Henry cannot sleep. For the first few hours of the night, car horns echo through the valley. Later it is filled with the sound of barking dogs. So many dogs, all yapping and howling at the same time, sometimes closer, sometimes further away. They follow each other around the lower edge of the valley, they gather at the top of the hills. His mother must hear them too. If not tonight then other nights. The wild dogs barking in the valley below and the wild dogs barking higher up, in the woodland near her window. On and on throughout the night. The last thing he hears is the horn of the train, as it pulls into the station at dawn. He sleeps then, and when he finally opens the long red curtains the day is white with fog.

~

Henry has been gone just over a week now. Every morning Charlotte stands by the living room window and waits for the post. She waits and waits and nothing comes. Then one day the postman lifts his hand and waves to her. After this she is careful to hide behind the curtains and look through the lace. Bills come, and the *Times Literary Supplement*, but nothing from Henry. She stacks the envelopes neatly on his desk and closes the door.

At lunchtime she takes the children to the river for a picnic. She makes sandwiches and they eat them in the sun. Ham and white bread. Strawberry jam. Cordial from one drink bottle. Milk from another. They pinch off the crusts of the sandwiches and throw them to the seagulls; the birds red-eyed, squawking. Arching and flapping their wings. Later the children nap in the pram, under the shade of the river trees. Charlotte sleeps on the blanket beside them. When they wake, the children play; there is a yellow ball, shells from the river, a bucket and spade.

Charlotte stands, brushes off her dress and walks towards the bushland that borders the water. 'I'll be back soon,' she says, then ducks under a low-hanging tree and onto a narrow path. A few steps in and there is no sight of the clearing behind. She follows what looks like an animal track, the leaves on the ground smoothed, beaten down by passing creatures going to and from the water. She has never been here before. In all these months. She thinks of Henry, far away. Up ahead is the sound of water, high tide slapping on rocks, but there is no sight of it. She bends down to pass beneath branches. Perhaps his letters have gone missing – overseas mail is often slow and wayward.

'*Mummy!*' May cries; the girls are somewhere behind her, in the clearing. '*Mummy!*' The child's fine, high voice drifts through the trees. A twig snaps beneath Charlotte's foot.

'Coming, sweetheart,' she calls back, but she walks onwards, towards the water, the path invisible behind her now. Part of her wishes to find Henry waiting when they arrive home. Then life would go on. Only, she is deep enough into it now to know that she does not really want this, the continuance. All about is the low, green-brown haze of shrub leaves, and spiky yellow flowers like gorse but which are not gorse. There are purple flowers like heather but which are not heather. Twists of black tree limbs rise up towards tufts of dangly eucalyptus foliage. Half a tree left after lightning. Contorted roots rise above ground. Something rustles in the purple grasses beside her.

'*Mummy?*'

'Coming,' she calls again, as she walks on still further. What did he feel, she wonders, when he left them, when he flew away? Three minutes, four, she has not gone far, but already she can't see her children. They have their sandwiches, she thinks. They are sitting on the blanket with their lunch and their toys. The bush thickens. The trees are taller here, the air shady and cool underneath, and all about is the smell of eucalypt, damp earth, rock and salt and river weed. She stumbles across the remains of a fire – a ring of stones, cans left behind. Rocks kids have pulled up to sit on. She rests on one and looks to the sky; a pelican flies overhead followed by a flock of yellow-tailed black cockatoos. She thinks of the history of this place, thinks that she has something in common with them after all – with the people before her who tried to understand it as home, while feeling they belonged elsewhere. Did they, she wonders, ever succeed? She would like to know them. She tries to imagine them.

'*Mummy!*' the two children call together.

'I'm here—' she calls. But where is here? The bush soon gives way to water. Rocks slope down to the tide edge. The surface of the rocks is covered in greenish algae and oyster shells. Dense mangrove trees lean out over the rocks, making the air briny, cool and dim. The only sound is the wind high in the trees and the water sloshing in and out of the small caves between the rocks. Shadows of leaf and tree branch tremble across the surface of the river. Beyond the shadows the water is bright.

'*Mummy!*' the children call again, frightened now, and Charlotte turns back.

HENRY'S MOTHER LINGERS for days. Nobody expects this. He sits at her bedside, reads to her, offers sweet food that she cannot eat. Time wears on: in a nearby room the staff chatter and drink tea. Beyond the window there is the forest. Henry comes and goes. He thought he'd be back in Delhi by now, making his way home. He misses the children. Soon he finds he no longer hurries to be at the nursing home before midday. He sleeps in, arrives late. Each day he takes his mother something – biscuits that sit untouched on a plate, a new book, an extra blanket for her bed. Today, he thinks, he will bring her flowers, remembering her bedroom graced with roses when he was a boy.

It is afternoon by the time Henry has dressed and eaten and left the hotel in search of the flower stall. The concierge told him it could be found behind the post office and gave Henry directions. Henry turns left up the hill, then veers right at the bend. From somewhere up ahead comes the tune of a brass army band, the call of the trumpets rolling out across the valley. Whistles join the trumpets in a marching beat and a series of cheers erupts from the ridge. He walks towards the music, passing numerous teacarts, market stalls selling fake pashmina shawls, chemists, the old bakery, the Maria Brothers antique bookshop, the public library, the brass statue of Gandhi, and a small girl sitting on a square of cardboard who says to him as he passes, 'Hello, Money. Hello, Money.' At the top of the mall stands a row of white horses available for hire. They are mottled with dust and mud and tethered to the fence. Many years ago one whole strip of the mall was kept for the horses. Children received an hour's ride for a small fee and the horses were led all around the hills. Henry remembers this. He remembers his mother handing him a chewy yellow sweet spotted with green pistachios before a man lifted him into the saddle. There was the smell of hay and horse dung and the sight of his mother standing below, waving as he set off on his adventure.

But no, it is not at all how it was before. Where is the cottage they lived in during the summer of '38? He thought it was further up, in Lower Jakhu, but now, standing in the centre of the mall looking about, he can't be sure. He's lost his bearings. There had been a fireplace, and his mother had collected sticks from outside, and his father had spent the day chopping wood so that in the evening they could burn great logs of sweet-smelling pine. The memory of the smell is clear, fleeting. It comes from nothing.

But he's walked too far. Henry turns and retraces his steps, the valley far below him and full of cloud. The blue peaks of the lower Himalayas stretch out into the distance, each rise paler than the last, a series of indigo shadows resting one behind another. At the back of the post office, two paths lead in opposite directions. On a whim he heads right, passing a line of coolies who carry impossible items upon their backs – a tank of gas, a wooden trunk, vast sacks of grain. There is a tiny porter balancing two enormous suitcases on his head, his arms hardly able to reach the top of them. Henry follows a stairway down and down but there are no flowers. There is the smell of shit and sweat and rotting bananas. A green and blue sari, the colours of a peacock tail, has been pegged out to dry on a length of wire. The path flattens and narrows. Lopsided wooden houses built by the British more than a century before hang over him, darkening his way. A rabid dog runs out and barks; Henry startles. Water drips onto his head from the buildings above. He has taken a wrong turn. He should have gone along the other path. No one told him. He is hot and sweaty and the hems of his trousers are wet with mud. Or is it sewage? There is a raw stink in the air. A man dressed all in white sits on his haunches in the alcove of a door. 'Flowers?' Henry asks, pointing down the dark path and imitating, with opening hands, the unfolding of a blossom. 'Flowers?' The man grunts and points the other way.

In the lower markets he finds what he is looking for – a tiny stall set up in the dirt beneath the verandah of a tall house. A wooden bench displays the vendor's wares: a yellow bucket holding carnations and red roses; another bucket with lilies, the bees dancing in and out of the brown and curling petals. A thin, short man steps out of the shadows, addressing him in Hindi, and Henry apologises, explaining that he does not know the language. The stallholder backs away in confusion, then returns when Henry nods his head and points, holding up his fingers to show he wants two bunches of carnations – one pink, one white – and at the last minute adds a small posy of roses.

He knows he's already taken too long. He must leave the nursing home by dusk, before the monkeys come down from the trees, and at this rate he won't get there until three. He holds out money for the flowers but the man does not take it. Instead he places the flowers carefully on the bench, picks up a single carnation and flicks open the petals as if dusting a tiny ornament. Henry expected to be handed the bouquets and then be off. But every flower is carefully tended to. The carnations are laid out in a row, then the roses flicked at and checked, one after another and another. The man gathers up the carnations and tapes their stems together. Then he disappears and comes back with a handful of greenery that he cuts and arranges and tapes to the carnations. The roses are pushed into the bunch, then they too are taped. Each time Henry thinks the production over, something else is introduced. Gold ribbons, silver glitter. More sellotape. Plastic wrapping, then a wrapping of old newspaper; a first, then a second spray of water. Passers-by stop to look. A woman asks the price of the roses, stands watching a while then walks on. After an interminable period of time – what has it been, ten minutes, twenty, half an hour? – Henry hands the man a bundle of notes, takes the flowers and walks up out of the markets towards the nursing home on the hill.

It is almost four when Henry arrives. He knocks, enters, and takes his place in the wicker chair beside his mother's bed. He leans forwards and rests his hands over hers. She does not appear to have moved since he saw her the day before. Perhaps they've rolled her over and rolled her back again. She does not open her eyes to see the flowers. A nurse comes and tends to her hipbone where a bedsore festers. Henry suspects this is done for his benefit – evidence of care in the face of obvious neglect. But they all know he is the one who left her here.

He knows he should speak to her, he knows she believes that the dead can hear everything said by the living. Of course she is not dead, but nor can he say that she is alive. He does not know what is keeping her. There is nothing here for her now. There is nothing to hold on to. 'It's me, Mother. I'm here. It's Henry.' The son who was named after a king of England. This was the plan: a line of boys all named after royalty. He squeezes her hand and for a moment thinks he feels a small movement in her fingers. 'It's Henry,' he says again. He pulls the chair closer and strokes her arm.

There is the shush shush of rain on the roof and the distant racket of car horns in the valley. Her breathing has been quiet but now it begins to change. Air rasps and drags at the back of her throat. In and out, out and in. The chair screeches on the floor as he pushes it back and stands and calls out for the nurse. At the same time he knows that it does not matter if something is wrong. Of course there is something wrong. She needs to die, he knows that, that's why he's come.

The nurse appears at his side. 'Shhh,' she says, pressing a hand against his shoulder and urging him to sit. He lowers himself slowly into the chair and takes his mother's hands in his. How terrible it is now that death is here, gurgling back and forth in her throat.

'It is all right,' he says. 'You can go now. I am here. I am here.' There ought to be something else to say, something more, but he doesn't know what. That he is sorry for buying the flowers. For taking so long. For staying away. For the years and years he has stayed away. Instead he repeats what he's said before: *It's all right. You can go now. I am here. I am here.* He strokes her hand, her arm. He knows it is too late. He knows he's waited until it is too late. Her breathing grows slower and more laboured. Henry leans closer still and strokes her hair. It is fine, thin hair and he can feel the bones of her head – the narrow band of her forehead, the rise of her skull. There is the dark hole of her mouth, the smell of her sour, meat-dank breath. It comes intermittently, her breath – long and rasping, then nothing. Then long again. Every time she falls quiet Henry starts forwards, thinking it is over. Then she breathes, the sign of life giving him fright. Henry sweats through his clothes. His trousers cling to his thighs, his shirt sticks to his back. He notices a breeze stirring the branches at the window, causing water to drip down onto the glass, tap tap tap, like the second hand of a clock. Thick cloud moves past, obscuring the trees, and when he looks back down he knows that she is gone. He holds her hands for a few moments longer, then lets go.

CHARLOTTE LOOKS UP at the clock on the kitchen wall and realises that it has stopped. It is the silence she notices. Henry usually winds the clocks before he goes to bed. At first Charlotte remembered to do this but at some point must have forgotten. It doesn't matter – somehow, in Henry's absence, time has changed, softened. The hours undulate rather than divide as they used to, an hour for this, half an hour for that, each day an equation. Now there is no one to check such progress, such efficiency. No one expects a packed lunch ready on the table by seven, dinner at six. Her watch is in the bedroom, but she will fetch it later, once she's finished the dishes.

She does not always dislike domestic duties. She enjoys bringing in dry washing that smells of clean air and feels warm with sunlight.

And she likes washing up at dusk, as she does now, the garden blackening and fading away, the bright interior of the room beginning to shine on the inside of the kitchen window. The girls are quiet in front of the television – they've both fallen ill and for the last few nights Charlotte has padded back and forth between the bedrooms, tending, tucking in, bringing milk or water or chamomile tea. Henry has been gone two weeks now. In the background the children sneeze and sniffle.

Charlotte is just lifting the saucepan out of the water when she hears a knock at the door. She looks around, then hears it again. Three taps once. Three taps twice. 'Just a minute!' she calls, wiping her hands on the tea towel and untying her apron.

Nicholas stands at the door. 'Oh,' Charlotte says, taken aback. 'I wasn't expecting you.'

'No. I thought I'd just drop by on my way home – I hope you don't mind.'

'Yes – I mean, no, ' she says, faltering. 'Henry's away, and the children are unwell. I haven't heard from you since, I thought maybe—'

'I'm sorry,' he says. 'I didn't realise you were on your own. Can I do anything? Get you anything?'

'No, no. We're fine, thank you,' replies Charlotte, pulling a crumpled handkerchief from her pocket and blowing her nose.

'Can I come in – at least let me make you a cup of tea? You could put your feet up a minute.'

'Oh,' Charlotte says, still barring the door with her arm. 'Well, no, I suppose not, I mean there's no reason not to come in.'

'You mean yes?'

'Yes, come in. That would be lovely. But let me make the tea.'

Henry pulls the sheet up over his mother's face and then returns to the hotel. He orders tea and drinks it sitting by the window. Seven sparrows perch in a row along the red awnings of a nearby building. Each time a new sparrow flies in to join the line, another sparrow flies off from the end, so that no matter how many new birds alight, there are only ever seven sitting on the roof. The fog lifted in the afternoon but now returns, rolling and creeping and floating down the hillside. Low-flying crows appear and disappear in its white depths. It is Monday. On Wednesday his mother will be buried in the British cemetery, as she requested, and Henry will not attend.

He falls asleep while there is still light outside and wakes, many hours later, to the sound of morning bells and chanting. He opens the curtains, looking for the parade, then realises that the music is coming from the church. Drums and bells and warbling voices.

It is time to go. He takes a car down to Kalka then boards an express train to Delhi. Fog engulfs the lower hills and then night swallows the plains. He is glad not to see the landscape beyond the window. The huts and the sheds and the rubbish and the mud – the catalogue that life is reduced to when moving at high speed over vast tracts of land. There is this and this and this. How simple it is to move forwards, and yet, in another way, how difficult, and how rare. Is he moving forwards now? It is hard to say. Later, he will remember things: three Indian women in iridescent saris emerging from roadside mists as if rising out of smoke. Bright pink and gold and violet. Then, lower down, on the narrow dusty roads, another woman, in black this time, carrying a tower of kindling on her head like some great crown of thorns, while two small children tug at her long skirt. The injured cow bleeding in the middle of the road. Stalls selling boxes of red and gold apples, each apple wrapped in paper. He thought of taking some home to the children, then remembered he could not. How he longs for them, and for Charlotte. The train judders over the tracks. A man in uniform pushes a tea trolley up and down the aisle. He pines for the sound of neighbourhood boys kicking a ball in the park, for the sight of couples walking hand in hand by the river in the evening, for the hushed nights when whole streets are sleeping peacefully. In this moment, as he passes through what he can only imagine are some of the poorest and ugliest stretches of the world, Henry longs for the ordinary suburban boredom that he's always thought somehow beneath him. It is unambitious, dull, so terribly average. But how comfortable it looks from this distance. From the dark window of his berth, that suburban universe seems the very pinnacle of civilised life. It is time to go home.

—

When he gets off the train he takes a taxi to the guesthouse near Lodi Gardens where he first stayed. He is given the room facing the rose garden and sleeps long and deep, waking to a fine gold morning, a haze of damp heat blurring the higher branches of the trees. Above this the sky is a pale brown, coloured by smog and desert dust. Birds of prey spiral slowly upwards like pieces of ash rising from an unseen disaster. Beneath them dart the yellow-winged dragonflies, while mynah birds watch on from the roof of the guesthouse, every now and then swooping through the low reaches of the neem tree. One for love, two for joy, three for success, four for boy. It is a song his mother used to sing him on the long trip up to his school in the hills. She didn't like to leave him, but there was no choice, so although the song sounded cheerful, it always made Henry sad. He had forgotten it and now, out of nowhere, the whole of it comes back. Five for silver, six for gold, seven for the secret never to be told.

He takes his morning tea on the lawn. Without warning the rain comes. It brings leaves and feathers down from the trees. It sends the squirrels into hiding. Parrots call from high branches and the guests rush to find shelter under the eaves. A tall Frenchwoman catches his attention – she has a small silver chain around her ankle with bells on it and they tinkle when she dashes in from the rain. The wicker chairs sit empty on the grass and turn black with water. It is not the season for visiting. Henry wants to be gone, but it turns out there's some trouble with the flights: something about weather conditions and staffing disputes. It might be another week, they told him earlier this morning, before he can get a flight home.

Henry returns to his room and writes to Charlotte, telling her of the delay and how he misses her. When he next looks up, the rain has stopped. The sun shines and bakes the grass dry.

Through the rosebushes Henry can see the gardener pushing a yellow lawnmower back and forth, back and forth. When this is done a second man comes out with a broom and sweeps the cut grass from the lawn. A third man crouches down with a smaller broom and sweeps the concrete terrace outside Henry's room where stray grass clippings have landed. He sweeps them into four neat piles. When he's almost finished a wind comes up out of nowhere and scatters the grass back across the terrace. The man stops his sweeping and looks up, watching the clippings being blown away. When the wind dies down he goes in search of them and slowly begins sweeping again. The sun is hot and Henry draws the blinds, lies down and closes his eyes. The fan whirrs above him and the sush sush of the brooms keeps on outside.

THE CHILDREN WORSEN; Lucie sweats and cries while May lies on Charlotte's chest and doesn't move – she can't lift her head or talk or drink. Her arms are floppy and her skin is hot to the touch. They have both been sick before but Charlotte has never seen a child like this. Henry wrote the number of his hotel on the calendar and Charlotte phones it – when Lucie starts vomiting and May won't open her eyes. But when she speaks to the man at reception she is told that Henry has checked out. Where is he? she asks. He didn't say? There must be a message for me.

The child screams all night. Over and over the child screams. Which child? She can't tell anymore. How many times has it screamed and for how many nights? She has lost count; she is too tired and she is too angry, unaccountably angry. There is no justifiable cause – she is simply worn out, and the fatigue turns somehow to rage, a shivering tide of rage that moves quickly now through her blood. If only they would stop crying and let her sleep. She is angry and afraid at the same time. Something must have happened to him. Has something happened to him? If only they'd stop crying. No, she will not go to them. Not again, please no. Please. *Mummy*, they call. 'Mummy's coming,' she calls back and like a huge wave rising and crashing and rising, she drags her body from her bed towards the children's room, the crying growing louder as she moves through the dark, towards them. This goes on night after night after night. One day. Two days, three days, four. She feels her way along the wall. There is no moon. She does not think to turn on a light. It is so black she can't see her arm as it reaches out in front of her. Where is the door? Further. This is the wall still. Now, here – the different wood of the door, the smooth glossy paint cold to the touch. Her hand slips down towards the low handle and she stands in the children's room, the crying coming closer now, and closer, and closer, until it is ringing down the tunnel of her ear, the child's hot wet face pressing against her cheek.

'Hush, hush. That's enough now. That's enough. It was just a dream. Just a dream. *Shhh, shhhhh*,' she tries again. 'There is nothing here. It's a fever. You're safe now. You're safe.' But at the sound of her mother's voice, May screams louder. She thrashes about in Charlotte's arms so that Charlotte can no longer hold her and drops her back down on the bed, letting her writhe. She is too tired to walk back to her own room, too tired to stand, so she slumps down against the wall and leaves May to grow hoarse. Her head pounds. The screams run deep through her bones. What does the child want from her? What? '*Stop it!*' she screams back. '*Stop it! Will you just stop it!*' She stands up then, quickly, searches out May's shape on the bed, picks her up under her arms and shakes her. 'Will you just stop it now! Now, I said! Now!' Then she throws her back onto the pillow. She hears the air push out of May's lungs as her little body lands. Silence fills the room and Charlotte stumbles out, feeling her way back to the bedroom, the dark behind her trembling with tiny, stifled whimpers.

By morning Charlotte too has come down with a fever. She knows she has to get to the doctor, but when she calls she's told he is out on his rounds and won't be able to attend to them until the evening. She can't find the keys so there is no option other than to walk the girls to the practice in the next suburb. She packs the pram and sets out, moving slowly, clutching the handles for balance, the ground rolling beneath her. Sweat beads on her forehead. The children cry. The inside of her mouth feels sticky and sour. Nausea comes over her in waves. May's face turns red and splotchy and her clothes soak through with sweat. They have not gone more than ten yards when Charlotte turns and very slowly walks back to the house. She unlocks the door, pushes the pram inside and lies down on the cold linoleum of the hallway.

Nicholas finds her there in the afternoon. He stops by to deliver biscuits and oranges for the children and when no one answers the door he tries the handle. He helps Charlotte into bed and puts the children in beside her, then he takes a flannel from the bathroom and wipes their faces. Later, Charlotte will remember him sponging her lips, the cool water running little by little into her mouth.

He leaves late in the night but returns the next day, the sun high, the bedroom full of slippery light. Charlotte has never been so glad of company. 'Come in, come in,' she whispers, the children just waking. Charlotte's fever has broken and she's eaten a little. He helps her dress the girls and together they go out into the garden. It is good to be outside. The sun is warm and the air fresh-smelling. They each carry a child. May rests her heavy, sleepy head on Charlotte's shoulder and Lucie rides on Nicholas's back. He talks to comfort Charlotte, telling her how he has begun reading Ruskin again. And how he is trying, once more, to figure out a way to paint the webs of light that waver beneath the surface of the river. This odd hobby of his.

'You never said,' Charlotte exclaims. 'Really?'

'*Nets of silver and gold have we, said Wynken, Blynken and Nod.* It's a rhyme I knew as a child. I've tried painting those bright lines for years, rather unsuccessfully I'm afraid. It's hard to capture the constant movement in a still image. Here,' he says, 'let me show you,' and the four of them walk slowly to the water.

They stand leaning over the edge of the jetty, Nicholas with his arms outstretched on either side of the railing, Charlotte in her wide-brimmed hat, holding May, Lucie sitting on the wooden planks and clinging to the hem of her mother's dress. Their shadows waver on the tan-coloured water. 'There are jellyfish down there,'

Nicholas says to the children. 'Can you see them?' Lucie watches, tracking the throbbing movements until the creatures disappear, their purplish bodies vanishing in deep water. Small waves from passing boats lap gently at the pylons and at the shore.

Charlotte has the strange feeling that she can tell him anything, anything at all, and he will understand. It frightens her, this feeling. It frightens her because it seems they do not even need to speak to understand. They can just stand here, watching the water, and it is as if they knew everything, as if everything that has ever mattered is immediately understood.

He stays for dinner, a small feast of fried eggs and grilled cheese on toast, then he helps ready the children for bed. Once they are asleep he and Charlotte step out the back door, into the tall grass. Charlotte's eyes are slow to adjust, the moon thin and the yard dark. She smells the cool draft of late wattle flower, and other smells particular to night: damp eucalypt leaves cold on the ground, left-over wood-smoke, ash, and the dirt-like, earthy smell of the cold night itself, black and fine and a little sour. She pulls two old wicker chairs out from under the house and places them square on the grass, then she and Nicholas sit side by side, leaning their heads back against the chairs so that they can better see the sky. Stars litter the dark. Charlotte's long white hands rest along the sides of the chair. They sit in silence, watching the night, and after a while Nicholas reaches out and touches the back of her wrist. Then he takes her hand in his, lifting it, pointing it with his own. 'There, the Southern Cross. There, Saturn. Do you see the shape of the bow and arrow?' he asks. No, not quite. Nicholas, still holding Charlotte's hand, traces it out. Then they sit quietly for a while. Charlotte watches for falling stars. She watches closely, her eyes open and watering in the cold. And then they come. Charlotte has never seen so many.

'Look!' she calls.

'And another!' Nicholas cries. The two of them are like children.

'You must make a wish,' she says. 'Each time you see one.'

His hands shake as he unties the scarf that she wears knotted at her throat. The coloured cloth falls to the floor as he pulls her gently towards him, running his fingers up through the fine hair at the nape of her neck. He bends to kiss the length of her collarbone then opens her dress while she seeks out his mouth with her fingers. They kiss for a long time. Later they make love in her bed, her feet hooked around his buttocks, her hands slipping on his damp back. She tastes sweat and musk on his mouth. His wide shoulders move above her face, wave-like, his head dipping towards hers. At the end she calls out to him while he makes a strange choking noise and drops his forehead on her shoulder. Their bodies tremble. She feels his stomach lifting and falling against hers, heavy and warm. They stay this way while he shrinks inside her, the slow suck of wet flesh coming away from wet flesh, then the cool leak and spread of semen against her inner thighs. She eases herself out from under him and rolls over; they lie beside one another then and she strokes his stomach – it reminds her of the belly of a dog, warm, the skin white-pink, tight but soft, the fine coating of hair. For some time they stay quite still, hands touching. Around them the room smells of old flowers, rotting and sweet, the green stems yellowing in the glass vase. White street light seeps in through the gaps in the curtains. The umbrella tree scrapes back and forth on the iron roof. Bird calls echo in the huge sky, the cluster of notes bouncing out and out and out until they vanish in distant air. There is the first hush of rain, then the jingling of a bell as a cat runs for shelter.

'You know I love you,' Nicholas says. 'You know that.'

Charlotte is quiet. She strokes the back of his hand. After a while she says, 'Yes,' although it is not clear whether this means yes, she knows, or yes, she loves him too.

'I want to be with you,' he says. Charlotte doesn't reply. 'I'm sorry,' he says.

'What for?' asks Charlotte. There is a long pause. Nicholas looks away, leans down and picks up his wallet from the floor. He takes out a scrap of paper and writes something on it.

'I'm afraid I'm returning to London,' he tells her, 'to sort out some business.' His voice is solid, factual. 'Nothing needs to happen here, but if you do go, if you do go back, I'll be there.' His voice softens. 'Take it,' he says, passing her the piece of paper. 'This is where you'll find me.'

'For how long?'

'I don't know yet.'

'And when?'

'Soon.'

A green silk nightdress hangs from a hook on the back of the bedroom door. Charlotte gets up, walks across the room and slips it on. 'I think you should go now,' she says.

When she makes the bed in the morning she finds money on the sheets. Silver and copper coins. They must have been in the pockets of his trousers. She rings once and he doesn't pick up. She rings twice and he doesn't pick up. She knocks on his door and he doesn't answer.

FOR DAYS HENRY wanders the city. Through Lodi Gardens and down towards Khan. There is the smell of frangipani after monsoon rain, of citrus flower and jasmine. It was a small home, this one – the little enclave of Anglo-India that he was hidden within as a boy. It was not the real India. That's what people said. But they said this about other parts of India too; they said it about New Delhi, with its wide, tree-lined streets and empty pavements – that was British India, they said. They said it about Calcutta. They are beginning to say the same thing about stretches of southern India, where the beaches are overrun by foreign tourists in bikinis. When Henry was a boy visiting Goa, he saw mongooses fighting cobras. Somehow between then and now even the behaviour of the animals has changed. No one sees such things anymore. What is the real

India? It is the poor India, the rural India. This is what people now talk of. But how narrow the idea of nationhood could become, how simple it could seem to those from elsewhere.

During the Raj it had been a common belief that Henry's fore-father, Colonel James Skinner, was the reincarnation of Alexander the Great. But by the time Henry was a boy no such high regard remained. Of course every Indian had wanted to be an Anglo-Indian, if only to garner British privileges, but when the British left, all that changed. Those of his kind who stayed did so as his mother did, in ghettos, kept company by yellowing portraits of the Queen.

Around him an afternoon storm is gathering. Mountains of clouds rise up behind the dense canopy of black plum and Indian beech. The sky darkens and the new green leaves glow in the yellow-grey light. A wind stirs and rain begins to fall, the drops slow and fat at first then faster and closer together. Henry runs through the rain and takes shelter in a tomb. It is dark inside. Black sparrows circle in the dome of the roof, tiny darting things rising up and up to the very top of the curved, mottled ceiling then swooping down again. Henry cranes his head to watch. Pigeons coo in the red stone alcoves as they look out over the wet trees. The tomb is peaceful – cool and quiet. It smells of dust and urine and birds. He feels like he could stay there for a long time. He feels this, although he knows that his time is up; he doesn't belong here anymore, and this sense of not belonging is made worse by the fact that he can well remember when he did – a sense of an original belonging. The belonging of a child who lives fully in whatever place he is. Now that he's come back and seen the place again and remembered, it seems as if everything that came after his early childhood was simple fabrication, history commanding him to become someone he wasn't meant to be, something so very different to what he was when he was born – first a British Indian, then an Englishman, now an Australian. What made him think he could reinvent himself so easily? But he hadn't the choice, he reminds himself, not always.

He walks back and forth, watching the way the world appears and disappears through the archways. He likes the darkness. He likes looking through the darkness of the tomb and out into the light of day. Something stirs inside him, a small memory. He has stood this way before. In the centre of their house in Australia, with the doors open, looking straight through into the front garden and the back. There is the darkness of the house, the lightness of the trees and the lawn outside. The pines swaying in the distance. The high clear sky. The sound of his children. These two places – inside him there are always two places.

The rain stops as quickly as it started. The trees look brighter, the air rinsed clean. All over the gardens, people begin to emerge from shelter. In the distance there is the sound of horns as taxis speed along Prithviraj Road carrying tourists to India Gate. He might have been happier, he thinks, if he had never left this place. His parents sent him to England so that he might benefit from new opportunities, and he moved his children from England to Australia for exactly the same reason. And although the benefits he experienced were no doubt many, to his own mind they seem vague, while the costs appear clear, now, as he grows older and understands that he will always be an outsider, that he will always live in a place he is not from. For a long time he thought that habit would counter this fact and custom would disguise it. He thought, in the beginning, that such things would not matter in the long run. But they did, they do, they always will.

Henry writes detailed letters to Charlotte telling her all this, explaining, but the letters are never sent. And he never gives them to her, because by the time he returns home she has gone.

FOR SEVERAL DAYS Charlotte sees no one but the children. Nicholas doesn't come back, another week passes and there is still no word from Henry. Charlotte doesn't know if she wants to hear from him; how will they resume, and must they? Meanwhile Carol has taken a job at the local library and so is out most of the time. It is as if the world has somehow been deserted; the suburb, with its neat lawns and lace curtains, is eerily quiet. Every day, all day, there is just her voice and the voices of the children. The birds. Then one afternoon a letter arrives from Henry. She tears open the envelope while the children whine and pull at her skirt. 'A letter from Daddy!' calls Lucie. 'Give me! Give!'

Dear Charlotte, Henry writes. *My mother died peacefully a few days ago. I went to come home straight away, but there have been troubles with the airline. They say it won't be long, a week perhaps. So hopefully by the time you receive this*—. She doesn't read to the end, but folds the letter up and puts it back in the envelope. She ought to be pleased at the news – there can be no doubt now. At the back of her mind had been the thought that perhaps he would not return, and that maybe this would be better, easier – an accidental parting of ways. But no. And it is unbearable, all of a sudden it is unbearable – to think of the days going on as they once did. Suffocating. She will make a show of it for the children though, because it is not their fault. 'Daddy will be home soon!' she says, as she pushes the envelope into the pocket of her dress.

To celebrate the news they make a cake, mixing flour and butter and eggs and popping it in a bundt pan because that is the shape the girls like. While it bakes they go out into the garden; there are weeds to pull and flowers to water. But Lucie trips and grazes her knee, then May gets a prickle stuck in her finger. Both girls wail, and while Charlotte tends to them the cake burns. When she opens the oven door, smoke billows out into the kitchen. It is too much: there is still dinner to cook and a bath to run then the bedtime stories to be read. Charlotte starts to cry. The cake was meant to change the feeling of the day, to make them happy. Dusk is coming. Charlotte takes a glass from the cabinet and pours herself a drink. She is exhausted: awake since three in the morning when May called out for her and she went, dutiful. But now she aches with tiredness – her eyes, the bones in her face. She is tired of the house, of the children, of Henry.

She hurries the girls through their dinner and their bath. And when she makes a simple request – *Please, put your nightie on now* – and Lucie staunchly refuses – *No, no I won't* – Charlotte's anger is instantaneous. She swoops down and yanks the red nightdress over her daughter's head, knowing the buttons are still fastened and that they have caught in her child's hair.

'Ow! It's hurting! Ow! You're hurting me!'

Charlotte forces the nightdress down, over her daughter's face. 'You will put this on! You. Will. Put. This. On!'

Lucie's eyes and cheeks burst through the opening before the top of her head, so that Charlotte has to tug the thing, making it drag at Lucie's throat. The child coughs and gags. 'Oh, stop making a show of it,' Charlotte snaps. It is too small, but it is the only one that is clean. Lucie screams and Charlotte yells at her, 'Hold still! Hold still! Would you damn well—You stupid child—You stupid—'

Lucie screams and screams then collapses between Charlotte's legs, lying on her belly with her face pressed into the floor, hollering and dribbling into the carpet. The nightie hangs loose around her neck; beneath it her legs are bare and pink from the heat of the bath. Charlotte pauses, looks down at those legs, at the soft pad of skin behind the knee, and hits them. She hits them once, twice, three times, a red print of her hand aglow on Lucie's pale skin. Then she turns out the light and slams the door. She returns to the kitchen to finish the dishes while Lucie wails.

Ten minutes later, Charlotte goes back to find her lying on the carpet in a puddle of urine. Now Lucie lets her mother dress her. Quiet as a mouse. Charlotte crouches down, soft now.

Lucie says, 'See the tears? See the tears on my face?'

'I do,' replies Charlotte, not looking. Lucie turns her back on her mother then twists her head around, slides her eyes in Charlotte's direction and holds her mother's gaze. Her brow furrows and she watches Charlotte until Charlotte cannot bear it anymore, the challenge, whatever it is, and looks away again, down into the floral twists of the carpet.

'I love apples,' Lucie says, her voice soft as though talking to herself. She is hiding now behind the curtains, her nose pressed to the cold window. 'I love strawberries. I love squeaky toys. I love Bessie. Bessie talk to Lucie?' she says, coming out from her hiding place. 'Bessie talk?' Bessie is the rag doll Lucie was given as a baby. In six months' time Lucie will be three; the rag doll is stained and losing her stuffing. 'Bessie talk!' she demands, holding the doll out to her mother.

The guilt Charlotte feels then, the need for atonement. 'And what does Bessie say?' she asks, kneeling down before her daughter. Charlotte aches to sleep. There is a terrible weight in her chest and in her feet. She feels giddy with the need for sleep. She bites her tongue deliberately, the pain sharpening her attention, keeping her awake. 'Bessie's going to the library,' says Charlotte. 'Off we go! We're going to get some books. Now, get in the car, Bessie. Okay. Broom-broom. We're at the library now. Out we get.'

How quickly Lucie has forgotten her mother's cruelty. But just as Charlotte thinks this, she makes some terrible, invisible error. 'No! Not like that. No! Noooo!' howls Lucie. 'Like that!'

'Like what, sweetheart?'

'Like that! Like that! Like that!'

Charlotte doesn't understand. She feels tears sting her eyes and tries to change the subject. 'Is Bessie hungry? Shall Bessie have something to eat instead? What about a cheese sandwich? Shall we all have a cheese sandwich?'

'Okay,' says Lucie. 'Bessie wants crusts off. And butter. Just butter. Not cheese, just butter. Make Bessie eat the sandwich.' Charlotte responds with the appropriate munching sounds. 'And ice cream. Now Bessie do a wee. And a fart. Bessie does a poo.' Charlotte hurries, trying to keep up with the commands. 'Now make Bessie talk. Talk to Lucie, Bessie.'

'And have you had a good day?' Bessie asks Lucie.

'Yes.'

'What have you done?'

'Umm . . . You tell Bessie,' Lucie says to Charlotte. 'You tell Bessie what Lucie has done.'

'Well,' begins Charlotte, in a squeaky little voice, 'today I . . . went to the park and I had a swing. I saw a dog running after a ball and—'

'No – not that! Not that!'

'What then?'

'Something else. Bessie do something else!'

'One more thing – the last thing – and then it's time for bed.'

'No, not the last thing! Not the very last thing!'

'Yes, the very last thing. Yes!'

The fantasy begins now. Just a quick flash of an image. A woman on her own, in a train, in a room. Somewhere else.

'I don't want to go to bed,' says Lucie. She is sitting on the floor nursing Bessie and shifts around, turning her back to Charlotte.

'That doesn't matter, it's bedtime.'

'No! Bessie – I want to talk to Bessie.'

'Bessie's tired, she's going to bed too,' says Charlotte, but this only makes Lucie wail once again. Charlotte picks her up and tries plugging her mouth with the teat of a bottle. Lucie wriggles and gags and cries louder, milk and spit running down her chin. She throws herself from Charlotte's lap onto the floor. May, who's been quietly watching television, comes into the bedroom and begins to wail as well, the two of them thrashing about, all legs and arms and red sweaty faces. Lucie gasps and howls and gasps until she vomits, milk and bits of half-digested meat coating her nightie.

Charlotte leaves them there, opens the front door and steps outside. How glorious is this release into cold dark air, the sensation of light rain fresh against her hot face, the smell of smoke and coal and damp leaves loose in the gutters, the smell of the river, the dank low tide and the rotting weed. Inside, the children continue to scream and flail. Charlotte walks down the steps and onto the grass, the sound of the children growing softer as she walks further and further away, right up to the front gate. The moon is behind the clouds and a wide panel of sky tilts over the black trees. She puts her hand to the latch, thinking of the river not far away, of Nicholas in his house above the sea.

She remembers a feeling from years before – a feeling of nascency, of potential, of openness to the world. Now she is a response but not a question; in all of this, she thinks, I am what comes after the event.

They don't know she is gone. They wouldn't know if she went. Not now. Not immediately. And they are young, too young – they would remember so little of their abandonment. She could just walk on now, through the gate, towards the train, or the river. Thunder booms in the distance and a great wave of cold wind pushes over and around her, sweeping the land clean and empty once again. Then she lifts her hand from the gate and turns back towards the house.

The moment she steps inside, the phone rings. 'I'm catching a plane in the morning,' he tells her. 'It gets in tomorrow night. No, don't worry, I'll make my own way.'

The trees stand very still in the dawn. White cabbage moths glint in the glassy air. A mist hovers over the grass. She has packed her bag and now pulls out her coat from the wardrobe, glimpsing the yellowed newspaper clipping that her mother sent shortly after Charlotte married, and which Charlotte has kept taped to the inside of the wardrobe door ever since. It started off as a joke between her and Henry; they used to laugh at it. She doesn't need to read it – after all these years she knows the words by heart:

The girl who marries must not expect to find the married state an enchanted garden of happiness, where never a weed nor a thorn grows. She will certainly have many times of trouble and weariness but she must, with brave heart and indomitable courage, face the new unknown life which, along with fuller joy than she has hitherto known, lies before her. She should do all in her power to make her home the daintiest, cosiest little nest imaginable, so that her husband should be only too glad to spend his evenings there instead of going off to his "Club". She must bear in mind that no man, even "the dearest fellow in the world", can bear with good temper being kept waiting twenty minutes for his dinner, or finding his shirts minus their complement of buttons or his socks full of holes. She should not forget that well-cooked daintily served meals go far to ensure household peace. No time is wasted that is spent as means to this desirable end. She should strive to be always as fresh and attractive as a newly opened daisy sparkling with the morning dew, and as sweet-tempered and loving a little wife as ever gladdened the heart of a husband.

Why had her mother sent her this piece? This fierce woman who for some unknown reason expected docility from her child. The wardrobe had belonged to Charlotte's father and his name is inscribed just below the clipping, written in pencil, in fine copperplate: *Mr. D. L. Thomas.* Although the wardrobe was given to Charlotte, she and Henry both hang their clothes here, and it is because of this, she supposes, that Henry chose to write his name below her father's. He meant to mark a simple change in ownership – the wardrobe was theirs now, it became theirs in the winter of 1961. But the appearance of her husband's name makes it seem as though the two men, together, are endorsing this strange comment sent to Charlotte by her mother. What kind of wife was her mother? This loyal woman who couldn't cook but who never admitted to such a thing. When her mother's Christmas cake sank in the middle she filled the hole with cold porridge before smothering it in royal icing. And how many burnt dinners were buried in the back garden? Charred roasts. Black potatoes. Her mother out there in the blue dusk with the spade, the kitchen thick with smoke. She thought that if she buried the ruined food her husband might never know.

Charlotte folds the coat over her suitcase then stands by the window waiting for the moment when it is time to wake the girls. Then she dresses them, feeds them and wipes their faces with a warm cloth. 'It's just for the day,' she says, biting down on her lip to stop herself from crying. 'And guess who'll be home to see you tonight!' She stands her children side by side and kneels before them. 'There now, let me get a good look at you,' she says, stroking May's tubby chest and straightening the collar of Lucie's blouse. The two girls sway slightly, little ships at anchor.

She leaves the suitcase to collect on her return, then hoists May onto her hip and takes Lucie by the hand. They walk towards Carol's house. It is Saturday, she will be home today. The morning sun is bright, the air cold. She is very conscious of the air all around her. The stretch of it. The thin gusting. The smell of fresh leaves and smoke. There is a flash of red in a neighbouring garden – Mr Oates bending down to water the flowers, then standing up and bending down again. Charlotte lets go of Lucie's hand and waves, Lucie's attention instantly diverted as she crouches down to inspect a row of marching ants. She pokes at them, watching one crawl over her small finger. 'Come, Lucie,' Charlotte says gently, taking Lucie by the wrist and lifting her to her feet.

The house rises up out of the shrubbery, the bungalow surrounded by bare frangipani and flame trees. Carol isn't expecting them. 'I've just got to go out for a bit,' Charlotte says to Carol. 'Would you mind?'

'Of course not,' Carol replies, looking at her strangely. 'Is there something I can help with?'

'No, Henry's back tonight, that's all.' As if this explains her appearance on Carol's doorstep. Errands, Carol must assume. A surprise, perhaps.

May reaches out her fat little arms and Carol takes her. 'Milk? Milk?' May asks, bouncing her head at her mother.

'Yes, darling,' Charlotte replies, running her palm over her daughter's soft hair. 'I'll bring more milk. I've packed them some lunch,' she says to Carol, passing her a bag.

'Oh, you didn't need to do that,' Carol says. 'There's always plenty here.'

'Hold me, Mummy. Hold me, hold me, hold me,' Lucie begs, tugging at Charlotte's dress. Charlotte picks her up, a tall heavy child now, and holds her tight. She breathes in the smell of her. Wax and butter and soap and clean clothes. She sets her down and crouches before her, kissing her softly on the nose. 'I love you, my poppet. I do love you,' she says, staring into her daughter's huge and shiny eyes. 'I do,' she says again, her voice cracking. She pushes her nose into May's squishy cheek and kisses her too, the warm sweet skin. Then she turns and walks down the hall. 'I won't be long,' she calls, dipping her head to button up her coat. 'You be good for Mrs Russell. And remember I want those sandwiches eaten by the time I get back!' Then she is gone, stepping out from the warm fug of the house and pulling the door shut behind her. A child's voice calls. There is the sound of small feet running across floorboards.

—

Henry pays the driver, walks up the path then stands in the open doorway, his suitcase hanging from one hand. 'Charlotte?' he calls, taking off his hat and holding it to his chest, but there is no answer. Perhaps she is sleeping, he thinks. He puts his bag down and goes quietly towards the bedroom, switching on the lights. 'Charlotte?' There is something about the air that tells him the house is empty. Even when Charlotte is asleep he can smell her presence, the loose note of rose that always strays from the complex source of her perfume, and somewhere below this there is always the residue of a morning's work in the kitchen – the smell of toast and coffee, onions and meat. At this time of night there is normally a cacophony of child noises as Lucie begs to stay in the bath and May cries.

He walks down the hallway, throwing open one door after another. 'Charlotte!' he calls again, louder this time. He checks the bathroom. He runs now, to the back of the house, to the laundry, out into the yard, scanning the dark mounds of the garden. 'Charlotte?' he calls, quieter now, and a little out of breath, his voice carrying across the wide, black stretch of lawn. The light from the laundry spills out into the yard. 'Charlotte?'

He finds her note on the kitchen table, scribbled on a piece of foolscap and held down by an orange. He reads it slowly, then reads it again and returns it to the table. She does not tell him where she has gone, only that she has gone and he must not – *please don't* – try to find her. Sure enough, some of her clothes are missing, her shoes, and a suitcase. He steps away from the wardrobe and pushes his hat onto his head.

CHARLOTTE'S PLANE LANDS in London and she takes a train to King's Cross. The concourse is thick with people: men bustling homewards, carrying fat briefcases, women balancing brown paper packages, small children being led by the hand. Charlotte makes her way to the ticket office and pays her fare. Then she steps up into the carriage, finds a seat and pushes the ticket into the pocket of her coat. She knew where she was going without ever having decided it; she simply understood, all along, where her life was to take her: away, back and away. She turns her face to the window, imagining her children awake and needing her, calling for her and wondering why she is taking so long. They will have slept and woken up again by now. Henry will be home. She imagines he will have lied to the children – told them, perhaps, that she has gone to visit a friend who is ill. 'But why?' Lucie will ask. 'Why? Where is she?' I don't know sweetheart. I don't know, Henry will reply. Charlotte stares out the window, blinking back her tears.

It is past eight at night when the train pulls into Cambridge. She takes a taxi into town, and walks from there – down Senate House Passage, past the library, along Adams Road and out through the fields into the nearby villages. She knows the way and the moon is bright. She shivers in her coat and pulls it tighter; the autumn air is cold. Eventually she reaches their old house, and although she knows she should walk on, she can't help but stop to look; the door has been painted blue, and new curtains hang in the windows. Her instinct then is to just lay herself down in the fields and never rise again. Her suitcase is heavy, her skin red where the handle rubs against her palm, her feet are swollen and aching in their tight shoes. She is cold. She wants a bath. She wants a pot of tea and a bath. But it is too late to book into a room, so she walks until she can't walk anymore, out through the fields leading towards Grantchester, past new-turned earth, brown and muddy, the smell of it in the air, the path edged by bare hedgerows and rosehips. She remembers living amid this mud and grass and feeling that all the world was held at bay, fields away from her. She remembers the first walk she and Henry took together when they moved into the little cottage, stopping in the dusk, the sky low and grey, and looking out over the ridges and furrows of the medieval fields, thinking about all the nights the fields had lain just so. All the rains that had drenched them. All the winds. All the frosts. The two of them full of a strange dim wonder as they tried to grasp the ancient nature of the place.

Australia is not just a different country; it is a different world in a different time, ahead, somehow, of the time she finds here, which will always be contained by time past, by the time of youth and childhood and all the vague grey time before that, the mists through which her family had come. Real future is not possible here, it seems. She's seen it, though – out there she lived in that other time, that broken time, that time that floats outside of all the times she'd known before, incommensurate. And now she's come back, forcing time to fold and pleat and become continuous again, the past and the future occurring once more in the same place, one on top of the other, one beside the other, and that great journey, that hot suburban life, is instantly reduced to one meagre experience among many. She wants her children now. She wants them in a way she has never wanted them before, her body aching with a kind of adolescent love, a pained adolescent craving. Only now does she think of how wrong she was. She was wrong to leave them. That is all she can think: she was wrong.

It starts to rain and the wind picks up. She knows she can't stay out all night, and even if she did make it back to town, nothing would be open at this hour. There is a little shed in the woods, just off the path into town. She used to pass it on her bicycle. It was once used to store old crates from the orchard. She heads towards the spot where she thinks the shed ought to be, slipping in the muddy drain beside the path and snagging her dress on the brambles. In summer this tract of woodland is thick with nettle and cow parsley and meadowsweet, full of soft green light. Now she stumbles about in the dark, leaning against trees, pushing through shrubbery. Then it is before her, a shape in the clearing. The door is open, and inside, yes, there are old wooden crates, tools for digging and pruning. She sits down on her suitcase and leans against the wall. Branches creak and drag on the roof. Foxes slink by, digging, sniffing. There is the call of an owl. Soon she drifts into a troubled sleep and dreams that she is to have a child, only it is to be born from her left breast and to give birth she must cut open the underside of her breast with a knife. Except when she does this, she finds not a child but the liver of a calf, whole and dark and slippery, and she understands that she must cut this open as well. Inside the liver lies a small, dead infant. She puts this child aside, slices open the soft skin beneath her right breast and finds there not a second, living child but three tiny and completely white tulips – stem and leaves and petals – all folded neatly together as if held fast in a locket.

She sees the advertisement in the morning, a sign written in neat white copperplate on a piece of black board and hung from the bars of the college gate. Charlotte stands in front of the sign, chewing her bottom lip and blinking. In different circumstances she might have done other things – she could have taught, or sought out commissions as she once did years ago, but she doesn't have the luxury of time, and has nowhere to stay. She hides her suitcase under some bushes outside and walks into the porters' lodge. She doesn't ask for the job, she begs. She looks a fright, she knows, damp all over and grey under the eyes. She lies about her experience but it is a petty lie that does not exaggerate her ability. And it is not exactly a lie, she reasons, to say that she has international experience, or that she has been, for nearly seven years, a housekeeper to a professor. Of course Henry is not that, but he will be eventually. The head porter is suitably impressed, and only when she knows she has the job does she apologise for her fatigued appearance, explaining that she's had the flu. 'But I am fine, really, and can start immediately.'

No one knows she is married: she removes her wedding ring when she signs the form setting out the terms of her employment. Six months initially, but they will be happy, they are certain, for her to stay on. It is surprisingly difficult, she is told, to come by a decent housekeeper these days. Another porter shows her to her apartment, a small set of rooms at the top of a large Georgian house. Once an attic, it was refurbished for housekeeping staff when the college acquired the building several years before, he explains. There is a bathroom, a small kitchen and a bedroom with a fireplace. Once he has left she puts her few clothes away in the wardrobe and hangs out her apron for the morning, when her duties are to begin. Then she runs the bath and lies there with her eyes closed until the water cools and her skin wrinkles and grows soft. Later she makes tea, and drinks it sitting by the fire. Her body is heavy with exhaustion but sleep will not come, so she stays sitting in the chair as the darkness drifts down all about. It is a relief, this blotting out of the world. It is so pleasant, she had forgotten how pleasant it could be, to see the busyness of other people's lives painted over by the night and to draw the curtains at four. The southern light is meant to be uplifting, but how soothing it is to be surrounded, now, by damp, close, low-lying dark, to hear the patter of rain on the glass, the windows rattling a little in the wind, the dark like a common tissue linking her to land and people. Charlotte closes her eyes and feels herself made of this same stuff, the shadowy inner reach of her own mind conterminous with the night. It is not unlike the comfort of floating in water, of feeling oneself adrift in a single substance, in contact with something into which one might meld and vanish if it were not for the border of skin. When she was a child she imagined her body to be black inside, because that was what she saw when she closed her eyes. Now it seems right once again. It is not dark because she closes her eyes to the light of the world; it is dark because that is what it is like inside.

THOSE FIRST HOURS pass, then after that more, and eventually she drifts off and wakes in the armchair at dawn. Soon, a whole day has gone by. Then a week. A month. At some point, a little further on, she looks up from the bucket she has just pushed the mop into and realises that she has not been thinking of her children. It is something she understands in retrospect: there is a small blank in her mind where that thought of her children should be. She doesn't know how long ago she stopped thinking of them, only that this is the first time such a thing has happened – the first time that she has ceased to consider them, the first time that they have been allowed to drop away from her consciousness, the first time since the day they were born. She thinks of that last night together. How after she came inside and answered the phone she went back to the bedroom to find May asleep on the floor. She picked her up and put her into bed, pulling the covers up, and kissing her forehead. Lucie was still awake. 'Moon! Moon! Go see moon?' she asked, pulling at Charlotte's skirt and peering at her with huge brown eyes. A full moon shone through the window.

'Yes, we'll go see the moon,' Charlotte said softly. 'Mummy will always show you the moon.'

The flyscreen banged shut as she and Lucie stepped outside. Somewhere behind the fence stood a fir tree. It went unnoticed by day, tucked away behind an olive haze of scrub. At night the pointed tip of its triangular mass stood taller than everything else before it, the long branches and clumps of needles blacker than the sky.

'I put my eye outside,' said Lucie, 'and I peek it.' She was talking about the moon still. Charlotte carried her deeper into the garden. They walked down through the grass, away from the light of the house.

'Where is it?' Lucie asked.

'Is it over there?' said Charlotte, pointing in the direction of the sea.

'No,' said Lucie.

'Is it over there?' Pointing this time towards the river.

Lucie looked. 'Just stars,' she replied. They crept down further, towards the back fence.

'Is it up there?' Charlotte said, pointing into the trees. And then they spied it, the huge, white, shining moon nesting behind a clump of leaves. They scurried forwards and the moon disappeared. Lucie threw her arms around her mother's neck and clung to her. Charlotte felt her daughter's breath against the side of her face, soft little gusts that smelled of butter and meat. Right then she wanted to stand in that dark garden with her forever. She wanted the world to stop. No, she thought, she wanted the world to never stop, but to go on and on, never letting this moment expire, never letting it change or end.

I thought I had come home, she writes in her diary. But home is never the same once you have left it for any length of time and come back. Home is a secret world that closes its door in your absence and never lets you find it again. *How do I get inside? No one can tell me.* She tries not to pay attention to the children playing in the street, but every now and then she sees a child who looks too much like one of her own, a blonde-haired baby in a pink jumper held high in its mother's arms. She has gone out to fetch bread and sees them at the roadside, waiting to cross. The baby leans backwards, its thin hair lifting in the wind, then drops its head against its mother's shoulder. Charlotte stares, unblinking, until it seems indecent, then forces herself to look away. How easy it is to imagine the round weight of the child, its nappied bottom on her hip, its tubby belly warm against the palm of her hand. The child's soft hair against her nose.

Meanwhile she repeats her housekeeping duties day after day, beginning with the beds in the north-east wing of Chapel Court, then the rooms and bathrooms, dusting, wiping, hoovering. After this comes the Hall, previously the nuns' refectory, where she mops the floors following breakfast. Someone else polishes the tables, others stack dishes in the kitchen. Outside, the gardeners tend the lawns and the beds of primroses, purple and yellow and pink. Later, she returns her mop and bucket to the closet and takes out the garbage. Then she unties her apron, folds it and slips it into her handbag before passing through Cloister Court on her way to the chapel, where she sits for a while, not praying but thinking, and watching the day play against the colours in the ancient windows. At last she stands up, walks slowly to the porters' lodge, ticks off her morning chores on the roster, then returns to her room, where she fixes a plate of food – peanut butter sandwiches or a fried egg on toast.

At night she sits in the armchair and knits. She works by a small candlestick lamp, soothed by the slip of needles and wool, the weight of the jumper pooling in her lap. She thinks of Henry then. 'Do you love me?' she asked him that last night when they were lying together in bed, just before he left for India.

'I do,' he said. 'You know I do.'

'Why do you love me?' she asked.

'Shhh,' he replied, 'it's late,' as if he didn't know the answer. Charlotte pushed her way through the sheets and took hold of his fingers. He squeezed her hand back, then let go, patted her arm and rolled away.

ON THE OTHER side of the world Henry waits. He waits through December and into January, past February and March. It is a long, hot, unbearable summer, dragging on past Easter. The lawn is scorched and little by little the greenery of the whole front yard dissolves into sand. Week in and week out he hopes for rain. By Easter, Charlotte has been gone over five months and in all that time they've had no more than two days of broken showers. Plane trees and maples are dying throughout the suburbs. The lemon tree has dropped its leaves. Dust rises from the ground when they walk. Each afternoon, clouds collect on the horizon, but then they slip quickly across the sky – moving inland – never giving rain. Wind rattles around the house and the floorboards creak and split from the dry heat. Often Henry thinks he hears someone in the house with him, someone other than the children. Or else he sees things;

out of the corner of his eye he catches sight of something moving in the breeze and is startled, thinking it is her, standing outside the window – her hair blowing back from her shoulders, her scarf – but it is just the peach-coloured sheet drying on the line, billowing back and forth.

By the end of April there is still no word from her. He tries to imagine her unhappiness, what she must have felt before she left. It is his fault, he thinks. If he hadn't been so preoccupied with his book, with work, with the garden, if he'd not gone back to India and left her here alone. If he'd not refused her. Or if he had told her that night, when she asked, why he loved her. What he loved.

He waits then in the only way he knows, immersing himself in his studies. The book that started as lecture notes on the ship flourishes. One essay links neatly into another and soon enough he has completed a draft. He reworks it, fiddles with it, plays the arguments back and forth.

During the day a woman comes in to look after the children. At night he bathes and feeds them, but he only knows how to cook three things: curry, which they won't eat, and spaghetti or sausages, which they will. So every night they eat spaghetti or sausages. One night Lucie asks for carrots and Henry realises that it has been months since he's cooked a vegetable to go with the meal. 'Of course, of course,' he says, pushing his chair back so quickly that it topples to the floor. But he can't even manage this. 'I'm sorry, sweetheart,' he says, peering into the almost empty fridge. 'We have a tomato, and look, here's an apple, would you like an apple?'

'No, no, no! I want a carrot!' She begins to cry.

He thinks often of the letter Charlotte left for him. *The story that starts a marriage*, she wrote, *is very often the same story that ends it.* Or rather, the seed of the end is planted in the beginning. It is the sadness of marriage that one can only learn where the end begins when it is too late; by then love is over and one is left bearing the various carapaces of wedlock – the little roof over our little house, the hat you wore on our honeymoon, the umbrellas we each carried of an English summer to keep us safe from unwanted rain. We err, she wrote, because we think happiness is a state in itself, when really it is only a symptom of love.

By the time the official envelope arrives it is June and Henry has forgotten that he ever made the application. The fine paper. The red, rectangular stamp of the college, the small black stamp of the post office. He'd applied for a research fellowship at Jesus College, to allow him to complete his manuscript, and the letter informs him of his success. He did it for Charlotte, when they were still together, and now she isn't here to know of this good news. It would have been all right, Henry wants to say. If you had just waited I would have given you what you wanted. Imagine that, imagine saying to her, 'Look, look at this, I'm taking you back to England.' Instead he thinks to himself, now I will find you. I will find you and I will love you and I will bring you home.

SHE IS ON her way back from cleaning the Bowery when she hears the sound. The small light notes of a child's voice. One child, then another. No, she thinks, it is not possible. It has happened before, this error – wrongly thinking that another child is her own. Nor is the mistake limited to human voices; she hears the call of her children in animals and inanimate objects – the distant howl of a dog, whining pipes. Surely not, she thinks, yet still she waits. All is quiet. Then comes the patter of feet and the small, rising notes of the voices again. Laughter, a curling, playful squeal. She steps off the path onto the damp grass and moves closer to the tree that stands at the edge of the courtyard. She presses her body against the tree and peers around, her heart thumping, the smooth cool bark against her cheek. There is the flash of blue cloth. The streamer of a pink hair ribbon. She tilts her face to see out across the lawn. Yes – yes. How could it be, but yes – the flash of their dark little eyes, the leap of leg over grass.

She feels her knees give and crouches down, biting her lip to keep from crying out. May is tugging off flower heads, squishing them between her fingers then rubbing them onto her wrist and sniffing. Lucie is building a house out of sticks and leaves; she runs back and forth between the trees, gathering supplies – mud, stones, twigs. Her old rag doll, Bessie, watches on, propped up against a purple-flowering hebe bush. Lucie runs and ferries and runs and ferries, her small cheeks red in the cold and her hair loose and damp. She is tall for a three-and-a-half-year-old. And she is a good little runner, her Lucie, fast and light, but her eyes are up in the sky, then casting back towards May, then darting left to where a gardener works up a pile of leaves for burning. She is not looking at the smooth, worn, tangled knot of roots rising up in her path. Just then Lucie's toe catches the loop of a tree root and her body crashes down. Charlotte pulls back, out of sight. May trots over to her sister and then there is the voice of a man. 'Are you okay there, sweetheart? Where's your mummy?' It is Mr Jones, the head gardener. Of course he does not know who they are, and if he did he would know that they have no mummy, or that they do not know where their mummy is. Charlotte hears May say exactly this: *I don't know.*

She knows she should leave before she is discovered but Lucie is squealing and holding her ankle as if it were sprained or broken.

Mr Jones is saying, 'There now, there now. Can you move it? It will be better soon, little one. Where's your daddy?'

From out of nowhere comes Henry's voice. *Luu-cie? Lu-cie!* He is running, taking great heavy strides, his voice bouncing in his chest then exploding over the grass. *Lucie!* Charlotte peeks around to see him hitching up his trousers and bending down, gathering Lucie into his arms. There he is, with our child, Charlotte says to herself, *with our child.* Lucie's long legs are bunched up in her father's lap, her red face pressed to the soft cloth of his shirt.

It only takes a few enquiries on Charlotte's part to discover what has brought the children to the garden. Henry has a small bedsit that looks out over that very courtyard and has been there now for two months. He has a book coming out, the porter tells her – a friendly man who prides himself on knowing such particulars – and is in Cambridge on a fellowship, making final changes to the manuscript while he works on a series of lectures that he is to deliver later in the year. Some annual series, a great privilege to be asked, and so on and so forth.

'Do you know him?' the porter asks.

'Oh no,' Charlotte says. 'No, I saw him with his children the other day and thought I recognised him for an old acquaintance, but it seems I was wrong.'

The following week the roster changes and she is assigned to clean his rooms. Charlotte suggests that she'd be of more use in the undergraduate rooms. 'Not at all,' the college manager says, thinking he is doing her a favour. 'You've got enough of those. Although if it's a question of too much work—'

'No, it's not that.'

'Well then,' he says, 'there's no problem?'

'No, sir, none at all.'

The next morning she takes her mop and bucket and waits under the archway until she sees Henry leave, one child hanging on to each hand and a rucksack of books on his back. Then she dashes up and cleans as fast as she can. It is not long before she learns their routine. They leave the college at eight thirty. At eight forty-five he rings the doorbell of a house on Adams Road. It is an enormous house set back from the footpath, the garden dense with apple trees and tall weeds. A woman comes to the door. Henry hugs and kisses the children, then hurries back to the library, where he works until a little after lunch. He and the girls return home in the afternoon and Henry carries on at his desk. If she is to trust the light in the window, he works late into the night. She reasons that if she arrives at nine each morning she could, at a push, be out by ten or ten thirty. This way they could run a little late or come home early and she will still be safe.

Henry's rooms smell like their house used to smell: old books, lemony washing powder, the fat from fried meat. Where to begin? she thinks. Should she begin? The carpet by his bed is covered in paper; there are piles of notes, pages of typed passages, several stacks of periodicals, books bent open to mark a place, cuttings from newspapers with notes scribbled in the margins. His belongings are in chaos, and she assumes that he cannot possibly know where anything is in all those mounds of paper. She imagines he does not even know the photograph is there, and because of this will not miss it. It only comes to her attention by accident. She is throwing the bottom sheet over the mattress, and as it billows out the breeze disturbs a stack of papers on the bedside table. The first few papers drift to the floor and as she tidies them up she notices the corner of a photo sticking out from the bottom of the pile. She eases it from its place and sits down on the bed. It is of the three of them, her and May and Lucie, just days after May's birth. May is wrapped up against Charlotte's chest while Lucie leans over to peek at her sister's scrunched-up face. Charlotte has one arm around Lucie, and another under May, her head tilted towards the older child and dropping down to gaze upon the new.

She can't remember seeing the photo before. It is clear from her dishevelled appearance that she did not know it was being taken, the milk leaking through her nightshirt, her hair unbrushed. She has no photos of them, of the children, or of Henry – she left everything behind, and how often she has regretted that decision. She peers closer, to better see the look of love on her own face. Then she presses the photo into the pocket of her apron, makes the bed and leaves as quickly as she can.

It is only a matter of time before her first theft leads to others. She takes a dress from Lucie's wardrobe, a ribbon from May's top drawer. She takes a book that she remembers as once belonging to her. She starts arriving earlier and leaving later, spending the extra time sifting through her children's possessions.

Charlotte has accrued quite a collection of items by the time Henry makes his complaint. Of course she denies it, and points out that the keys to the college rooms are available to a great many staff.

'But you are the only one,' the head porter points out, 'who has regular access to the rooms.'

'May I ask what is missing?' she says.

'Items of a personal nature,' he replies.

'How do you know Dr Blackwood hasn't simply misplaced them? He is on his own, you know, with those children. Things get lost,' Charlotte says. 'And he is not exactly orderly.'

'I don't care what is missing, or why,' the porter tells her. 'We can't have this kind of incident. If you don't know where the things are, then I suggest you find out. You have until Friday,' he says, then picks up his bangle of keys and waddles out the door.

The complaint was made on Monday. This exchange takes place on Tuesday. Charlotte is too afraid to clean his room on Wednesday, and come Thursday she stands trembling in the archway, awaiting Henry's departure for the day. It is freezing. Soon, she thinks, there will be snow.

Twenty minutes pass, half an hour. A lamp glows in the window. She doesn't see them leave; it is late, perhaps they've gone out already and forgotten to switch off the light. She is about to drop the box of stolen items outside the front door, then all of a sudden she knocks. It is a small, accidental knock, a thing of habit. She pulls her hand back as if she's touched something hot. Quickly she turns to go, her coat swinging out as she makes for the stairs, but just as she steps away she hears a key click in the lock. The door opens.

'Charlotte?' Henry says. 'Charlotte?'

The girls are sick. Of course he is at home.

'Yes, Henry,' she replies, turning slowly back to face him. 'I came to return your things.'

SHE WOULD HAVE walked, only Henry said no. The footpaths are treacherous, he told her, and I don't want you slipping and injuring yourself when I've just found you alive and well. The snow has come early and the cold is fierce. No, he said, I'll come and collect you and bring you back here, to the hotel near the river. There wasn't room for them all in his bedsit and Charlotte didn't want the college knowing of their situation, so Henry had booked rooms at the Royal. He'll be driving past the river now, she thinks, checking her watch. Her husband, ever punctual. The water a dark stripe in the corner of his vision. He'll see it as he drives straight ahead, lose it as he turns left then right. On the river there will be rowboats – the faint sound of blades smacking and cutting at the water, the creak of hull and oarlock, the call of boys.

Charlotte opens the window and pushes her face into the cold. Outside, the college grounds are empty – the air filled with the whirr of falling snow. There are no bird calls, no lawnmowers, no hum of the London train, no movement other than this drift of white. The wind gusts towards her and she steps back into the dim room. Although there is not much more to pack, her stamina has vanished. There is a glass paperweight from the market, a small blue vase for the flowers she gathered on her tramps through the fields, the photograph she stole from Henry. But the effort required to wrap these last things and place them in the box seems monumental. She crouches on the ground, tugs a sheet of newspaper from the pile and stuffs it into the vase. She slips the photograph of the children into her handbag. Altogether there is less than she expected, just a couple of boxes and a suitcase. Henry will be surprised.

Another gust blows snow into the room. Charlotte gets up to close the window and sees his car parked beside the hedge. How had she not heard his arrival? The purr of the engine and the slow crunch of wheels over gravel and ice. She had kept the window open so that she might catch the sound of these things. She didn't expect this. He will be here any moment now. She had meant to watch for the car and use those last minutes to compose herself. To be ready; to know what to say. She starts to sweat. There is the smell of it. This frightened animal called woman. Her hands shake as she lifts the small round mirror to her face and tries to fix a smudge of blue eye shadow. She rubs a hand against the centre of her chest and walks a nervous circle, to the door and back, her heart skittering beneath her palm. Should she let him in, and invite him to sit down, or should she wait by the window and call out – *It's open* – when he knocks? Then they'll walk towards each other. Or will he find her with her back to him; she'll turn, and each will pause, unsure of who should make the first approach. He'll brush the snow from his coat. He'll take off his hat. And the children? Where are they? The children.

What Henry noticed most was the smell of geraniums, sharp and sweet in Charlotte's warm, stuffy little room. They crowded the windowsills and the middle rung of the bookshelf: two with common brick-red flowers, one with wild purple blooms and another with a pale pink bud on a stem that shot up like a tree, reminding him of the blossom on a crabapple. While he waited for her to close the last box he bent down and rubbed a scented leaf between thumb and finger. The plants on the windowsill reached sideways towards the light. The leaves of others trailed down onto the ground to be crushed underfoot. All over the floor were spots of crimson and pink where the petals had dropped and been smudged into the carpet.

As he drives he rubs at his jaw and catches the smell of the leaf still on his fingers. The windscreen wipers skid and drag over the ice. Henry manages to clear a small circle in front of his face but the rest of the window remains opaque.

'I had a dream, you know,' he says, keeping his eyes on the slippery road. 'That this happened. Not me finding you again, but before, everything that came before. It was a long time ago now, one of those dreams that I didn't know was a dream. I dreamed, like this – very real – that you were in love with him.'

Charlotte raises her voice in protest. 'That's not the reason, and it wasn't—' she says. But Henry holds out his hand to silence her.

'I know,' he says. 'I mean I knew. Of course I knew. I am not a fool. Although I suppose that's what everyone says and then we go and do foolish things.' He pauses a moment, checking the side mirror before veering right.

'That's not why—' Charlotte begins, but Henry talks over her.

'It was a very simple dream,' he says. 'We were out together, you and I, and we met Nicholas, just by chance. He'd been eating a cake of some kind and there was icing sugar on his cheek. We were all talking. Or Nicholas and I were talking. You, I think, were standing quietly beside me, with your arm through mine, looking at the ground. There was grass on the ground, worn down, with patches of mud showing through. Perhaps we were at a market. I don't know. Anyway, Nicholas and I were talking when you reached over and brushed his cheek, to clean the sugar from it. You did it very slowly, and carefully, little strokes with the fingers of your left hand. Nicholas and I stopped talking, and then, after a moment, he dropped his gaze from mine. I'd been politely pretending I hadn't seen it, the sugar – the sign of this indulgence of his. But you insisted. I remember thinking, in the dream, that I couldn't tell whether you were touching him like a mother would, or as a lover might. I didn't know, I couldn't make up my mind, although it seemed obvious that the point was not to wipe his cheek clean. The sugar just gave you an excuse to put your hand to his face. Then I dreamed that we were in a boat that was sinking, half of it torn away and filling with water. I had to save the girls. I didn't know where you were. And then I woke up and I knew. I just knew.'

'It was only a dream.'

'But it told me the truth, didn't it?'

'Some of it, not all.' Charlotte stares out the window; he has misunderstood her.

Henry flicks the indicator, then throws a glance over his shoulder before turning left. He drives slowly, carefully. 'Almost there now,' he says gently, as if they've been on a terribly long journey that is finally coming to an end.

'And the girls?' she asks. 'What have you told them?'

'That you have been unwell. That you were unwell and that you'd come back when you were better.'

'What did they say?'

'What could they say? You were gone. You've been gone for a year.'

'And now?'

'I haven't said anything.'

'You haven't told them?'

'I didn't know how, and I thought it didn't matter, that it wouldn't help. They'll see you. You'll be there. That's enough. You left without explanation. You're returning that way.'

'Is that how you think of it?'

'What do you mean?'

'You make it sound like we are moving backwards, resuming something old.'

'I don't know how else to think of it. I loved you. I love you still.'

'Yes,' Charlotte says, but does not know quite what she is agreeing to. Love? Something old? Old love, perhaps. She wants to be with them all, more than anything, but he must know she is not the same, that they are not the same and that she can't return to that country, to that suburb, to that house. But he must know this, surely he must.

They pull up on the street, opposite the entrance to the hotel. Henry walks around to the other side of the car and opens the door for her. Charlotte pauses a moment then swings her legs out, letting him take her by the elbow. His hands are large on her – she had forgotten this. They dip their heads against the wind and step slowly over the black ice, Charlotte lifting her face at the kerb to catch sight of a waiter through the front window. He is positioning serviettes beside the place settings. A tower of folded white cloths rests on his left forearm and with his right hand he carefully peels them away, one by one, leaning towards the table just enough to drop the serviette into place without disturbing the white tower. Around and around the tables he goes, like a wind-up doll. A smoking room is visible through the next window, the back wall lined with rows of pale leather-bound books. She feels Henry steer her leftwards. Then he nods to the doorman, removes his hat, and they step inside.

His room is two flights up. He takes the keys from his trouser pocket as they make their way through the entrance hall. The keys hang from a plain metal loop. Henry hooks this over his finger and Charlotte follows him up the stairs.

When they arrive he gestures for her to enter first, then closes the door quietly behind them, unwrapping his scarf from his neck as he clicks the lock. He pushes the keys back into his pocket and with his free hand yokes his scarf over a spare hook on the hatstand. Then he shakes his jacket from his shoulders and hangs it up too. Until this moment he has looked almost robust, but without the padding of the corduroy and the thick weave of the wool he looks frail, shrunken, his shoulders narrow, his back a little hunched.

Charlotte drops her gaze to her hands, and with her handbag still slung over the crook of her arm tugs at the fingers of her gloves. She pulls off the left glove and holds it crushed in her palm while loosening her fingers from the fit of the right. Then she undoes the clasp of her bag and pushes the gloves inside. She does not know what is meant to happen next. She thinks she should put the bag down, only she doesn't know where. She has not yet taken off her coat.

'They're through there,' he says, pointing to the door of a small adjoining room. She steps forwards, Henry close behind. 'Go on,' he says. The door creaks as she pushes it open, then she stands in the shadow against the wall and searches out their figures. Bit by bit her sight adjusts to the dimness and she sees them, tucked up in bed. She can hear Henry breathing, somewhere behind her. Then his voice coming from the far side of the room. 'Please,' he says. 'Go to them. All they have wanted is you.'

She steps forwards once more and kneels down beside their bed. She tries to quieten her breathing. Her palms sweat. The two of them, close enough to touch: May with her round arms thrown above her head, Lucie pressed against the wall with her sweaty feet sticking out of the covers. Charlotte bends down, closer, and closer still, until she can feel May's puffs of breath warm on her cheek.

'I'm sorry,' Henry says. 'I tried to keep them awake so they could see you, but they were so tired.'

'No, it's better this way.'

Charlotte looks down at their long bodies, at Lucie's thinning face, her fat baby cheeks gone, and she understands, by dint of evidence, how life masses together to become life. She had forgotten. She gazes down at them and feels something beneath the surface of her skin ache and stretch, as though she were being drawn forwards by a magnetic force. Henry stands in the doorway and blocks the light. Then she hears him moving up behind her. His wide, warm hand comes to rest on the back of her neck. From the corner of her eye she can see his other hand bunched in his pocket.

She remembers the letter she left him. What had it said? *I know you think there something poor in my motherly constitution. And I suppose there must be, there is. Is guilt something I feel? Yes, but bewilderment more so. I know I ought to feel differently. I wish I did. I wish you could understand this. It has always struck me that you have deliberately not understood so many things. Why? You've always seemed so intent on dismissing my complaints about this place and my affection for the old one. I say this calmly, but I can't begin to explain the pain this has caused. To be told that such things do not matter.*

I don't expect you to understand. There was always something about you I couldn't fathom, some quality that seemed strange. Now I think I know what it is — it is homelessness, a grown-up version of the restlessness you must have learned as a child, and it means you can pretend to be at home anywhere. I cannot. There is a chance, of course, that my leaving will make us the same — both wanderers, both alone.

'You should eat,' comes his voice. 'Are you hungry?'

'Yes, a little.'

'What would you like? I can order some food up.'

'Oh, anything. A sandwich. Some toast.'

'You need more than that.'

'You choose then.'

Henry lingers behind her, watching Charlotte kneel at the bedside. May lies closest to her. The child takes a quick, deep breath and sighs, turning towards Charlotte and pressing her soft warm nose to her mother's breastbone. Charlotte puts her mouth to the whorl at the crown of May's head: she smells warm fur, skin and soap, remembering, again, in this one deep breath, the whole of her child's existence. She strokes May's silky hair and feels her stir. The child mutters something in her sleep, rolls over and kicks the covers away. Then her eyes open slowly, close, then open again. 'Mummy?' she says. 'Mummy?'

'Yes, sweetheart,' Charlotte whispers. 'I'm here.'

Lucie hears the voice and wakes too. She opens her eyes, sits up and stares at Charlotte as if she doesn't quite know who she is. She blinks once, twice, then scrambles across the bed and throws herself against Charlotte's chest, knotting her arms around her neck. Charlotte had forgotten the weight and warmth of her child; she holds her tight. There is, again, the feeling of being made whole by this simple proximity. It feels like the first flush of love: the burning need to touch and be near. May begins to cry and Charlotte pulls her close. Lucie pushes her face to Charlotte's skin and says, 'You still smell of Mummy.'

'Yes,' says Charlotte, kissing Lucie's head. The children clamber over each other to get nearer to her. May's hair flaps at Charlotte's face while Lucie wraps her arms tighter and tighter around Charlotte's neck. They wriggle and twist. Charlotte's breathing becomes shallow and rapid – the children's hands on her hair, her forehead, her throat, stroking, patting, fiddling, their bony limbs digging into the softness of her stomach. For an instant she feels buried beneath them and fights the instinct to buck them off, the way a small dog might be flicked from the ankle. Of course, she thinks, this is how it has always been: the great need for them, the great love. Then the swift feeling of being overcome, smothered. Henry is saying something but she cannot hear him because the children are yelping at her ears, vying for attention.

'What was that?' she calls to him.

'Nothing,' he replies, as Lucie gains better purchase on Charlotte's neck and tugs her down towards the bed. Charlotte feels her mind turning in smaller and smaller circles – she does not know if she can bear this all over again, the closeness, the constant pressing in, the airlessness. The need for her own resignation, the desire for her own space.

As if sensing this, Lucie stops her wriggling and pulls away. 'Where were you?' she asks, as if Charlotte's absence had been brief.

'I went away.'

'Why?'

What did her father used to say? Y is a crooked letter that cannot be fixed. They have grown up so much. Now they are children, tearing through a green world. It will be one of her most enduring memories, the sudden sight of them in that courtyard, one of those memories that will make her feel so happy and so sad at the same time – these two girls chasing each other over the grass, their legs racing, their faces upturned and grinning, not looking where they are going as they gallop in arcs and zigzags, slightly knock-kneed, their hair flipping behind them, their cardigans falling from their shoulders, the two of them breathless from running and still trying to laugh so that they gasp and smile and sigh and gasp again.

'Thank you for coming back to see me,' says Lucie.

Charlotte laughs, alarmed by the formality of the phrase. It makes her return seem temporary, generous and unexpected – a gift, not a demand, not a necessity. A surprise, of course it is a surprise. 'You're very welcome,' Charlotte replies.

'Did you miss me?' Lucie asks.

'Oh, darling, I did. Of course I did,' Charlotte says, tucking her arm around Lucie's shoulders, but Lucie resists.

Henry goes to fix Charlotte a drink. When he comes back he sets the glass down on the bedside table.

What did he say on the way over? Give them time. But it is not the same. What made her think it could be? There is always the fantasy of maternal love, but it does not accommodate a mother's fear of her children. Lucie and May stop touching her, sit back and stare. They stare at her as though they have never seen her before, as if she does not belong here, as if she has no right to belong, not now, not after so much time apart.

She has seen it before, this look – when she once walked in on Lucie and Henry playing together with Lucie's dolls. She was an interruption, an interloper in a new world. Lucie froze and stared. Then she uttered her command: *Go away*. The force of it was so unexpected that Charlotte could only laugh and do as her daughter told her. She waited outside the door a moment, then retreated to the kitchen, the sound of the game recommencing as she moved down the hall, one doll talking to another in the quick, high voice that Henry reserved for his children's play. Now both girls look at her with these strange wide eyes. They look, unblinking, until Charlotte flinches and turns away.

Henry comes up behind her and puts his hands on her shoulders. 'It will be all right,' he whispers, 'just be patient.' But she did not expect this. They seem to understand so much while knowing so little. One can pretend with a child but one cannot lie. It is true, she is a stranger. She does not belong here anymore. Not now, not like this.

'Ah,' she says, 'I almost forgot – I have something for you both.' She reaches down to the floor and picks up her handbag, dipping her fingers in and fishing about. In an instant she has their attention.

'What is it? What is it! A present? Mummy's got me a present!' they both chime at once. 'Is it a present from England?' Lucie asks.

'Wait, here it is – no, that's not it,' says Charlotte. 'It must have fallen out in the car. Just wait a moment and I'll go see if I left it behind.'

'No!' Lucie cries. 'No, stay here!'

'I won't be a minute,' says Charlotte, 'and I'll be back with a treat.'

'No!' Lucie's eyes well with tears.

'Stay with them,' Henry says, 'and I'll get it – if you tell me what I'm looking for.'

'But that would spoil the surprise,' Charlotte says, standing up and putting out her hand for the keys. 'I'll be as quick as I can.'

She hurries down the stairs and out into the cold. The car is on the other side of the street: she goes quickly, slipping on the ice, then unlocks the driver's door and ducks into the vehicle. A few moments later Henry appears at the entrance to the hotel. Charlotte sinks down behind the steering wheel. Henry looks towards the car but doesn't see her. Charlotte watches: he is talking to the doorman, describing the curve of her hat with his hands and pointing. No, the doorman seems to indicate, shaking his head.

The gifts have slipped underneath the passenger seat: two small picture books and a bottle of boiled sweets. She knows Henry thinks she is lying and that there are no gifts – why else would he chase after her? And now it is as if he has given her the idea. Of course it was always there as a possibility; he must have feared it all along. She sees that now – the little sideways glances, the questions, the constant holding of her hand, the touching of her shoulders, her neck. Of course it is natural, that suspicion – it is what she deserves. She pushes the presents into her pockets and turns them over and over in her hands. Then she opens the door and steps out of the car.

Snow whirls slowly beneath the orange street lamps, and all about is the long hollow moan of wind and ice. Pedestrians hide from the sound, hunching their necks into the high collars of their coats, tugging their hats down over their ears. Across the road the lights shine in the upstairs windows of the hotel. She could have been back inside with them by now. Instead she finds herself standing on the pavement and waiting. The tissue paper in which the presents are wrapped turns soft beneath her sweaty palms.

New eras of life always begin as something imaginary: new countries, new motherhood, marriage. It seems that at some point such things should cease being imaginary and become real, the dream leading naturally, easily, into the life that is built in its wake. But for some reason this never happens, the imagined version always hovering behind the real life that one falls into, so that the two never merge. She has the overwhelming desire to lie down with her daughters in the dark, the children asleep on either side of her, her skin in contact with theirs as they breathe, like the surface of water clinging to a lifting fingertip. Oh, to remember the complete happiness of this, the peace, how it stops all wanting, all thought. But this – now it is so plain to her – this feeling belongs to a time before. It was always fleeting. Always inconstant. A momentary bliss that is now simply part of her history.

There is a feeling, at the end of something, of going forwards into the rest of your life. She knows she will not be forgiven. She knows she must never expect forgiveness, however much she might hope for it. What will they remember most? Her jewel-like glass bottle filled with the perfume of violets. The fox fur in the wardrobe that Lucie used for dress-ups. The slippery pink bedspread, the smell of Imperial Leather soap and talcum powder on her skin. *Tomorrow*, he whispered, when she turned away from the staring children and he came up behind her, *tomorrow we'll start over. Everything is different now. You'll see.*

Through a window across the street Charlotte sees the shape of a mother bending down to kiss her child; she hovers a moment, then reaches out and touches the stem of a lamp, making the room dark. Where does sorrow come from? It seems a magical thing, no matter how terrible, perhaps more so when it is very terrible – so deep and loose and slippery. How to correct this but return to those children and live in the shadow of error, in the general disappointment of her own imperfect love? Ever since they emigrated she has felt they needed something she could not give, and that this failure was not innate but part of the place he'd taken her to. And now what? Her failure has changed her.

Without warning the snow turns to fine rain. In the distance she hears the sound of a bell calling out the hour. How many? Nine, perhaps ten. Her feet are numb in her shoes, and the damp seeps through the lining of her coat. She takes shelter beneath the branches of a tree, cold and sorrow sickening her as she watches the upstairs windows of the hotel, their bright rectangles of light blurring in the rain. She thinks of the car windscreen and the streetlights seen through the crust of snow. Henry's blue gloves slipping down the sides of the steering wheel as they turned the corner. Henry beside her, saying nothing. 'You should say something,' she had said. 'Now is the moment when you are meant to reassure me.'

'What do you want me to say?'

'Anything.'

'I'm driving. There is snow.'

'Then tell me I'm wrong. Tell me it will all be okay.'

'I don't know, Charlotte. I don't know what to say.'

There is the sound of rain hitting the leaves. Then wind blowing the branches. Then leaves shaking the water off. Pitter patter pitter patter patter pitter. Drops fall above and to the sides, for it is a high tree, a wide tree. A purple-leafed birch, with what Henry would call a weeping habit. She does not remember hearing the bells again. But they must have rung, the sound must have swarmed around her while she stood there, waiting.

For a brief moment she thinks of Nicholas. He is here somewhere, in England. She could hold out her hand and a taxi would take her to him. He'd made her that offer, after all. 'I will be there,' he'd said. 'I'll wait for you.' But does she want that? This seems hardly the question. She doesn't know what she wants. She only knows what she cannot bear.

'Go to them,' Henry said. 'Go.' And now she cannot. 'Why?' he'd asked, when they were driving towards the hotel. 'If you could just tell me why.' Silence filled the car. She watched the windscreen wipers catching and dragging on the ice, and thought, *How is it that you can ask me that question? To not understand. After all the time we've had to understand things.* Then he said, without looking at her, 'How could you?'

When she came back to England it was to visit a remembered place. To return to a remembered place. She had thought this was what she needed, this homecoming. She could not have known that such a return would never be simple, never complete, and that her feelings for England came from a remembered time that was itself gone, uninhabitable. The era before their departure. The countless dusks when she stood still in the fields, rocking the pram, when time seemed lost, ancient, unmoving. What is the difference, she thinks, between a time and a place? Children, she thinks, looking up at the windows of the hotel – her children are like this. They are places in time, a mother's first memory of new personhood retrieved through the body of the child. She always cherishes the remnants of the baby in the expressions of the girl. How sad this is.

How lovely. How strange it is to see, every day, the stark evidence of a person's disappearance, quite indistinguishable from a person's becoming. Those early versions of ourselves, she thinks, that vanish over an ordinary course of days.

'I was not myself,' she had explained to him, her eyes turned towards the river.

'What was that?' he asked. She could hear the fast ticking of the indicator. She felt the car veering right.

'Nothing,' she said. 'It doesn't matter.' If he couldn't understand, if he must insist that she make it plain. And then she was holding Lucie to her chest. And Henry stood quietly, watching, and now she knows that he will never ask for another explanation, that he will never have the chance, never again. 'When I was sleeping I saw pictures in my eyes,' said Lucie, her nose pressed to Charlotte's collarbone. 'What did you see?' asked Charlotte. Her child dreaming, the miracle of it.

'I saw you,' Lucie said. 'You and me.'

Charlotte pushes the gifts deep into her pockets and steps out into the street.

Acknowledgements

THIS STORY WAS inspired by the migrations of my grandparents. I would like to thank them for their willingness to talk about their lives and share their story with me. Thank you also to my mother, Rosemary Bishop, for sharing her memories. Although the book is fiction, and this story is not the same as that lived out by my grandparents, I have drawn on these oral histories and used them for my own imaginative purposes. In the course of writing this book I have consulted a great many texts and have used these similarly. I am especially indebted to the following: A.J. Hammerton's and Alistair Thomson's *Ten Pound Poms: Australia's Invisible Migrants* (Manchester University Press, 2005), Reg Appleyard's *The Ten Pound Immigrants* (Boxtree,1988), Thomas Jenkins's *We Came to Australia* (Constable, 1969), Elizabeth and Derek Tribe's *Postmark Australia:*

The Land and its People Through English Eyes (Cheshire, 1963), Nonja Peter's *Milk and Honey – But No Gold: Postwar Migration to Western Australia. 1945-1964* (University of Western Australia Press, 2001), Margarate Hill's Corrugated Castles (Seaview Press, 2005), Marie M. de Lepervanche's *Indians in a White Australia* (Allen and Unwin, 1984), Coralie Younger's *Anglo Indians: Neglected Children of the Raj* (1987, BR publishing Corporation), Blair R. Williams's *Anglo Indians: Vanishing Remnants of a Bygone Era* (Calcutta Tilljallah Relief, 2002), Gloria Jean Moore's *The Anglo Indian Vision* (Australasian Educa Press, 1986), Lionel Caplan's *Children of Colonialism: Anglo-Indians in a Postcolonial World* (Oxford 2001), Joyce Westrip's and Peggy Holroyde's *Colonial Cousins: A Surprising History of Connections Between India and Australia* (Wakefield Press, 2010)

I would like to thank the staff at the University Library Cambridge and the State Library of Western Australia. I would also like to thank the Australia Council for the Arts for a New Work Grant, and Asialink, the Department of Culture and the Arts, Western Australia and the Australia-India Council for an Asialink Fellowship. Thank you to Himachal Pradesh University in Shimla and to my host Pankaj K. Singh. Henry's island musings rightly belong to Elizabeth MacMahon and her work on the island imaginary. Thank you Liz, for lending them.

I am indebted to a great many people who've encouraged and supported this work over many years. Thank you to Alice Nelson – without your friendship and wise eye the book would never have made it. Thank you to D.S. for talking to me about portraits. Thank you Sylvia Karastathi for those early conversations on women, fiction and painting and for pondering characters in galleries: that moment is yours. Thank you Diana for good company and cake. Thank you to Catherine Therese for pointing me in the right direction. Thank you to the brilliant people at Tinder Press and most especially, thanks to Mary-Anne Harrington: your passion for this project and your understanding of it has meant so much. Thank you to my wonderful editor Elizabeth Cowell.

The greatest thanks are to my family: to Milla for your companionship and your beautiful questions, and to Dashiell for joining us in the last stages and making us all laugh. Above all, thank you Boyd – for your fortitude, love and care. This is for you.